SWEET AS SIN

ANA JOLENE

For Auntie Juliet
I will always remember your kindness and generosity

A NOTE TO READERS

Hutch Happa-Hewitt is definitely one of my favorite heroes that I've written so I knew it would take a special woman to tame him. Maison Lane's sweet ways manages to snag his attention, proving that kindness and hard work go a long way. I hope you enjoy their story as much as I have enjoyed writing it. You'll see more of the Happa-Hewitts in the rest of the Moonrise Beach series. However, make sure you don't miss Dacey and Greyson's love story in CLOSE TO YOU, the first book of the Moonrise Beach series too. Each book is written to stand alone, but will be part of a larger series for your enjoyment.

If you enjoy this book, please sign up for my newsletter so you don't miss out on any future Moonrise Beach releases on my website: www.anajolene.com. And if you like darker, more grittier stories, my New Adult Dystopian series, Glory MC, might be the thing for you! There are several books already available in the series (GLORY, ORIGIN, and NIRVANA) with plans for more to come this year!

Happy Reading!
—Ana

ONE

DIRTY, BLOODY BATTLE.

For most people, it was something to fear. However, Hutch Happa-Hewitt *loved* it. He loved everything about being in the Army. He loved the strategy, the training, and the hard work. He loved the blood, the sweat, and the tears involved. And he loved being out there, fighting for what he'd always believed in.

However, he would no longer be living out his dream. Since the attack, his life had drastically changed. It'd been so quick and unexpected that only brief moments had stuck with him. He'd been the only one in the Stryker vehicle when the explosion happened, and as a result, his entire right side had been hit. As fire ripped through his system, he'd been forced to act quickly.

No amount of training would've prepared Hutch for the kind of pain and agony. Knowledge meant nothing when you could smell your own flesh burning.

Teeth gritted against the pain, he'd done his best to hold on, to stay conscious. He remembered hearing the sounds of gunfire before help came. It'd felt like eternity ago, and yet, the phantom pain of it still stayed with him.

He remembered waking up in a hospital, screaming at the top of his lungs. His whole body was on fire, but it centered in his right leg the most. He'd done his best to lift up his head, but he was weak and his movements were limited; his head slammed back hard against the pillow.

When he woke again, it was to find someone before him. It took him a while to realize that it was a nurse asking him about his family. She wanted to know if she could call someone to be here with him so that he wouldn't be alone and to help him through his recovery. But as far as he was concerned, he was alone, and he would always be.

There was no one he wanted to call, no one that would help him through this mess. If he wanted to get out of here, he'd have to do it on his own.

His family wouldn't help him. They wouldn't come to see him, and even if they did, what good would their presence do? He didn't want them to see him like this anyway.

Pain.

Pain was all he felt now. Pain and anger.

"Why doesn't he call his family?" he heard one nurse whisper when they'd thought he was asleep.

"He doesn't have any."

"Yes, he does. He just chooses not to let them know."

He could hear the confusion in the other nurse's voice. "Why wouldn't he want their support?"

"Maybe they're not close. Maybe they wouldn't come."

Now confusion was replaced with pity. "How terrible."

Hutch was tempted to open his eyes but instead he lay there as still as a corpse with only one thought running through his mind.

Get better.

Need to return.

But he didn't mean returning home. No, he fully intended to go back to the Army where he belonged.

It wasn't until weeks later when he realized that he no longer had half his right leg that he fully grasped his new situation.

He couldn't go back. Not like this.

He couldn't even manage sitting up on his own without feeling excruciating pain. Still, his stubborn attitude hadn't allowed him to give up. He spent months in recovery, relearning how to move, how to walk. It'd been the toughest experience of his life but pain and anger had motivated him and kept him alive.

Too bad that it still wasn't enough. When he'd tried to come back, they'd refused him. He'd lost his speed and stamina and they'd deemed him unfit to serve. All those months of pushing himself hadn't been enough to get him back to where he used to be. Now, he'd be forced to go home. But Hutch would've preferred to die on the battlefield than return to Moonrise Beach.

And wasn't that fucked up?

Hadn't he had enough already? Hadn't losing his leg been enough for him to stop and try to live a peaceful civilian life? Was he so messed up that he still longed for that adrenaline rush despite the fact that he'd almost died?

He'd been a damn good soldier though. He'd earned every ounce of what he'd had. No one could ever say that his father had given him this; he'd climbed the ranks on his own. People had long ago stopped asking who he was because the simple answer was that he was a soldier.

Now he was simply an amputee.

Get a fucking grip, man. He had to stop feeling sorry for himself. He was acting like such a pussy. People used to praise him on how tough he was, but the truth was, he didn't feel tough at all. He felt raw and vulnerable and he wanted nothing more than to drown himself in alcohol.

Too bad that there was no whiskey left. He'd drunk it all yesterday. Now he'd have to go hunting for something around the house.

It was already late in the evening, but time held no meaning for him. Since he was out of a job, he could stay up all night if that was what he wanted. Except staying awake, staying conscious made the days feel longer. Everything was like one long torture session that never ended. Right now, Hutch wanted peace. He wanted oblivion and he knew he would find it once he had another bottle in his hand.

He searched the kitchen, finding it surprisingly empty. The wine cellar didn't have any of the hard stuff that he was craving either so he went to the place where he knew he'd have some luck.

Luckily, his father's office wasn't locked so Hutch stumbled his way in, cursing his leg when he got caught on the expensive Aubusson rug. He headed straight for Matthew's secret stash, whispering "jackpot" when his cold hands wrapped around the bottle of whiskey.

Snatching up a shot glass, Hutch dropped himself on the chaise and poured himself a shot. The first one was sweet nectar on his tongue so he drank some more, greedy for the oblivion this drink would give him.

After shooting back five in a row, he stopped to gaze around the room. It was dark; he hadn't bothered with turning on the lights when he'd come in, so the only source of illumination was the moon.

He poured himself another shot, luxuriating in the feeling of his body already heating up.

He'd put a lifetime of sweat and blood into the Army so having it taken away was a crushing blow. He was going to have a difficult time living life in Moonrise Beach without losing who he was.

Hutch stared at the shot glass in the moonlight. He knew he shouldn't be doing this. His father would no doubt rip him a new one if he found him here, but despite the threat, he continued to drink. He was that desperate for release. He wanted to escape the pain, to escape the memories, and escape the loss that wouldn't let him go.

The more he drank, the faster the world spun around him. Soon the tension in his body lessened and Hutch took another shot, feeling his chest relax even more.

With his next shot, his pain was blissfully, gratefully . . .

Gone.

TWO

THERE WAS NO REST FOR THE WICKED.

Letting out a weary sigh, Maison Lane stared at her computer screen, blinking blearily as she tried to get some moisture back into her eyes. She was no longer seeing the text before her. Her focus and sense of concentration had deserted her about an hour ago. Now, she was busy *trying* to look like she was working because Matthew Hewitt, her lovely boss that she was so fond of, currently sat beside her.

They'd been at it the entire day, working diligently on an important project that they still hadn't yet been able to complete. So when the workday had finished, instead of going home to relax like any other normal person would, Maison followed her boss to his expensive pad and set up shop here, continuing their grueling work for another few hours.

They'd been able to get a few more things done, but it was becoming apparent that no matter how much they tried, they wouldn't be able to complete everything tonight.

Maison yawned, sitting back in her chair as she picked up her coffee mug and brought it to her lips. "*Ugh.*" There was nothing but cold grossness inside it now. Over her laptop screen, she caught Matthew's eyes. "Want another cup?"

Matthew glanced down at his own empty cup. "Sure. That'd be great."

Wonderful. She now had an excuse to take a small break. As Maison reached for the mug he gave her, she couldn't help but notice the darkness beneath her boss's eyes. Clearly Matthew was just as tired as she was, but he was pushing through it. The more work they could get done tonight, the better. And another cup of java would certainly help them get the jumpstart they needed.

As Maison made her way into the kitchen, she tried to keep her jealousy at bay. All white marble and stainless steel, the place was like something out of a catalog. It was a shame the room was rarely used as the only people living here were all men who didn't cook. She would run wild if she had a kitchen this size. Too bad she wasn't swimming in money like the Happa-Hewitts, otherwise she'd be tempted to deck her own kitchen out like this. As she started another pot of coffee, Maison leaned back against the countertop and continued to admire the house's interior.

That was when the loud shouting started and three little boys rushed into the kitchen. Matthew's only grandchild, Owen, was having a sleepover with his friends. While it made working in the dining room a little bit difficult with all their yelling and excited squeals, Maison didn't mind too much. She *loved* children and it beat the quiet silence that made up most of her nights.

She guessed that the kids had consumed sugar earlier because their feet were bouncing happily as they danced in front of her. Amused, she could do nothing else but laugh as they proceeded to show off the "cool" gun they each had. She was pleased to notice that they all wore matching Spider-Man pajamas and she wondered for a moment if they'd planned that or it'd been a funny coincidence. Knowing Hunter though, he'd probably done it all on purpose. He'd always been really good at planning parties like that.

Hunter came into the kitchen then. "Owen! It's time for bed!" He wore a simple black T-shirt and gym shorts and his eyes lit up when he saw her standing with the kids. "Oh, hey, Maison. You're still here." He glanced at the clock. "It's a little late to be working, don't you think?"

Maison shot him a smile. "We've still got a lot to do."

Hunter's mouth turned down in a frown. "Yeah, well. Doesn't hurt to take a break and get a bit of rest, right?" He shook his head. "Geez, Dad works you to the bone!"

Maison shrugged. "I don't mind it actually." She'd heard this a million times before, but she actually preferred the busy schedule of working late nights. At least here she had some company.

Hunter nodded. "Well, if you need to stay, just let me know."

"Thank you, but that won't be necessary." While she often stayed late at the Hewitt house, she *never* spent the night. "I'll be heading out soon."

"You could join our sleepover!" Owen chimed.

Maison grinned at the little guy. "Thank you for the invitation but won't it be better without a grown-up around?"

Owen grabbed Hunter's hand. "No, Daddy's going to be there and he's fun." When she grinned up at Hunter, he had this proud smile on his face.

"Well, maybe next time then," she promised him.

"Yay!"

"Okay, guys," Hunter said. "It's time for the actual *sleeping* part of the sleepover now."

Owen pouted. "Aw! Do we have to?"

"But we're in the middle of an epic fight!" one of his friends whined.

Hunter employed his brook-no-argument tone. "It's late, and we still have a big day tomorrow. You do still want to go to the movies, don't you?" All three boys nodded. "In that case, we need our rest so we can play hard tomorrow, okay?"

There was less grumbling this time and as the kids headed upstairs, Maison was left smiling to herself in the kitchen. "I'll see you later," Hunter said before he followed them upstairs.

No matter how much Hunter complained about the struggles of being a single father, Maison thought he was doing a pretty good job of raising Owen.

Speaking of jobs, she probably should get back to work . . .

After refilling both mugs with fresh brew, she returned to the dining room. Matthew looked relieved to see her again and accepted his cup with a thank-you. "So how are we doing?" she asked him.

Matthew shook his head. "Thought we'd have made more progress by now." He glanced down at the expensive watch on his wrist and rubbed his eye with a palm of his hand. "But it's late. You should go home and get some rest. I'll need you ready to work a full day again tomorrow." He turned back to his laptop. "In the meantime, I'll keep at it for a couple more hours."

"I don't mind staying longer." *God, what was she saying? Her boss was giving her permission to leave! Why wasn't she grabbing her things and running for the door?*

"Are you sure?" Even with the dim lighting in the room, she could make out the fine lines around the corner of Matthew's eyes. His face was pinched with frustration or worry—she wasn't sure which—and it made her feel a pang of sympathy. They were both exhausted with the day they'd had already, but it didn't feel right to leave him here swamped with their work.

"Yes, I'm sure. Do you need me to do anything specifically?"

Matthew seemed surprised by her decision, but he'd never say no to her help. "Actually, yes." He set his mug down and started shuffling through the many pages of documents and folders scattered across the table. "Might be the fatigue, but

I can't seem to find the papers on this account." He pointed at another piece of paper before him. "Have you seen them?" Maison frowned, glancing down at the mountain of paperwork in front of them. She'd gone through these files twice already today and didn't recall seeing those in the pile.

As she relayed that information, Matthew frowned and scratched his head. "Maybe I forgot it in my office then." *Damn. She was afraid of that.* She tried hiding her dread at having to return to the office this late in the evening when Matthew said, "Wait a minute. I think I may have a copy in my home office."

Oh good. "I'll go get it," she said before Matthew could get up.

"Are you sure?"

"Yeah, just let me know where it is."

"It's in the filing cabinet. The one beside—"

"Beside the desk." She shot him a grin. "Thanks. I think I've got it. Just sit tight while I go grab it."

Matthew's grin was magnificent. "What would I do without you?"

"Definitely not as much," she drawled as she turned for his office.

Since Maison had been in here many times before, she knew her way around pretty well. She'd be in and out quickly so she didn't bother with switching the lights on.

Thankfully, the large window behind the desk had its drapes pulled back, allowing the cool gleam of the moonlight to flow into the room. It made it easier to finger through the various folders in the filing cabinet. Maison frowned when she couldn't find what she was looking for.

What the hell? Where'd he put it?

She spotted another filing cabinet located on the other side of the desk. Had Matthew done some reorganizing around here and moved things over? Trying her luck, Maison quickly went around the desk to check. "Nope . . . Not it . . . Not it either . . . Where the hell is it?" she grumbled.

A low groan made her yelp. She spun around. "Who's there?" she whispered into the dark.

Her attention was so focused on finding the missing files that she hadn't realized she wasn't the only person in the room. A hot hand wrapped around her calf, scaring the crap out of her. "Could you stop making so much noise?"

Maison yelped in surprise and crashed against the front of the desk. How the hell had she not seen someone sprawled out on the chaise? She squinted in the darkness until a figure came into focus. "*Hutch?* What the hell are you doing here?"

Another groan was her answer. Her heart gave a little lurch at seeing him so hapless before her. She moved to him, intending to sit beside him but she tripped when her foot caught on something on the floor. As she was launched forward, she braced herself for impact. But instead of feeling pain with the crash landing, she found herself pressed up against a hard, warm body. "Whoa," she breathed. *What the hell?*

Hutch gripping her hard and she became intensely aware of where their bodies touched. Her heart started a rhythmic pounding in her chest. Rich, brown eyes gazed at her and she promptly lost her ability to breathe.

Wow. He had the most beautiful eyes she'd ever seen. A deep chocolate in color, she'd never seen anything so arresting. Maison felt her body tighten.

But it was also very clear that something was also wrong with him. "Hutch? Are you okay?" He didn't look like it. In fact, he probably looked the worst she'd ever seen him. "What happened to you?"

Instead of answering, he released her and settled back onto

the couch, throwing one big forearm over his eyes. Maison could only stare down at him in puzzlement.

It was then that she finally took in what she hadn't before. Hutch had ditched his shirt sometime during the night, and now, his muscled torso and thick arms were on full display. His hair was mussed up from sleep and his jaw sported some sexy scruff that told her that he hadn't shaved for days. He was by far the most disheveled thing in this ornate office, but Maison still couldn't take her eyes off of him.

Lowering to her knees, she reached out to gently touch his forehead. He didn't look sick but he was a little sweaty and warm. There was no question that he was drunk. "What have you done to yourself?" she murmured as she slicked his hair back from his face and proceeded to check him over. That was when she realized that his lower leg was missing. "Where's your prosthesis?"

When another groan was her response, she rose to her feet and searched the room. She'd been so caught up by his proximity that it'd taken her a while to see what was wrong with him. Now she wondered what had happened to him that made him drink himself into a stupor.

She'd only just begun to search for his prosthesis when Hutch reached out and grabbed a hold of her arm, pulling her until she was lying on top of him. "Hey, what the hell are you doing?" She pushed against his chest but his hold on her only tightened. "Let me go!"

Momentary alarm kicked in, but then so did something else. Arousal hit her like a freight train when the sultry scent of his skin filled her nostrils. He smelled of something calming and uplifting, accompanied by fresh soap.

She stiffened when he returned the gesture and dipped his head and sniffed her. His murmured words of "You smell good, you know" nearly undid her.

"What?" Maison glanced down at him to find that his eyes were shut.

She tried pushing off him again, but he wasn't going to let her go. *Did he really think she smelled good?* God, why did she even care what he thought? It wasn't like he'd ever go for a woman like her.

Hutch Happa-Hewitt was a renowned rebel. A bad boy and a ladies' man for sure. And yet in all the years that she'd known the guy, Hutch had always been a perfect gentleman to her. She knew it was because she wasn't as pretty as all the other women he'd dated. Hell, Hutch had probably never looked twice at her. But she enjoyed imagining what it would be like pressed up against his hard body and have him look down at her with those dark, mysterious eyes.

Maison shook her head. She needed to kick that daydream to the curb. It was never going to happen. Not in this lifetime. *Not ever.*

She pushed hard at him but Hutch only gripped her tighter. "Let me go find your leg."

"No, stay with me."

Her eyes flew wide when his hand glided up her arms. Immediately, goose bumps sprouted all over her skin. Then, Hutch then drew his hands down, running them down her arms again. Maison stiffened. *What the hell was he doing? Did Hutch think she was someone else?*

He had to be. That was why he was acting so strangely and probably why he'd gotten himself drunk. Had something happen to him with one of his lovers?

Annoyance sprouted at that thought and she tried pushing off him. Her efforts only tangled them together further and their breaths mingled.

Over her shoulder, she caught sight of an empty bottle of whiskey at the other end of the chaise. *Oh God, had he drunk all of that himself?*

She forced herself to look down at him. "Hutch, it's me. Maison. I'm not . . ." Her words sounded pathetic to her own ears. "I'm not whoever you think I am." Not his girlfriend or whatever.

She had no idea why she was suddenly in a bad mood. She didn't want to acknowledge that she was jealous because that would mean that she actually thought she had a shot with him.

"Hutch, I'm going to get help, okay?" He was clearly out of it and she wouldn't be able to help him alone.

His hands tightened around her and Maison felt her anxieties return in a rush. "No," he growled. "Don't leave me."

Oh God, he now had his arms around her hips! Could he feel how big she was? Could he feel how much extra weight she was carrying there? Mortification filled her but overriding that was her concern for him.

"What happened to you?" she asked.

When he refused to answer, Maison pursed her lips together. What else could she do to help him? She had no experience with this kind of stuff. In college, she had totally avoided parties and hardly ever drank. "Let me call your brother," she said. Hunter would know what to do.

"No! Don't call him. I just want you." *Me?* she thought. What the hell would he want with her? His voice sounded so fragile and broken that she refused to argue anymore with him.

"Okay, fine. I won't."

"Thank you." Hutch seemed to relax a little bit. He even burrowed his head into her hair and let out a sigh. Maison froze as his mouth brushed her neck.

Oh my God! Did he just kiss her?

No, no, he hadn't. He was just really close. But she now felt like her entire neck was on fire. *What would it be like to be kissed by Hutch Happa-Hewitt?*

Since the first moment she'd set eyes on Hutch, she'd been enamored by his beauty, but Maison knew better than to believe that he'd have an interest in her. It still hadn't stopped her from fantasizing about him.

She'd be so helpless to him. There would be no denying entry; she knew she'd melt for him the first moment he'd touch her. Hell, even now just being in his arms was turning her into a pile of goo.

If only he knew just how desperate she was for it. She wouldn't stop him if he wanted to lay her out on this chaise and have his wicked way with her. God, even just thinking about it made her want to sigh! How much more titillating would it be knowing his father was just a few rooms down, waiting for her?

"You feel amazing," Hutch groaned.

"Really?" She couldn't hide her shock. No man had ever said that to her. She didn't have the type of figure that men usually found attractive.

Maison looked down at herself. Her big boobs were squished against his chest and her eyes went wide with fear. *Oh God! Was she crushing him?* She'd gained a few pounds recently. She doubted she felt light on top of him!

"Stay," he said again when she tried to push off him. "Please." Rich, brown eyes drowned her.

"No, I can't do this! I'm heavy! I'm going to crush you!"

"You're not heavy, Maison."

She stiffened. *Wait. So he knew it was her!* Why then was he holding her like they were lovers, like someone he was comfortable with?

"Why won't you tell me what's wrong?" she pleaded. "At

least tell me what you're thinking."

His laugh surprised her. It was airy and light, and so different than his previous darker moods. "I think you can guess what I'm thinking."

Maison searched his face, noticing the dark glint in his eyes. Her body buzzed with electricity, shooting through her entire body. *Oh my God! Did he mean—*

She let out a nervous laugh.

Okay, this was *so* not what she was expecting. Whatever expression she had on her face had Hutch chuckling and her body responded to his deep laughter. "Okay, that's enough." She pushed off him but she accidentally grazed her hand over the hard ridge of his arousal. "Oh my God!" she squeaked as she pulled her hand back.

Hutch chuckled again.

"Stop doing that!" she snapped.

"Doing what?"

"Stop laughing. It . . . It's . . . distracting." It was turning her on, that was what.

Maison straightened. "Okay, time to get out of here. I'll help you up to bed."

"You don't want to stay with me?"

The truth was, she did. She was currently scared out of her mind, but she was also pretty sure Hutch was flirting with her. But then she remembered that he was also really, really drunk. Maybe he had no idea what the hell he was doing after all.

"You'll get over it once you're in your own bed." Ignoring his pout, Maison helped him up into a sitting position. It turned out to be a little more difficult than she expected, but once he was upright, Hutch couldn't stop staring at her.

"Why are you looking at me like that?" He'd never looked at her like that before.

He pointed at his crotch and the bulge beneath his jeans. "That's for you, you know."

Maison felt her cheeks flush from embarrassment. *Liar.* She hated liars. And now she hated Hutch for playing with her.

Even inebriated his flirting was lethal. She really hoped he forgot this conversation in the morning.

"Stop it, you're drunk." And she didn't appreciate how he was toying with her.

"Sorry," he mumbled.

Still, Maison couldn't bear to leave him here alone so she helped him put his leg back on in awkward silence. Once she had him standing, she slung one arm over her shoulder.

His father walked into the office. "What the hell is taking so long?" Matthew came to a stop as he caught sight of them. "Jesus Christ, what the hell happened to him?"

"He's drunk."

"No, I'm not," Hutch protested.

Her boss's gaze cut from his son to the empty bottle of whiskey behind them. "Did you drink all that?"

Hutch hiccupped. "No."

"But you came into my office to drink what was left, right?"

Hutch rolled his eyes. "Relax. I'll buy you another bottle." Despite her protests, he pushed off her and headed for the door by himself.

"Hutch, wait!" Maison called out.

But he only paused briefly by the door. "I'll be fine," he said, his voice softening only for her. A lank piece of dark hair fell into his eyes before he pushed it away. "Thank you for staying with me."

And with those words, he was gone.

THREE

Hutch Happa-Hewitt woke feeling like twin horns were sprouting from his temples, and he wasn't exactly in an angelic mood either as he attempted to get up and realized that he was no longer in his father's office anymore. *What the hell? How did he get here?*

When the events of last night finally came back to him, he cursed. What the hell had he done? He clutched his pounding head as he thought of poor Maison. He'd acted like a complete lunatic with her! His father's assistant would no doubt be terrified of him now that he'd been all over her.

Last night clearly hadn't been one of his best nights. Actually, he'd been in a crappy mood a lot lately since he learned that there was no possibility that he would be able to rejoin the Army, but last night had been particularly rough for him.

Because he was more than a little drunk, he'd acted without really thinking. Now, he was regretting his behavior. Not only had he likely frightened Maison, but he'd probably confused her as well. He knew he'd said some things to her that he'd never said before. What did she think of him now? Was his behavior bad enough to change her opinion of him?

Shit. He really shouldn't have touched her. He'd hate it if she suddenly avoided him.

Not that she seemed particularly fond of him to begin with. Every time he complimented her, she seemed to think he was lying to her. Why? He'd complimented many women before, but none of them ever look at him like she couldn't believe his words.

Hutch recalled his father and the words they'd exchanged. Ever since he'd come to live here with his father, their relationship had been strained. No matter how much time they spent together, they could never get along. Hutch felt like a prisoner in his own home where his every action was questioned and he was constantly being watched by his father or brother.

It also didn't help that he'd disappeared for a few days without telling anyone about his whereabouts so his family seemed to be watching him more intently now, possibly anticipating that he would try to leave them again. But where would he go?

The only place he wanted to be was back in the Army, but that was never going to happen now after he'd lost his leg.

Hutch pushed himself up until he was sitting. His body ached with every movement and his head felt like a sonic blast every time he tried to move.

He needed coffee. *Stat.*

He reached for his prosthetic leg, thankful that it wasn't located halfway across the room this time. As he started the long process of putting it back on, he did his best to bite back the frustration. No use in bitching about what he couldn't change. This was his life now. He just had to accept it.

Still, a curse sat on the tip of his tongue as he started with the thick neoprene liner. He hated wearing the damn thing. It made him feel hot and sweaty and it often caused sores if he had it on for long periods of time. But again, it was a necessary nuisance if he wanted to walk around.

After covering his leg with that, he popped on his prosthesis. Then, he slid on the long, elastic sleeve that extended up to his thigh before putting his pants on. After that, the rest of his clothes went on easier. He moved for the door.

The stairs were a workout for his calves. He was breathing

hard by the time he got into the kitchen and froze when he realized that he wasn't the only one running late this morning. "What are you doing here?" he asked his father.

Matthew shot him a glare over his coffee cup. "I live here," he said simply. Okay, yeah. He knew that. Maybe that was a stupid question to ask. But at least now Hutch knew that his father was still pissed at him. "Sit down," Matthew ordered.

"Wait, I need some coffee first." If he was going to get a tongue lashing, he wanted to be prepared first. "Last night nearly killed me."

"That's exactly what I want to talk to you about."

Uh oh. Here we go. "Look, last night was just—"

"You need to get a job," Matthew interrupted.

"A job?" What the hell? Of all the things he expected his father to say, he wasn't expecting *that.* "Why?" he asked. He wasn't exactly broke. In the Army, he'd been making good coin and he hadn't really had time to spend any of it since coming to Moonrise Beach.

"To give you something to do," his father answered. "You can't just stay at home and mope around."

"Mope around? I'm not moping." *Okay, maybe last night he'd been but—*

"Here's what I propose," Matthew announced as if he were in a business meeting. "Since I think having a job is so import-ant, I'll let you move out if you get one."

Hutch blinked at his father. What the—"Really?" He'd let him leave? That was what he wanted from the very first mo-ment his brother had dragged him here in the first place.

Matthew nodded. "Yes. But you need a job first."

"Okay, fine." *Get a job. How hard could that be?*

"But I don't want you to work at any old place," his father said. "I want you to come to work at Gleam with me."

"*What?*" Hutch was already shaking his head. "No. *No way*." There was no way he was going to work for his father! As the CEO of Gleam Enterprises, it would be so easy for his father to get him a good position. But Hutch didn't want that *or* the attention he'd get if he started working there. He had enough on his plate to deal with already. "Why can't I find my own place to work at?"

Matthew shook his head. "That's the deal. If you work at Gleam then you can live wherever you want."

He shook his head. "It doesn't really sound like a good deal to me." Either way, his father would be breathing down his neck!

"Sorry, but I have to keep an eye on you somehow."

"Dad, I'm fine. I'm just—"

"We both know you're not fine. You're heartbroken and still adjusting to civilian life. It's not an abnormal thing to experience that after everything you've—"

"Stop. I know exactly what I've been through." He saw it every night in his dreams and didn't need a reminder. "But I can find my own job, thank you very much."

Matthew shrugged and turned away. "Guess you'll be living here for a while longer then."

"Dad!"

He turned back around. "Sorry, but those are my conditions."

"I can't believe you're forcing me to stay here like I'm some troubled teenager! I'm an adult, you know."

"And I'm your father," Matthew shot back. "And I still worry about you. After you didn't tell us about your accident, there's no way I'm letting you out of my sight until I know you're okay."

"I told you, I'm fine," he gritted.

"Then prove it."

Hutch stared at his father. Why the hell wouldn't he drop this? Things would be so much easier if he'd just left him alone. But Matthew stared right back at him. Hutch could feel the tension between them rising, but neither one of them said anything more.

His father wasn't giving him very many options. There was already no privacy around this house. If he was going to stay in Moonrise Beach, he'd want his own place. If he agreed to his father's terms and worked at Gleam, that would mean he'd only be spending eight hours with him instead of every minute of his freaking life. Maybe that wouldn't be so bad after all.

"I'll think about it," he said as he took a sip of his coffee. He wasn't stupid. He knew that he'd have to get on with his life. He'd already spent enough time "moping around" as his father had called it. So maybe it was time to try and return to the land of the living and stop acting like he was dead already.

Matthew nodded and smiled. "Good. It's about time you start living your life again."

* * *

Hutch felt much better after he took some pills to help ease his headache. By the time he was pulling up in his best friend's driveway, he could actually smile without it physically paining him.

"What the hell?" he muttered as he caught sight of Sam in her front yard. "What the hell is she doing?" Cutting off the engine, he quickly rounded his car and pulled out his cell phone. *Click click.*

He'd managed to snap two photos of her before Sam whirled around. "What the hell are you doing?" she snapped.

"I think I should be the one asking you that question." He peered over her shoulder and grinned. "Are you planting flowers?"

"So what if I am?" Her chin jutted out in defiance.

Hutch grinned wider and he glanced back down at his phone. "I'm putting this shit on Facebook."

"No! Don't!"

But it was already too late. Now all their friends would be seeing tough girl Sam Cosi planting petunias in her garden. After pocketing his phone again, he asked, "Want to tell me why you're planting petunias?"

"They're not petunias, you idiot. They're peonies."

"Whatever." His knowledge of flowers was restricted only to petunias and roses. "Still doesn't answer why you're doing it."

Sam sighed. "I'm doing it for my neighbors."

"Your neighbors?" That didn't make any sense.

"Yeah. I'm trying to make my place look a little more like everyone else's." Hutch craned his head down the street and realized that the other houses did indeed have full bushes of colorful flowers.

He shook his head. "I still don't see why it's necessary."

Sam sighed. "Unlike some people I know, I'm trying to fit in and make friends." *Make friends? Since when did Sam Cosi care about making friends?* "Stop looking at me like that and help me dig a hole for this tree," she snapped.

Hutch laughed. "All right, all right, I'll help you," he said before she could take a crack at him again. "But if you think for one moment that you're actually capable of making friends, you're delusional."

Sam punched him. *Hard.* But she had a smile in place for him as he took the shovel from her. "Right here?" he asked right before he started digging.

"Yup. Let me bring over the tree." Sam gripped the base and let out a grunt, carrying it over to him. If it was any other woman, Hutch would've offered a hand but he knew Sam was more than capable of doing it herself. Plus, since it was still a sapling, he knew it wasn't that heavy.

His best friend was six feet tall and had an athletic build. In addition to that, Sam also had a few tattoos that often intimidated a lot of other women, especially the housewife variety. That was why he thought it was hilarious that she'd chose to live here where all her female neighbors were housewives. If she wanted to fit in more, Sam should've lived closer to a biker club.

But Sam's dreams had apparently changed after she'd tried to get into the Army. In the beginning, she'd been the whole reason why he'd joined the Army in the first place. It'd been her dream initially and after she kept talking about it so much, it began to interest him as well.

However, things hadn't gone down the way they'd planned. They'd both known that the standards were high and that there was no leniency made for women, but it was still a hard pill to swallow when he learned that Sam wouldn't be by his side.

Her departure had nearly killed him, and while he hated not having her by his side, he knew she would hate him more if he threw away the opportunity because of her.

Now that they were both out, however, it seemed like he was the only one suffering. After he'd been discharged, he'd come to stay with her instead of going home to his family. Somehow he knew seeing Sam would be easier than explaining what had happened to his family. Plus, he'd been such an emotional wreck that the last thing he wanted was to get into another argument with his father.

Sam was the same. Her own family hadn't approved of her

decision to join the Army. They'd actually been ecstatic that she hadn't made it in and that had only caused more hurt for Sam. Because of that, she lived alone instead of living closer to her family.

So whenever Sam was having one of her rough times, Hutch always made sure that he was available for her to cry on. She'd been a pillar of support for him every time he felt down that he considered her as one of the most important people in his life.

Sam was the only one who understood his fucked-up desire to return to war and that was why he valued her friendship above all others. They simply understood each other on a level that no one else did.

Hutch stepped back from the hole he'd dug. "Okay, how does that look?"

Sam peered down the hole. "I guess that will work. My neighbor, Amara, was actually the one that gave me this tree. We've been talking about gardening a lot lately."

"Gardening? I never knew you were interested in that kind of stuff."

"Yeah, I've gotten really into it recently."

"Well, it's nice that you've got a new hobby." Maybe it was time he found something he enjoyed as much.

"I'm going to pop this in there." As Sam worked on loosening the tree from its pot, Hutch went inside to grab something to drink. It was hot today and all that shoveling had made him thirsty. As he grabbed a beer from the fridge, a picture stuck on its door caught his attention. It was an old one of him and Sam together, long before they had enlisted and he'd lost his leg. He looked so lanky next to her, and Hutch frowned at how much he had changed.

It was depressing to think that he'd never be able to turn

back time and go back to that point in his life where he'd been happy. Things were just too fucked up now and he honestly had no idea how he was going to find some semblance of happiness as a civilian.

But he didn't really have much of a choice. His options were taken away from him once the explosion had occurred, and now, he'd have to find something of his own to get him through.

Hutch meant to turn around to go back outside when pain sliced up his leg. Damn, he hated when that happened, but it couldn't be helped. No matter how much time passed since the accident, his pain would always be with him.

Teeth gritted, Hutch set his beer down and found the nearest chair. After planting his ass on it, he bent over to check his leg.

His father's words came back to him.

You can come work at Gleam with me.

God, was he really going to consider his father's offer? At first he'd just said the words to get his father off his back, but now after seeing Sam, he felt like he needed to find something of his own that he was passionate about. If she was able to get over her grief of not making it into the Army, then he should too.

He knew he had limited options. A combination of PTSD and a dark desire to get back in the field made him unstable. Finding any old job might be difficult for him. For years, he'd considered himself a soldier. He'd need a little more time to get used to life here as a civilian.

Sam walked into the kitchen. "You're done already?" he asked. That was quick.

Sam snorted and grabbed a beer from the fridge. "No way, are you kidding me? It's too hot to be outside right now." As he laughed, Sam chuckled along with him. But then her expression sobered as she saw him rubbing his leg. "Are you okay?"

"I'm fine. Just feeling a little bit uncomfortable."

Sam nodded in understanding but didn't fuss over him. He was thankful for that. The last thing he needed was her nagging him also. Hutch sighed loudly. "My dad wants me to work for him." As soon as he said it, Sam choked on her beer, sending spittle everywhere. "Hey!" he cried, moving out of range.

"Sorry," she said as laughter consumed her. "But that's crazy talk!"

"I know." Sam was already well aware of how badly he and his family got along. He wasn't even sure why his father had suggested it in the first place. Did he really want him bothering him at work?

"So why does he want you to work for him?" Sam asked.

"He says it'll give me something to do."

"Ah. He still thinks you're just bumming around and feeling sorry for yourself, huh?"

"Yeah. I mean, I only lost half of my leg, right?"

Sam smirked and settled down beside him. "Hey, you never know. It might actually be a good idea. I'm serious!" she said when he narrowed his eyes at her. "A job is a good thing! It takes your mind off things and gives you a sense of purpose."

"Were you this enthusiastic when you started your PI business?" he asked.

"No. Definitely not. But now that I have my own business, I can say that it is worth it."

"But it wasn't what you really wanted." How could she be okay with that?

"No," she admitted. "It wasn't my first choice. I still wish I was good enough for the Army but being your own boss isn't bad either."

Hutch shook his head. "Except I won't be the boss. My dad is."

"Oh, stop it. How hard is it to wear a suit all day?"

"I don't know. I don't wear suits." They were hot and stuffy and not his style at all. "But he said if I worked for him, I could move out."

"Hutch, you can move out anytime. Your father is just worried about you, that's all. He wants to keep an eye on you."

"That's what everyone's been telling me." But he couldn't help but feel caged in.

"So, are you going to do it?" Sam finally asked.

"We'll see." He wasn't sold on the idea yet, but like Sam said, it might actually be a good idea. Who knows, it might actually be the first step in trying to acclimate here. "Come on." He rose to his feet and polished off the rest of his beer, shelving the conversation for the moment. "Let's go finish planting that fucking tree."

FOUR

M AISON HAD ALREADY BEEN AT THE OFFICE working for nearly forty minutes. It wasn't out of the ordinary for her to be in early before everyone else. Sometimes, she just liked being able to enjoy her mornings and hang around the office before her colleagues started pouring in. It gave her the chance to set up her week in her planner. Ever since Dacey's boyfriend, Greyson, had given her one for her birthday, she'd been decorating it weekly with stickers and other cute stuff. Not only did it work in keeping herself and Matthew organized, but it also allowed her to be a little more creative in her daily life. She was just filling out her week with a pen when her phone rang. She answered it immediately. "Maison Lane speaking . . ."

Matthew's smooth voice carried over the line. "Maison."

"Oh, Mr. Hewitt. I didn't know you were already in." What was happening that required Matthew to be in so early? She checked her planner again. She hadn't marked anything important down.

"Do you mind stepping into the office for a moment, please?" Matthew asked.

"Sure." Brows pinched together, Maison tried to not look confused as she knocked on the door and let herself in. She really hoped that she hadn't forgotten something important today.

As per usual, her boss sat behind his desk, wearing a crisp, white shirt. It looked impeccable, all pressed and pristine compared to her own blouse she wore now. Matthew's light hair was combed back away from his face, bringing attention to his angular facial features and high cheekbones. In the last few years, his hair had turned gray at the temples, but instead of looking old or haggard, the gray only added to Matthew Hewitt's distinguished looks.

Matthew smiled at her. "Have a seat, Maison."

Her confusion was swiftly replaced by shock. "Oh," she breathed. "I didn't realize you were here too."

On the other side of the desk, Matthew gave a little chuckle.

Hutch rose to his full height and shot her a grin. As if trained by his actions, the butterflies in her stomach took flight as she remembered the events of the other night. "G-good morning."

"Good morning." Hutch was dressed up in a pair of navy slacks and a light-blue shirt that complemented his tanned arms nicely. The sleeves were rolled up, giving him that effortless, casual feel that was still very much work appropriate. That silky voice, whispered low, sent a shiver through her body and goose bumps sprouted along her arms, just like it had the night he'd pulled her into his arms and ran his hands over her.

What the hell was he doing here? And why was he smiling at her like that?

"Um." She glanced back at Matthew.

"Please sit down," Matthew instructed. As they both sat, Maison tried hard not to flush. The events of the other night were still fresh in her mind. Was that why Hutch was here?

"What's going on?" she finally asked.

"Hutch is going to be working with us."

Maison couldn't contain her shock. *"What?"* She blushed fiercely as she realized she'd said it out loud. *But how could that be? Hutch didn't even have any interest in working at Gleam before! Why now?*

She glanced at Hutch, shooting him an apologetic smile when she realized that he was staring at her. "I mean, that's great."

But it wasn't great. If Hutch was going to be working here, she'd never get anything done! She'd be walking around nervously, acting like a scared little rabbit, especially now that she was taking extra precautions to avoid him after the other day.

"He's going to need a little bit of your guidance as he gets acquainted with how we do things here," Matthew said. "Since this is his first office job, I'd really appreciate it if you can take him under your wing. Maybe he can even help us with our latest work."

Maison nodded slowly. "Ookayyy." Inside, however, she was reeling. *Dammit, why didn't Matthew tell her about this beforehand?*

Matthew addressed his son. "You're going to work under Maison as her assistant."

"*What?*" Maison exploded.

"I am?" Hutch arched a dark brow and then cut a glance at her. He looked just as surprised as she was. "Are you sure you want to do that?" Hutch asked his father.

"Yes. Of course. Maison is my most competent employee. She'll know how to handle you." Matthew turned to her. "Isn't that right, Maison?"

The blow had still to wear off but Maison did her best to recover. "Uh. Yes, sir."

Hutch shrugged. "I just figured that when I agreed to this that you'd start low and give me a filing job."

"No, of course not. You're my son. People would talk."

Hutch looked conflicted but then he nodded. "Okay then. As long as Maison is fine with it, then I'll do it." He glanced at her and Maison felt herself flare with heat. *Oh God! What was she going to do?*

Maison forced herself to swallow back her anxiety and nod. "Sure. I'll get him settled."

"Good. Thank you. Now if you'll excuse me, I have some other work to do."

Maison didn't wait for Hutch as she made a beeline for the doors. The office suddenly felt too small and she was having a difficult time with breathing.

As soon as she was out, she breathed in deep but the huge gulps of air weren't working in calming her down. She still couldn't believe that Hutch was going to be working at Gleam! *As her assistant!* What the hell was she going to do?

Why had Hutch agreed to work here anyway? He didn't seem like a suit and tie kind of guy. Was this because of what had happened the other night? Was he trying to torture her some more?

He seemed to enjoy seeing her squirm for him. Maybe he got a kick out of seeing her redden with embarrassment and see her stutter over her words whenever she spoke to him.

But if Hutch wanted to work here, he would have to actually *work*. She wasn't about to jeopardize her own job just to babysit him.

A second later, he was by her side and she stiffened. "So," he drawled, a wolfish smile playing across his lips. "What do you want me to do first, *boss?*"

Maison had given him a quick tour of the building, dumping him with a pile of paperwork before returning to her own desk. When she'd asked him to start inputting the numbers in a spreadsheet for her, he'd gotten straight to work. And for the first hour or so, he was doing well. But now his focus was slipping and he was getting bored. Was this all they did here? Although he wasn't expecting a party when he arrived, he thought that Maison would at least give him some more guidance on his first day. However, it seemed that she wanted to stay away from him as much as possible. Was it because she was upset with him because of the other night? Maybe he should apologize to her.

He turned over to see what she was doing. As expected, she was at her desk, busily typing away at her computer. He called out her name and she looked up at him but didn't stop her typing. "Are you done already?" she asked.

"Ah, no. I'm just taking a break." Man, he felt lame saying that when it was only his first day here. And by the way Maison was moving a mile a minute, he knew she had to be busy. Now he felt like an ass for bothering her.

Maison glanced at the clock. "You've only been working for twenty minutes."

Damn, really? How was that possible? He was sure half the day had gone by already. At this rate, he'd gouge his eyes out before the day was over!

At least they'd given him his own workspace and computer. Maybe he could check his email and send a greeting to Sam. Not that she would respond anyway, but he was getting desperate here. His eyes were already dried up from staring at the screen and his ass was going numb in this chair. He threw his arms up, letting out a long groan as he stretched his back.

Maison's eyes lifted to meet his and he couldn't help but wink at her. In response, she rolled her eyes. Yeah, she was definitely annoyed by him. "So what exactly are these numbers that I'm putting in here?" he asked.

"That's our expenses report."

"Oh, okay. Don't you guys have a department that is

supposed to be doing this kind of stuff?"

"We do, but I like to do it myself just to make sure nothing goes wrong."

"So why am I doing it?" he retorted.

Maison's mouth opened, but no words came out. He let out a chuckle as her face reddened. "It's because I didn't know you were coming in today."

He frowned. "Are you mad at me?" It was so like his father to forget to tell Maison about him coming.

His question seemed to catch her off guard because she stopped her typing and looked at him. "N-no."

"No? You sound unsure."

"No. I'm not mad at you. I'm just—"

"Look, I'm sorry about how I acted the other night. I wasn't myself. I apologize if I made you uncomfortable." Her face reddened even further and he realized it was because many of their other colleagues could overhear them. "Sorry," he added.

"It's okay. Nothing happened."

No, technically nothing had, but he did remember how she'd felt in his arms. How warm she'd been pressed up against his body. And he also remembered his own body's reaction to hers. He still couldn't believe he'd gotten a hard-on!

His smile widened. "Well, since I'm here now, feel free to dump the work you don't like to do on me."

But Maison didn't return his smile like he expected. "Actually, I like to do things myself," she said. "That way I know things get done right the first time."

Ouch. Okay, so she didn't have much faith in him. That wasn't so surprising since he was more accustomed to being on a battlefield than behind a desk, but he was determined to prove himself to her even though he still wasn't sure why.

With a smile, Hutch turned back to his computer and began to work.

Maison cursed her earlier words. What the hell was wrong with her? Why had she said those mean things to him? She knew Hutch was just trying to make conversation but she had to go and assume that he'd do everything wrong. She just wasn't good under pressure! While she usually exceled at her job, having him around was making her fumble around like a fool.

She had to be better at keeping her gaze firmly on the screen before her and not on him. If she did happen to glance up at him, she'd get wrapped up under his spell and forget all about her responsibilities. But she couldn't afford to be more behind on her work than she already was.

It was nearing midday, and so far, Hutch hadn't said another word to her. She worried for a moment that he was mad at her. Had she hurt his feelings when she'd said those words to him? Maison made the mistake of glancing up at him.

Damn, he was beautiful. With his dark hair and that strong jaw, there was no doubt that her female colleagues would notice him. As a matter of fact, a few of them were already fawning over him in the corner.

Hutch didn't seem to notice though. He was silently staring at his computer screen, looking to be hard at work. His brows were slightly knitted, and he was leaning his head on one of his hands. He was also biting down on his lower lip in this way that made her think of sex. His words from the other night came back to her. *You smell good.*

God, what the hell was wrong with her? She had to stop thinking about that night! When Hutch had brought it up earlier, she'd flushed so red that she was sure she looked like a tomato. What was it about this guy that made her stomach feel like they were on a merry-go-round going at a warped speed?

At the thought of her stomach, Maison realized that it was time for lunch. Maybe taking a break would get her mind off of him too. Saving the document she'd been working on, she hit Print and made her way over to the printer.

It was then that she realized that she'd totally forgotten to tell Hutch that he could go for lunch any time he wanted. Intending to do so, she turned to him and promptly felt her jaw drop. "Are you—*Are you playing solitaire?*"

Hutch craned his head up to look at her. "Huh? Oh yeah, check out what level I'm on!"

"Hutch!" Had he been playing all this time?

"I know. I'm awesome, right?" His grin was so dazzling it almost made her forget about her anger. *Almost.*

"What about my expense report?" she exclaimed. "I need that done by the end of the day! You're supposed to be helping me! Not be playing a stupid computer game!" If he didn't have it done by the end of the day, she'd have to work through her lunch break to get it done now. This was why she never let others help her with her work. They always slacked off, or never did things right and then she'd have to redo everything herself!

"Maison, relax, okay?" Hutch said calmly.

Relax? How could she relax with him around? It was bad enough that she kept tripping over her words around him.

"Look." Hutch shoved some papers into her face. "I'm actually done with the report." She smacked it away from her, unable to believe that he managed to finish a report in a couple of hours. "Seriously." He shook the pages in front of her face. "I'm done. Take a look at it."

Maison glanced down at the papers. "What the—"

At first glance, it all looked right, but surely there were errors riddled all over the place. Snatching the papers from him, she returned to her desk to check it against her own records, just to make sure that her eyes were working correctly.

"So what do you think?" Hutch prompted when she remained silent.

"Oh my God." *She couldn't believe it!* Everything looked exactly as it was supposed to! He'd even formatted it so that it looked nice and presentable.

Hutch shot her a cocky grin that took her breath away. "Looks good, huh?"

"Um, yeah." She nodded, impressed. "It actually does. How did you do it so fast?"

"I've always been pretty efficient, so I can usually get a lot of things done." So he was a quick worker, huh? Guess that wasn't surprising, really. He'd no doubt have to have good reflexes with his previous job.

Maison felt herself flush. "I guess I owe you an apology. I shouldn't have assumed that you'd do a bad job."

Hutch shrugged. "No worries."

But she still felt terrible now for assuming the worst. "It's just that every time I rely on someone else to do something for me, they always mess things up even more and I end up spending more time fixing their mistakes when I should've just done it myself."

"That's all right. It's our first day working together so how would you know?" He was being nice to her. Why was he being nice to her when she'd been such a bitch to him all day? Hutch rested a hand on her shoulder, and to her surprise, the simple touch was enough to get her blood popping and fizzing like a can of soda.

Just like that, she recalled the other night. While Hutch looked different, he still smelled the same. Like mint and eucalyptus. He wasn't nearly as disheveled as he'd been the other day and now he actually looked like a much younger version of his father, just with darker hair and eyes.

"Thanks. I promise not to be so harsh next time. Since you're all done, why don't you go for lunch?"

Hutch clapped his hands together. "Great. Do you want to have lunch with me?"

Maison blinked. Hutch wanted to have lunch with *her?* Her first reaction was to say no. There was no way she could eat in front of him. Even talking to him made her feel strangely nervous since the other night. But wouldn't his father expect her to? Especially since it was his first day?

"I-I don't know," she whispered. If she did, people would talk and she didn't want any more scrutiny from others. She was sure Hutch could handle himself. "I'm sorry, but I can't go with you."

Hutch frowned. "How come? You're not still mad at me, are you?"

"I told you already, I'm not mad at you. I'm just on a diet." The words sounded pathetic even to her own ears. Oh God. Now that she'd mentioned that, he was probably thinking about her weight and how heavy she must've been when she'd lain on top of him the other night.

But all Hutch said was, "Why do you need to go on a diet? You have a perfect figure."

Maison shook her head. He was just saying that to make her feel better. "I'm fat."

"*Fat?* Sweetheart, you're not fat at all." The wink he shot her had her blushing. "Come on, come eat with me."

"I can't. Maybe next time." Or maybe never. She felt too self-conscious around him already and she'd feel even more anxious eating around him.

Hutch's face fell. "All right then. But if you change your

mind, I'll be at the taco place down the road, okay?"

Maison nodded and forced a smile. "Okay. Enjoy your lunch."

"See you in a bit."

She let out a long breath as he started to walk away. She was insane for turning him down. And she was an even greater fool because she couldn't stop herself from checking his ass out in his slacks.

"God, you're an idiot," she muttered to herself, wishing she had more to look forward to than a spinach salad.

FIVE

AFTER RETURNING FROM LUNCH, HUTCH WENT OVER to Maison's desk, not at all surprised to see her munching on some rabbit food. He really wished she'd taken him up on his offer to have lunch with him.

"Did you enjoy your lunch?" he asked her. He'd timed asking the question so she had just shoved a mouthful of spinach into her mouth and couldn't answer. "Here, have this." He shoved the extra taco he'd bought into her face.

"Wha—" Maison swallowed. "Hutch, I can't have this! I'm on a diet, remember?"

Fuck, she was cute. And she was also delusional if she thought she needed to be on a stupid diet. "And I told you that you don't need to be on one."

As he expected, Maison started shaking her head. "No, I can't. I need to stay on track."

He shrugged. "Fine. Suit yourself." Maybe he could convince her to share it with him later for a snack. "So, what else do you need me to do?"

Maison looked around her desk and Hutch did his best to bite back a smile. "Sorry, I'm a little bit disorganized. I wasn't expecting you to be here today."

"No need to apologize. I'm here to help you, remember?"

She seemed to flush at the reminder. Man, he would never get tired of seeing her blush. "I have some paperwork you can help me with. Do you think you're up for that?"

"Sure. Bring it on."

"I'll email it to you."

"Good." At least now she trusted him with some of her work. It was a good thing too. She was always working; it'd be nice if he could get her to relax a little.

Hutch returned to his desk and waited for the email to appear in his inbox. He had to admit, he thought it'd been cute when she'd gone off on him earlier. The Maison he knew all his life was sweet as honey and usually really shy, but he was quickly learning that she could sting like a bee if you pissed her off. She took her job seriously and had obviously gained a good reputation here at Gleam. It wasn't a surprise to know that everyone liked her.

A ping sounded and Hutch checked his inbox. He had no idea why but he liked seeing her name on his screen and he smiled a secret smile before opening her email.

She'd outline exactly what she wanted from him. Not surprisingly, the email was highly detailed and very specific. She'd even given him step-by-step instructions on what to do so he'd have no problem downloading the attachments and getting started immediately.

Just as he was about to do that, his concentration was disturbed when one of the parcel carriers arrived with a package. The man walked up to Maison, shooting her a smile that immediately put him on guard.

From past experiences, Hutch could tell when another man was interested in a woman and this guy clearly had a thing for sweetness because he was smiling at Maison like she was a princess. Maison greeted him with a smile. "Hey, Conrad."

"Hey, sweetheart. Got another one for you." He handed her the package.

Sweetheart? How well did this guy know her to call her sweetheart? Hutch had known her for a long time but had never addressed her with anything other than her name.

Maison flashed him another smile, looking sweeter than a glazed donut. She quickly signed the form and handed it back to him, taking the package with her.

"Thanks." As Maison rose from her chair and turned to put the package on a nearby table behind her, Hutch couldn't help but notice how Conrad's eyes landed on her ass. He immediately straightened but then caught himself. *What the hell was he doing? Was he jealous?*

When the guy's eyes met his, Hutch forced himself to smile back. However, it came out strained, looking more like Jack Nicholson in The Shining than the nice guy he was pretending to be.

When Conrad left, Hutch's gaze returned to Maison. She seemed to be completely oblivious to everything that had just occurred because she was back at her computer, typing away at her keyboard. Once again, he had proof that she didn't need to go on a diet. Men liked how she looked just fine.

Including him.

While he'd never done anything to indicate his feelings for her before the other night, Hutch had noticed her a long time before that. However, since she was his father's assistant, he hadn't done anything about it.

Besides, Maison was too good of a person for him. That was why Hutch tended to go for women who were more on his level. No use to aim high when he'd just make a fool out of himself.

Hutch forced himself back in his seat and focused on the screen before him. But all he could think about was Maison. Had other guys at work asked her out to lunch before? Had she gone out with them? "Hey, Maison," he heard himself say. "Have you ever dated anyone from the office?"

Maison looked completely shocked by the idea. "No, of course not." Once again, the people around them stopped to look at him. He shot them a smile and turned back to Maison.

"Really? So you'd never go out with anyone who you know from around here?"

"No, absolutely not. Why?" Her gaze turned suspicious. "Did you hear something?"

"No. Not at all. Just curious. That's all."

"Good. I don't want people spreading rumors about me."

His lips curled into a smile. Maison was continuing to surprise him. Apparently, she cared about what people thought about her. Was that also why she was so self-conscious? "No. I don't think anyone would dare try."

Just then, the doors to his father's office opened and Matthew stepped out. His father didn't even bother glancing in his direction and that was totally fine by him. Hutch was used to that, but by the looks from the people around him, they'd obviously expected more interaction between them. Instead, Matthew walked straight up to Maison's desk and started barking orders.

Hutch simply watched, knowing that if he were on the receiving end of his father's orders, he would probably keel over and play dead. Surprisingly, Maison looked interested and engaged, nodding and smiling at Matthew as he listed all the things he needed from her.

It was then that he realized that Maison acted differently around him than she did with others. He thought of how she'd been with Conrad. She'd smiled at him. But Maison never smiled at him when he spoke to her. She was always looking down, never meeting his eyes for long.

What did that mean? Did he make her nervous? Had his actions the other night frightened her? Was that why she was acting differently with him now?

After a lengthy conversation, Matthew turned back around and slammed his office door behind him. "What was that all about?" he asked Maison.

"Oh, you know. Just some more work." Again, no eye contact.

"Does he always do that to you?"

"Do what?" There. A brief look up but then she turned away again.

"March out, bark orders, and expect everything to be done?"

"Yup."

"And that doesn't bother you?"

"Not at all. I am his assistant. That's what he hired me for."

Wow. Hutch had no idea how she managed to do that and still function like a normal human being. For all he knew, he'd probably be passed out by midday with all the demands his father threw her way.

That or he'd bite back and surely get his ass fired. He had no idea how she managed to do all that and still keep a happy face on all day.

Now all Hutch wanted to do was to get Maison to smile at him again.

When he'd left and spent a few days with Sam, his entire family had thought he'd left them. He hadn't expected them to worry so much when they could barely stand each other when they were together. So he'd been surprised when he'd returned after a few days and was greeted with hugs.

It'd also been Maison's thirtieth birthday. He'd been so surprised when she'd thrown herself at him in front of all her colleagues. Was that why they were all looking at him? Because they suspected something was going on between them?

If only he were so lucky. Maison was way too good a person for him. But that day had really spurred on his fantasies about her. He wanted to see her smile again, to hold her in his arms and breathe in her glorious scent. To do that, he had to charm his way into her heart. He pinned her with a wide smile. "Now that he's gone, why don't you tell me what you really think about him?"

Maison blinked at him. "What do you mean?"

"There must be some things you hate about my dad. And don't worry, I won't tell a soul."

Instead of smiling like he hoped, Maison lifted her shoulders in a shrug. "What's there to complain about? He's a great boss."

Okay, so maybe this would be tougher than he thought. He straightened in his chair. "I'm sorry, I think I misheard you. Did you just say you think he's great?"

"I did. Why is that so hard to believe?"

He pointed at the closed door Matthew was behind. "Are we talking about the same person here?"

Her lips twitched but he didn't consider that a smile. "He's not as terrible as you make him out to be."

"Oh, really?" He found that hard to believe. "Tell me one thing that makes him a good boss."

Maison's response was automatic. "He makes great donations to charities."

Hutch rolled his eyes. "Please. Everyone donates nowadays. Give me something else."

"Well, I guess in being his son, you probably don't see him the way I do. But trust me, there are worse people out there."

"You mean like Hitler?"

"Hutch!"

His laughter had other people stopping and staring at

them and they smiled when he grinned at them. Only Maison had yet to smile. "He's probably worse than that, huh?"

"No!" Maison covered her mouth and giggled behind her hand. When she pulled her hand away, he was hit with the brilliance of her beautiful smile.

Ah, there it was. *Exquisite.*

Maison grinned even wider. "God, why am I even having this conversation with you?"

"Sorry." But he really wasn't. He loved making Maison laugh. And would do it again and again just to see her pretty smile. "I'm just trying to figure out why you're still hanging around here. You're clearly better than this place."

And better than him.

"I like it here." Her eyes glittered with her words. "The pay is amazing and I really feel like I have a purpose here. I'd be a fool to leave here after all these years."

True. She worked harder than any other person he knew. Maybe even more than his father. He just hoped that he hadn't messed up their friendship by pawing all over her while he'd been drunk. He'd apologized once, but he wanted to make sure again. "Hey, Maison," he said, searching for her eyes.

"Hmm?" She was facing her computer screen again and when he didn't say anything, she was forced to look at him. "I just want to make sure we're okay."

A frown appeared. "What do you mean?"

"I mean about the other night. I'm really sorry for—"

"Hutch, I already told you it's fine. I was just concerned for you, that's all. So as long as you're all right, I'm okay."

"I'm fine."

"Maybe you should just take it easy next time. Don't drink so much."

Now it was his turn to flush. "Right. Yeah. I'll take better care." Truth was, he liked that she cared about him. It made him feel that little bit less lonely inside.

"It's almost time to go home. Why don't you pack up?"

That snapped him out of his thoughts. "Oh. I didn't realize it was that late already." While the minutes had dragged by earlier, now Hutch realized that he didn't want to leave. "Do you need a ride home?"

"No, thanks. I've got my own car."

"So I guess I'll see you tomorrow then?"

"Yes."

"Great. Have a good night."

He turned to gather his things when she called out, "Hey, don't forget. We've got an early morning meeting tomorrow. I need you to be there early."

"A meeting? Oh sure, no problem. I'll be there."

"Okay, thanks. Have a good night." Maison smiled at him again and Hutch felt his chest tighten.

As he grabbed his things and turned to leave, he couldn't help one last glance back at her. To his surprise, Maison was in the midst of pulling a pair of sneakers out of her bag. *Now why would Maison need to keep a pair of sneakers in her bag? Where was she going?*

He watched her leave, wondering about her next destination before he headed home himself.

SIX

MAISON ARRIVED EARLY AT THE FERLITO-JONESES' household. Funny, she never thought she'd find herself walking towards the house of a convicted felon, but here she was.

Taking a deep breath, Maison slicked down the front of her blouse and pressed the doorbell. A moment later, an older woman with graying hair answered the door. "Hi, Mrs. Ferlito," she greeted.

"Ah, Maison, you're here! Come on in." Despite her anxiety, she smiled. This was the first time she'd come to Rissa's house to meet her. Rissa was a young teenager living with her mother and grandmother. And for the last two months, she was Maison's Little Sister.

Maison had joined the Big Sisters program because she wanted to do something good for her community. Work had been the center of her life for so long that she wanted something more to look forward to after work hours. Joining a program such as this one was a great way to give back to the community while also keeping her from feeling so lonely when she wasn't working. So here she was again, trying to do some good for a family who needed it. The only problem was, Maison got the feeling that Rissa didn't like her.

Well, she actually wasn't sure if that was really the case, but Rissa was having some trouble opening up to her and Maison wondered if it was because something was happening at home.

That was why she was here now. She wanted to check in on

her family and see what was happening behind closed doors.

Rissa's grandmother called for the teen, and a second later, Maison heard her running footsteps above her. "She'll be down in a minute," Mrs. Ferlito said. "Do you want something to drink?"

"Oh no, thanks. I'm fine." As the older woman headed for the kitchen, Maison took that opportunity to explore the house. She knew from Rissa that her family liked to move a lot so Rissa was never in a single school for long. She wondered how that affected her grades and her social life. It must be hard to constantly be the new girl at school.

After Rissa's father had been incarcerated, her mother seemed to have given up on raising her, which was why her grandmother was the one who was constantly around. Their family income had dropped as well, as it usually did when a parent was incarcerated. Rissa had even told her that she'd visited her father at three different prisons already. So there was no doubt that Rissa Ferlito-Jones was living a tough childhood, but Maison didn't want to accept that this was always how it was going to be for her.

"Hi, Maison."

Maison spun around to find her Little Sister standing at the bottom of the stairs. Tall for a fifteen-year-old, Rissa already stood at five nine. Since her father was African-American and her mother was Hispanic, Rissa was an exotic blend of the two. She had a smooth, warm complexion that Maison would never be able to get no matter how many hours she stayed in the sun. Not to mention that Rissa had an abundance of natural curls that she usually needed tools to create in her own hair. Maison smiled at her. "Hey, Rissa. Are you ready to go?" They'd planned to watch a movie tonight of a popular Young Adult series.

"Yeah." Rissa hopped down the last step. "Let me just tell my grandma I'm leaving."

"Sure. Is your mom around?" Maison knew it was unlikely, but it wouldn't hurt to ask. Rissa pinned her with a look that said *what do you think?* "Guess not," she mumbled as the girl disappeared into the kitchen.

Maison tried not to feel so glum. Why wasn't Rissa's mother around more? Fifteen was a very vulnerable time and Rissa would likely need her mother's guidance. Well, at least she had her grandmother to turn to if she needed help. And she would do her best to be there for her too.

When Rissa and her grandmother returned, Maison smiled brightly for the both of them. "I hope you two have fun tonight."

"Oh, thank you, Mrs. Ferlito."

The older woman made a face. "Please call me Aba."

"Aba." Maison grinned. "Okay, Aba. We won't be long. We're just going to catch a movie, okay?"

"Sounds great. Have fun, girls!"

"Bye, Aba!" Rissa chimed.

"Bye!"

"So how have you been doing?" Maison asked once they were alone. She was hoping that Rissa would open up to her tonight.

"I'm okay," the teen answered.

She waited to see if she'd say anything more. But when it was clear that Rissa had nothing to add, Maison frowned.

She couldn't deny that there was a major age difference between them. There were also the cultural differences to consider as well. But Maison wasn't about to give up yet.

A lot of people had given up on Rissa already. Her father, her mother . . . Only her grandmother seemed like she was interested in the teen's well-being. So no, Maison wasn't going to turn away just because she was having some difficulty getting through to her. She believed she would in time. She just had to be patient. And sooner or later, Rissa would trust her enough to open up to her.

Hutch expected to find Sam outside gardening again when he pulled up to her house, but he was only faced with the beautiful blooming flowers and tree that they'd planted together the other day.

With his first day at Gleam finished, he wanted to come and tell Sam about it. However, he hadn't considered that she might still be out working. Private investigators tended to have different work hours than at the office.

Pulling out his phone, he quickly called her. When the phone rang but no one answered, Hutch got out of the car and walked over to the flowers. He was surprised to see that they hadn't died. He didn't have a green thumb and usually anything he planted died within a few days. Luckily, Sam was taking good care of them.

As he passed by the large window in the front of the house, he frowned. He could hear something from within. Was that Sam's cell phone ringing? Maybe she was home already and was taking a nap.

He hung up and called her again, listening for the ringing inside the house. When the shrill sound echoed from inside, Hutch made his way to the front door. He banged on it once. "Yo, Sam, it's me. Open up!" He knew Sam kept odd hours so it was entirely likely that she'd stayed up all night again working on a case and still hadn't gotten out of bed yet. When the door cracked open slightly, Hutch peered in. "You okay?" He found Sam standing there, wearing a tight tank top and a pair of boxer shorts. She held her phone in one hand and was rubbing at her sleepy eyes with the other. "Did you just get out of bed?"

"No . . . Maybe." They both moved for the living room where Sam flopped back onto the couch and covered her legs with a throw blanket.

Hutch had seen her naked plenty of times before, but unlike with other women, seeing her skin didn't rile him up. While he was a typical hot-blooded male, his relationship with Sam wasn't like that at all. They'd always been strictly friends. Plus, he knew too much about Sam to ever see her as anything other than a good friend, or at most, a sister.

Easing back, Hutch let out a sigh and started to loosen a couple of the top buttons of his dress shirt. He still wasn't sure about the office dress code. He'd much rather spend his days in his band T-shirts and sneakers. "So how did work go?" Sam asked.

Hutch shrugged and reached for the remote. "It wasn't too bad actually." He'd enjoyed spending the day with Maison even if she refused to have lunch with him. And while the work hours could be a little grueling at times, he could actually see himself having a good time as long as Maison was around.

"Wow, I'm surprised. I thought you'd want to quit."

"I can't quit." He'd only just started. Plus, if he wanted no complaints from his father when he moved out, then he'd have to endure longer than a day. "I'll admit, the hours suck but at least I don't actually have to work under my dad."

"Wait. What do you mean? He owns Gleam, so technically you do too."

"Yeah, but he's assigned me to be Maison's assistant."

"Maison? Your father's assistant?"

"Yup. I'm an assistant for an assistant."

Sam laughed. "Well that's something."

Hutch cut a glance at her. "What's that's supposed to mean?"

Sam shook her head. "Nothing. I guess that means you'll be spending a lot of time with Maison then."

Yeah, he would be. He was excited about it.

Sam laughed and shook her head. "Poor girl. She has no idea what she's gotten herself into."

"Hey!" he protested.

Sam smirked at him and got up to walk into the kitchen. He could hear her rummaging through the fridge for food. Pulling out a microwavable meal, she ripped off the cover and shoved it in the microwave. As she waited for it to heat up, she turned back to him, smiling as she crossed her arms over her chest.

Seeing her this way, Hutch couldn't help but compare her to Maison. The two were polar opposites. He couldn't see them ever being friends, not even in an alternate world. They were just too different in personality. While Maison was shy and sweet, Sam liked to kill her food before she ate it.

Still, Hutch knew the tough girl had her own vulnerabilities. As a private investigator, most people came to Sam with their problems, expecting her to do some research and hash it out. Nine times out of ten Sam prevailed, but there'd been a few instances where Sam almost hadn't made it.

Hutch would never admit it to her but he worried about her. She didn't have a solid relationship with her family, and instead of staying with them, she had opted for living alone here. While he knew that Sam was capable of handling herself, Hutch still didn't like that she lived here alone. That was why he came here so often. He wanted to check on her and make sure she was okay. Plus, there was no other person in the world who he could relate to better than Sam. Instead of seeing him as less of a man because of his missing leg, she envied him because he got the opportunity to do something that she was never able to do herself.

"Stop staring at me, you perv."

He grinned at her tone. "Don't flatter yourself. You're not my type."

"Oh, so smart, independent women don't get you hot? I wonder what does then."

Actually, they did. But instead of the skinny women he'd used to date forming in his mind, there was only one buxom blonde that took center stage in Hutch's mind.

Maison.

SEVEN

"He's late!" Maison gritted her teeth at the frustration she felt. "I already told him not to be late!" She checked her watch again, hoping that by some miracle Hutch would appear before her. But nope. He wasn't in front of her when she looked back up.

Matthew sat on her right side, silently sipping his coffee. "Did you remind him to come yesterday?" he asked.

Maison stiffened. "Of course I did." She never would've forgotten that. She'd reminded him right before he'd left for the day.

"Well, he didn't come home last night," Matthew informed her.

"*What?*" She swung on her boss. *He hadn't? Then where the hell had he gone?*

Matthew shook his head. "I should've expected him to do something like this." Annoyance and disappointment laced his tone. "But there's no time." He rose, moving to the front of the room. "We have to start the meeting."

Maison could only purse her lips together. "Dammit, Hutch!" she muttered. She'd been counting on him to be here. That had been his job, right? To help her? Had she been so impressed by his work yesterday that she'd been too lenient on him? She hadn't bothered to send him a formal memo about the meeting, so maybe this was her fault.

Silence spread over the room before Matthew started speaking. "Good morning, everyone . . ."

Maison glanced back at the door but Hutch was still no-where to be seen. Swallowing her annoyance, she focused her attention on Matthew at the front of the room.

After over an hour of taking notes, her hand ached. Normally she used a laptop to take her notes, but she'd actually been counting on Hutch to bring his and be the one doing it.

Thank goodness the meeting was now over. She could at least rest her hand for a bit. But she knew she would eventually have to type up the report all over again. *Great. More work to add to her already mile-long to-do list.*

So much for trusting the guy to keep his word. Just because Hutch had done one good thing for her, she'd allowed herself to believe that she could count on him. *Big mistake.* Maybe she'd been right all long. Maybe she couldn't count on anyone to do things for her.

With his absence though, she could at least focus on her work without any distraction. Having him around yesterday had totally knocked her off-kilter. Although Matthew had apologized about dumping his son onto her like that, Maison believed the root of her trouble wasn't that she wasn't prepared for his appearance but because being around Hutch made her nervous.

For as long as she'd been working for Matthew Hewitt, she'd always kept a respectable distance from the rest of his family. She was still friendly with them but things had start-ed to change when Matthew's wife, Camilla, had died. Now she was spending more time with Matthew because he began working longer hours and would sometimes take his work home with him.

Maison had spent countless evenings in their living room pouring over their latest work, and when Hunter and Hutch had begun living with Matthew again, she'd started seeing a lot more of them too.

It wasn't until her birthday that she realized how close she'd become to the Happa-Hewitt family. Hell, she felt like she was spending more time with them than her own family.

They'd been kind enough to throw her a surprise party and she'd never been more thankful. That day, Hutch had also come back too and she'd been so relieved to see him again that she'd thrown herself against him. To this day, she still didn't know what had gotten into her. She'd *never* done that before!

To make matters worse, she'd seen the way Hutch looked. He'd been so surprised that it'd taken him a moment before he'd wrapped his arms around her. Warmth had spread over her at knowing he was safe. But then she quickly realized that they weren't alone. Not only had she thrown herself at him in front of his family, but all her colleagues from work had seen it too.

They'd asked her about it after and she'd quickly said it was nothing. The truth was, she'd been embarrassed by her actions. All this time she'd been harboring feelings for Hutch but she never allowed herself to act on it. Not until that day. After that, she promised to keep her distance from him. He was her boss's son. People would talk.

When she'd found him in his father's office, looking pitiful and drunk, her heart had clenched for him. Despite her fear, she helped him. What she hadn't expected was for him to pull her into his arms and ask her to stay.

Maison felt goose bumps sprout all over her arms. Damn, even just thinking about it caused her body to react. She had to stop thinking of him that way. Nothing would come of it. Did she really believe that she had a shot with him? She couldn't even complete a proper sentence with him around since that night!

Her frustrated growl was so loud in the room that everyone

turned to look at her. "Sorry," she muttered.

As the meeting ended and everyone left, Matthew and a couple other people remained at the front of the room. "Did Hutch show up yet?" he asked her.

Maison shook her head. "No."

Clive Davenport, Gleam Enterprises' other co-founder, huffed a laugh. "I haven't even seen him yet. Have you lost track of him already?"

Maison felt her cheeks flush with embarrassment as she made her way towards them. Thankfully Matthew was there to quickly draw the attention from her. "He's probably with some woman." He gave a shake of his head. "I can't seem to control that boy."

Clive laughed again. "Well, I guess Maison here needs to do more to keep his attention." He gave her a good-hearted wink and excused himself. Once she was left alone with Matthew, Maison could relax. At least now the meeting was over.

She caught Matthew's worried expression and asked, "Are you okay?"

Matthew shook his head. "I can't believe that kid. I thought he'd at least have the decency to tell me that the deal was off."

"What deal?"

Matthew blew out a long breath. "You're probably well-aware that Hutch is a little bit of a rebel."

"A little?" she teased, trying to pull a smile from her boss.

Matthew smirked before he said, "I can never get him to do what I want. So I offered him this job so that I could keep an eye on him. He needs something to keep him busy and keep his mind off of what's upsetting him, but I'd hoped he'd last longer than this."

Maison was about to ask how he thought he was doing when Hutch walked through the doors. He was still wearing the same clothes as yesterday and he looked a little frumpled. His hair was messy around his face, but at least his eyes looked alert.

"Well, look who decided to show up. Where the hell have you been?" Maison winced at Matthew's tone. She'd become well acquainted with that tone over the years and it only came out when her boss was really upset.

"I'm so sorry," Hutch started. "I didn't realize—"

"I don't want to hear any excuses. You're my son and I understand that this is my company but I still expect you to behave like a responsible human being. Maison was counting on you to be here and you let her down. Now she'll have extra work to do because you weren't here. How does that make you feel?"

Hutch cut a glance to her and Maison felt her stomach do a flip. Although she'd been upset with him earlier, she felt terrible for the tongue-lashing he was currently getting.

Whenever Matthew got like this, his voice rose and sometimes you could hear it across the various floors. She glanced around them and realized that several other people were watching them already. Dammit, she had to stop this. "It's okay," she said with more firmness than she expected to come from herself. "I'll handle it."

Surprised, Matthew turned to her. "You will?"

She gave a nod. "Yes, sir. You don't have to worry about anything."

"Well, at least Maison is more forgiving," he said to Hutch. After gathering his things, he left her alone with Hutch.

"Maison, I'm sorry—" he started.

"Stow it." She wasn't going to show any mercy today. "Why were you late? I told you before you left that you needed to be here early."

"I'm sorry. I spent the night at a friend's house and didn't realize what time it was."

She felt her heart clench with his words. *I spent the night at a friend's house.* "*That's* the reason why you were late? Because you spent the night with some woman?"

"I don't mean it like that. She's just a friend."

What a liar. Maison *hated* liars. Quickly gathering her notes, she ignored the pained expression on Hutch's face. "I've got to go. I need to type these notes up."

Hutch followed her back to their desks, and on the way, Clive caught sight of them. "Oh, look who decided to show up," he drawled. He extended a hand for Hutch to shake. "I was looking for you earlier."

Hutch shook the man's hand. "Nice to see you again, Mr. Davenport."

"Please, call me Clive. How many times do I have to tell you that?"

Hutch offered him a small smile. "Okay, Clive."

"So I hear you're working alongside Maison."

"Actually, I'm working *under* Maison."

"Is that so?" A brow arched on his too-perfect face. "Well, you're in good hands. Maison is excellent at her job." She accepted his compliment with a smile.

"If you'll excuse me," she said, pushing her way past them in the hallway, "but I have some work to do."

"Right. See you later."

"Later," Hutch said.

But Maison was already walking towards her desk.

Hutch watched as Maison dumped a pile of papers on her desk and settled down in her chair. Within moments, she had organized the pile and was documenting them on a new Word file. She did all this with an ease and confidence, all while also ignoring him.

Shit. He'd really done it now, hadn't he? He hadn't meant to be late but instead of going home to shower and sleep, he'd spent his entire night with Sam.

He'd slept on her couch while she'd gone to bed in her bedroom. They'd done this countless times before but he really should've considered his early morning when he made the decision to stay. Now he was paying for it and seeing Maison angry at him made Hutch feel terrible.

"Do you need some help?" he offered. Maison's only response was the soft clicking of her nails against the keyboard.

Damn, was this what Hunter meant when he'd warned him to not piss Maison off? He couldn't imagine her mad. He'd never seen her get upset at anyone. But she was clearly upset with him now.

"Look, Maison. I'm sorry for being late. I should've called. I know it's my fault for not being responsible and making sure I was on time. But please, don't be mad at me. I really am sorry."

He waited for her response. But she simply continued typing. Hutch rubbed his neck, feeling his panic start to rise. Shit, what was he going to do? Maison wasn't talking to him!

Sighing, Hutch went back to his desk and proceeded to continue apologizing to her in an email. After blabbering on for four paragraphs, he sent it, holding his breath for her reaction. However, when minutes passed and he didn't receive a response, he gave up hope.

Maison was really mad at him and nothing he did seemed like it was going to help. Instead of wasting more time, he started on the work that he knew she might need to do later. That way she'd have less to do. He knew he'd messed up big-time but he was going to do everything to get her to smile at him again.

EIGHT

After work, Maison went to pick up Rissa. They'd been texting all day and she seemed to be in a much better mood today. Maison wasn't sure if it was the movie yesterday, or perhaps it was something going on in her personal life that was lifting up her spirits, but she was just glad to see the younger girl smiling for once. Unfortunately, her day hadn't gone too well and her own mood wasn't up to par with hers.

They'd already gone through the mall once, stopping at all of Rissa's favorite shops, and while Maison was trying to enjoy herself, her mind kept wandering off. Even with flats on, her feet were killing her and she really hoped that this was going to be the last time they went around the mall. "What's going on with you?" Rissa finally asked.

"Huh?" Maison cut a glance at her friend and noticed the furrow in her brow. "Oh, it's nothing."

"Yeah, right. That's the kind of answer I give Mom whenever she asks about something that I don't want to talk about."

Maison flashed an apologetic smile. The truth was, she *didn't* want to talk about it, but then she was reminded that this was also the first time that Rissa had ever started a conversation with her. Usually she was the one trying to pry out information from her. "Sorry. I don't mean to be a downer but something at work happened and—"

God, what the hell was she doing? She shouldn't be telling Rissa this! First of all, the focus should be on *Rissa*, and secondly, this was hardly the type of conversation she should have with her Litter Sister.

"Did someone make you mad?" Rissa asked.

Maison cut another glance at her. It was clear that she wasn't going to drop the subject. "Yeah," she finally admitted. "Someone made me mad."

"Who?"

Oh, what the hell. What harm could it do? "Well, there's this new guy at work. He's actually my boss's son." She checked to see if Rissa was still listening. To her surprise, the teen was glued to her story, eyes bright with interest. "We had this meeting this morning and he was late for it . . ." As she recalled the rest of what happened, Rissa sipped at her drink, all the while asking questions that spurred Maison into telling her more about Hutch.

"So do you like him?" she finally asked her.

Maison felt herself stiffen. How was she supposed to answer that question? She shouldn't really be talking to Rissa about this. But there was also a part of her that wanted to spill everything. God, why had she said those things to him? She felt terrible!

She caught Rissa smiling at her and groaned. "All right, time for a subject change. What about *you*? How are things going at school?"

Rissa shrugged. "It's okay."

"That's it? Just *okay*? There's nothing else fun happening at all?"

Rissa gave her a small smile. "Well, there's this one guy . . ."

Maison's eyes lit up. *Was Rissa finally opening up to her?* Before she'd felt so crummy that she had no smiles for anyone but now excitement had her grinning at Rissa. "Oh, reeeally . . ." she drawled. "Since I told you mine, now let's hear yours . . ."

That evening at dinner, the table was strained. Hutch had done his best to avoid his father for most of the day, but dinnertime was the only time when he couldn't.

Now he sat beside Matthew while his older brother, Hunter, and his nephew, Owen, rounded out the rest of the table. Damn, he wished Dacey were here. His sister typically had his back more than Hunter did and if his father decided to hassle him some more, at least he'd have someone around to defend him. He also wanted to talk to Dacey about her time working at Gleam.

She'd recently quit her job after working there for years. And although she'd worked in a completely different department and floor as their father, Hutch figured that he could get some advice on how to handle things from her. However, Dacey was super busy working on her new career, and he'd likely have to go to the beach house where she was currently staying to see her.

His brother didn't seem to notice the tension between them. Or maybe Hunter was just used to it. Seemed like his family argued more than they got along these days.

"I want more," Owen chimed from beside his brother.

Everyone turned to see what he was asking for and when Owen jabbed his fork at the mashed potatoes, Hunter asked him to pass over the dish. That was when his father reached for it at the same time. As their hands collided, their eyes met.

Not surprisingly, Matthew looked pissed.

He grabbed the dish and handed it to Hunter without a word. "Thanks," he said, before plopping a couple more scoops onto Owen's plate.

Hutch resumed his eating. He was nearly finished with his meal when his father cleared his throat and said, "You know, you really disappointed Maison today."

Hutch stiffened. When he lifted his head, Hunter and Owen were looking at him with twin expressions of confusion.

"I know you're only working there because of the deal we had, but I still expect you to try," Matthew said.

"I *am* trying," he gritted.

"You're not trying hard enough. Maison is the hardest worker I know. That's why she's my assistant. I trust her to do things correctly and get things done." Hutch didn't understand why they were making such a big deal out of this. All he'd done was miss a single meeting. "She was counting on you and you let her down."

Hutch bit down on his molars. *Damn, he was right.* He'd just left Maison high and dry without even calling to tell her that he was running late.

"Things work differently around here. If you don't take responsibility—"

"I get it," he gritted. Matthew didn't need to talk to him about that. He'd had enough responsibilities in the Army and had handled it just fine.

The thing that was eating at him was Maison. He knew just how hard she worked and he also knew that she cared a lot about what other people thought about her. That was why she'd been so concerned when he'd asked her if she'd ever dated anyone from work. He would hate it if people started talking shit about her because of his actions.

Hutch stood up in a jolt. Damn, he had to apologize to her.

"Where the hell do you think you're going?" his father snapped.

"I'm going to see Maison."

"Have you even been to her place before?" his brother called out.

No. This would be the first. But he wouldn't be able to think about anything else until Maison forgave him.

* * *

Her house was dark when he arrived. As Hutch got out of his car and walked towards the front door, he realized that Maison's house was a direct reflection of her.

The beige stucco walls were well maintained and clean, and the concrete terra-cotta roofing made it look sturdy and competent. There were bits of elegant details here and there that accented it beautifully, but Maison kept things mostly functional.

On his way over, he'd gone through his speech in his head, hoping that it would be enough for her to forgive him. He'd never realized it before but he'd always had a sweet spot for Maison.

He liked her because she never judged him. There had been times when she'd been present to see his fights with his father, and despite how horrible some of them had been, she had never held it against him. Similarly, he'd never taken his anger for his father out on her either. How could he when she was usually just following his orders? But that also meant that she probably knew more about him than he did of her.

Even after years of knowing her, Hutch was ashamed to say that he hardly knew anything about Maison. She was also so private about her personal life.

He knew she was a single child but that was the extent of his knowledge of her. He didn't even know she liked planning until he'd seen her decked-out planner on her desk. Somehow

Greyson had known it before he had and had gotten her an a5-sized leather planner for her birthday. What the hell had he gotten her?

Nothing.

God, he was such a douche.

Once he reached the front door, he rang the doorbell and waited. When minutes passed and no one answered, he gazed at the windows.

Pitch black. *Was she not home?*

He thought back to the last time he'd seen her at work. She'd been pretty upset with him at the time, but he remembered that she'd been texting someone right before she left the office. Was she making plans? Did she have a date?

Hutch fisted his hands at his sides. He had no idea where that surge of jealously had come from but it'd been wholly unexpected. First of all, he couldn't even remember when he'd started developing feelings for Maison. This wasn't like him and she certainly wasn't his usual type. Even Sam had commented on how weird it was.

Whatever. That was something he could figure out later. What was important was making sure Maison knew how sorry he was. He never planned on letting her down again.

Grounding down on his molars, Hutch turned back to his car. His intentions now were useless if Maison wasn't even home. *Where the hell was she?* He checked his watch and noted that it was nearly nine. Was she out on a date? For some reason, that thought made him sad.

Sliding back into his car, Hutch keyed the ignition but instead of heading back home, he turned the other way towards Sam's place. He needed some cheering up and Sam was the only person who could do it.

When Sam opened her front door, she wasn't surprised to see Hutch standing there. "What the hell are you doing here again?" She made a face as he stepped inside. "Sooner or later people are going to think we're dating."

A reluctant smile appeared. "That would be a jump for you," he shot back.

Hutch made his way to her living room and plopped down on the couch. She made shooing motions with her hand. "Get off, can't you see I'm doing something here?" She'd just started cleaning it when he arrived.

"Fine." Pouting, Hutch moved to sit in another chair while she cleaned. For a moment, she was too consumed with tidying up that she failed to notice the mood he was in.

Turning to him, Sam finally asked, "What happened?"

Hutch let out a sigh. "My dad got on me for pissing Maison off."

Wait, what? "You pissed her off? How'd you do that?"

After Hutch explained what happened, she laughed. "She was that upset because you missed one silly meeting?"

"Yeah, but I guess I should've expected that. Maison takes her job very seriously." Well, that made the two of them. "I feel like I've really let her down."

Sam frowned at Hutch's sudden sadness. "Hutch, are you okay? You don't normally get upset about stuff like this."

"I went to her house to apologize but she wasn't home."

"Wait. You went to her house?"

Hutch glanced up at her. "Should I have not done that?"

"Well, I don't know." But that wasn't like Hutch. He rarely chased women. He didn't need to. "I don't really know her, but even if your father was upset about it, I didn't think you'd care that much." Especially when it concerned a woman he wasn't even interested in.

Unless . . .

Sam shook her head. *No, Maison wasn't even Hutch's type. How could he have feelings for her?*

But as she took in the way Hutch's eyes darkened, she realized that maybe there was a possibility that he liked this chick.

Sam continued to study him from her seat. Once again Hutch was dressed in his favorite band T-shirt and jeans. She much preferred this casual look to his dressed-up one he had on yesterday. It suited him better, and if she was being honest, Sam didn't think he belonged there at Gleam.

But she also understood that he was still in the process of adjusting to civilian life. Unfortunately, acclimating would be more difficult for him after what he'd been through.

Hutch rubbed a hand over his face, his frustration clear in the way his strong jaw tightened. "I've got to get my shit together," he said as he stood up. "I don't want her thinking I'm some useless bum. Everyone else thinks I am already."

"I don't think you're a bum."

Hutch grinned at her, but the usual spark of mischief was absent in his eyes. "Thanks, but your opinion doesn't count."

"Hey!" She threw a cushion at him and it hit him hard in the face.

"*Ow!*"

"That was your own fault. You should know not to disrespect me in my own house!"

This time Hutch's smile was genuine. "You're right. I'm sorry. So have you got any advice on how to fix this situation I'm in?"

Sam shook her head. "Sorry, but I hardly know the girl. You're going to have to figure that out yourself."

"Dammit." The muscles in his arms bulged and he tightened his fist.

Drawn in by the sight, Sam couldn't help but think that he'd lost some of his bulk since returning from service. Hutch was still big, but he'd definitely lost some definition. What else had he allowed to go soft since coming back? A thought occurred to her and she smiled. "You know what, I think I know of something that might help you."

Hutch eyed her warily. "What is it?"

Her smile was both cocky and mischievous. "Come around tomorrow and I'll show you."

NINE

EARLY THE NEXT MORNING, MAISON WAS SURPRISED TO see Hutch already at his desk when she arrived. Upon seeing her, he flashed her a grin that sent shivers through her entire body. "Good morning."

"G-good morning," she returned. "What are you doing here so early?"

"I'm not early. I'm just on time for once."

"Oh." She guessed he was right. But what did that mean? Was he still sorry for what happened yesterday?

She definitely was. She'd acted out of character. While she normally stumbled and stuttered her way through her conversations with Hutch, yesterday's events had turned her into a raging bitch. She was surprised he was even talking to her. Today she was going to make the extra effort to be nice to him.

Feeling embarrassed, she quickly made her way to her desk and started to unload her bag. She'd just checked her to-do list in her planner when she made the mistake of glancing over at Hutch again.

His gaze was fixed intently on the computer screen. His jaw rested in the palm of one hand while his other moved on the mouse. Once again, he wore a dress shirt and the sight was enough to give her heart palpitations. Through the thin material, she could see his bulging biceps.

All her swooning came to an abrupt stop when she spotted Belinda, one of their colleagues, walking up to him. "Good morning," she chirped, that ever-present grin in place.

Hutch tore his gaze from his screen to dazzle her with one of those panty-melting smiles. "Hey, Belinda, how's it going?"

Ugh.

"Not good," Belinda started.

"Why?"

"My car broke down last night so I don't have a ride anymore."

"Oh, that sucks." Maison tuned herself out of the rest of their conversation. She really didn't want to hear Hutch offering to give her a ride home. Because he would. He was a gentleman like that. And there was no doubt that Belinda would want an altogether different kind of ride from him after.

Flushing with anger, Maison turned back to her screen but her attention wasn't on the words before her. She realized with annoyance that she wanted to know what Hutch would say.

A smile split her face when she realized that he wasn't going to give Belinda a ride at all. He had simply told Belinda that he was sorry to hear about her car troubles and hoped that she got her car back sooner rather than later.

As Belinda left, looking suddenly sullen, Hutch caught her gaze. He winked at her before turning back to his work. God, when had she turned into such a terrible person? Was she actually happy that Hutch hadn't made a move for Belinda?

Rissa's earlier words came back to her. *Do you like him?*

The answer was very obvious now.

Yes, she did like him. She liked him enough that when other women came within five feet of him, she turned into a jealous maniac.

"Hey, Maison," Hutch called out. "Could you come over here for a second? I just have a question about something . . ."

Maison quickly made her way towards him. "Sure. What's the problem?"

Hutch pointed at the screen. "Tell me what you think of this. I moved things around a little bit. I hope you don't mind."

Maison took a quick glance over his work, surprised to see that he'd accomplished so much. "Wow. It looks really good." So much better than what she could've done on her own.

"Really? So you don't hate it?" He'd moved forward and the scent of his cologne hit her like a tidal wave.

Maison suddenly found it hard to concentrate. She was well aware of how close they stood and she wasn't sure why but the heat coming off his body was akin to sitting by a fire; it warmed and comforted her.

"Maison?"

"Huh? Oh sorry. What were you saying?"

The corner of his lips tipped up. "Thinking about your date last night?"

"Date?" She frowned. *What the hell was he talking about?*

"Yeah. You left early yesterday. And you didn't come home until late."

Maison felt herself stiffen. How did he know that? She and Rissa had such a good time chatting that she'd lost track of time.

"Sorry," Hutch said when he noticed her reaction. "I should say that I came by your house yesterday to apologize."

"Y-you did?" She couldn't hide her shock.

"Uh huh." He unleashed the full effect of his dark gaze on her. "I really am sorry."

"It's okay," she said quickly, breaking the contact. God, now her heart was *really* pumping. Why was she always so nervous around him?

Knowing herself, she'd probably start tripping over her words again and make a big fool out of herself. "So this is okay?" he asked again.

Maison nodded quickly. "It's perfect. Keep up the good

work." And then she scuttled back to her desk to hide behind her computer screen.

Dammit, what the hell was wrong with her? She should've apologized to him as well. She couldn't believe that he'd actually come by her house last night! It was probably best that she wasn't home to receive him. She wouldn't know what to do with herself then.

Maison picked up her pen and stared down at her to-do list in her planner. *Dammit.* Her hands were still shaking.

On a breath, she quickly added another task to her list.

Get your shit together.

Otherwise, she'd never stop falling over herself with Hutch around.

"So what's this thing you wanted to show me?" Hutch sat beside Sam in her car after work, feeling a little claustrophobic in the small, cramped space. He had no idea why she kept this matchbox Honda around. Not only was it too small for anyone but Sam to ride in but it'd also seen better days. Unfortunately, Sam had grown attached to the thing, and no matter how many times it broke down and refuse to start, she still kept the piece of shit around.

"Relax. You're going to like it, I promise."

Yeah right. "The last time you said that, you took me to some kid's bar mitzvah."

As Sam laughed, Hutch shook his head. "So how was work today? Did you get to talk to Maison?"

He nodded. "It was way better than yesterday." What a relief. He wasn't sure what he'd do if she'd continued to ignore him. But he still couldn't help but believe that she was trying to avoid him. She had run back to her desk without even a word of departure. Had he said something to upset her again?

As Sam drove, Hutch took in the beautiful scenery. The sun was out and shining, which meant that inside the car it was boiling. He'd already rolled the windows down because the a/c in the car didn't work and the warm breeze was making his hair fly all around his face.

His gaze found the horizon and the setting sun. At this hour, the sky was a gorgeous wash of yellow and orange hues and the colors reminded him so much of Maison's hair. She had beautiful blonde locks that reached her shoulders. Oftentimes she'd curl her hair, giving herself that buxom babe look all the while looking effortless in the process.

As they turned at a bend in the road, Hutch caught a glimpse of the ocean. Beautiful blue extended as far as he could see. Again, the colors reminded him of Maison.

The ocean looked just like her eyes. Pretty, with darker bits of navy. Maison's eyes were just as captivating as the waves.

Man, he missed her. And that was a ridiculous thought since he'd spent the majority of the day with her already. But they'd been working, only speaking when he had a question to ask.

Hutch was determined to get back on her good side again and not cause any more trouble for her. But that also meant he had to reel in his feelings and act professional. That was a huge hardship when what he really wanted wasn't professional at all.

"Here we are," Sam said suddenly, forcing him to return to the present.

When he saw what was in front of him, he balked. "What the hell? This is what you've been doing?"

"Yup. It keeps me sharp."

Hutch was in awe. Why the hell hadn't he thought of this? As he got out of the car and walked towards the shooting range, Hutch felt a bolt of adrenaline go through him. Man, he hadn't felt that rush in a long time! Excitement bloomed in his chest. "Oh man, I can't wait to try this."

Sam beamed. "You're going to love it." How had she known that this was what he'd needed? He'd spent too much time trying to adjust himself to civilian life and conforming to other people's standard of living that he'd never even thought about looking for something here that might get his blood pumping again. Although this wasn't exactly typical for everyone, it was something he could do to get his adrenaline going again.

Hutch was surprised to find that the owners knew Sam by her first name. Apparently, she'd been here a lot because she knew every person in the establishment. Why hadn't she shown this to him earlier? He'd have to ask her later. Within minutes, he was ready to begin thanks to Sam's help.

This particular facility had two independent shooting bays. Both ranges were twenty-five meters in distance. The first range was a pistol caliber range, which accommodated any pistol caliber up to .500SW and the second was a rifle range, which accommodated any caliber up to .50BMG.

Excitement filled Hutch as he stood there, hearing the other people firing their guns at the targets. Was this what Sam did to keep sharp? Had she been coming here all these years while he'd been away? No wonder she'd been able to keep her skills after all these years. She'd been practicing.

Sudden worry consumed him. He hadn't touched a firearm in months. What if he forgot everything? What if the accident had damaged something else he wasn't aware of and he couldn't shoot for shit either?

That was when Sam appeared beside him. She held two rifles in her arms and handed one to him with a grin. "So what do you think?"

"I think it's amazing," he said despite the anxiety running

through him.

"Good. I thought you'd like it."

He did. He really did. "Thanks for taking me here."

Sam rolled her eyes. "All right, all right. No need to get all sappy on me."

He couldn't help but smile at her. "You ready to get your ass kicked?"

Hutch saw the glimmer of challenge in her eyes and felt his heart begin to race. "You're the one that needs to watch it," she shot back. "They don't call me Annie Oakley around here for nothing."

Hutch grinned. "Bring it on."

TEN

Hutch hadn't had that much fun in a really long time. It'd been nice to be able to talk some trash and joke around like he'd used to. He couldn't even remember the last time he'd had such a good time with Sam. It actually reminded him a lot of their early days together.

Had he really been that out of the loop though? Sam had adjusted fine after having her heart broken. Not only did she have a new career that she enjoyed but she still managed to stay on top of her game by practicing at the gun range. He would've been impressed if he wasn't so jealous.

Just like he expected, he'd been rusty. Although many would consider him an expert in what he did, Sam had totally killed him.

Guess I need to practice some more, he thought with a grin. At least now he had something to look forward to.

He was still smiling as he entered the Gleam offices the next morning, not at all surprised to see Maison already there. He could see that she had her planner out in front of her and she was in the process of pulling out stickers when he came to stand beside her. "Wow, busy week, huh?"

Maison glanced up at him, surprised to see him there. Had she been so caught up in her planning that she hadn't seen him? For some reason, that brought a smile to his face. He liked that she was so focused on everything that she did. He only wished that she focused more of her attention on him.

No, wait. He was supposed to keep his distance from her!

That was the only way to maintain a professional relationship.

Maison smiled at him and Hutch felt his heart skip a beat. Yeah, staying away from her was going to be a real challenge.

But just as quickly as that smile had appeared, Maison's nervousness took over once again. "H-hey." She glanced down at her spread.

Hutch could see that she'd made notes for herself everywhere, using stickers to denote the most important tasks and events. He pointed to a note she'd made further along the week. "What's that?" he asked. She'd marked down that she had to pack. Was she planning on going somewhere? Take a vacation perhaps?

"Oh, that? I'm going to London with your father for a conference presentation."

Hutch blinked. *London? How come he hadn't known about this earlier?*

His confusion must've shown on his face because Maison said, "Sorry, have I not mention it before? We've had it scheduled for months."

"No worries." He hadn't been working at Gleam for long. He still needed to make himself more acquainted with how things were around here. "So does that mean I'll be having those days off?" he asked jokingly. If his dad and Maison were going to be out of town, there wouldn't be much for him to do.

He watched as Maison frowned. "Oh, you're right. I didn't think to ask him about what we were going to do with you."

Ouch. Had she really forgotten all about him? Hutch tried not to look so offended. Maison shot him another smile. Could it be that she was getting used to his presence? "I think I'll ask him after he's done with his first meeting."

"Great. Thanks."

He turned for his desk, his earlier bright mood dimming.

What was he going to do if they were both gone? He'd still probably have to work and the thought was not as appealing without Maison around. But like she'd said, they had this planned months ahead. How could he expect them to change that just because he was now around?

He'd just have to do his best without them. It would be a good chance to prove that he was not only competent but also reliable to her and his father. And then maybe, Maison would actually have a good reason to notice him.

It was nearly lunchtime when Maison remembered that she needed to talk to Matthew. He'd been in meetings all morning, and although she'd promised Hutch she'd speak to his father about him after his first one, she'd lost track of time and had totally forgot to ask.

She wasn't exactly sure, but Hutch seemed to be disappointed when he'd learned about their trip. She wasn't sure why. It wasn't like they were going off to some exotic place on a vacation. They'd be going to London, England, once again for this year's conference. Matthew would be making an appearance before thousands of people to speak about Gleam and how he'd been able to build it from the ground up. To many, he was a genius and a lot of other entrepreneurs wanted to learn from him. Maison attended it with him because it usually spanned a couple of days.

But now that Hutch was around, she wasn't sure how this time would pan out. Matthew had never given *her* an assistant before. She'd always been able to complete her tasks. Sometimes she'd make it right before deadlines, but at least she got things done.

More recently, however, she was feeling more overwhelmed by her work. Matthew was still a great boss, but with

Gleam doing so well, that meant there was more work for her and Matthew to do. So while she'd been shocked to hear that Hutch was going to work with her, she was actually quite glad that he was here. If only she wasn't so nervous around him then maybe she could actually enjoy his company too.

Behind her, the door opened and Matthew stepped out. He'd obviously intended to take his lunch but Maison shot to her feet and rushed over to him. "Sir, can I talk to you for a second?"

"What is it?" Matthew asked.

Maison glanced over her shoulder at Hutch, who was still at his desk, working. "It's about Hutch."

Matthew peered at his son over her shoulder and then nodded. "Come inside." As he closed the door behind them, Maison spun around. "What happened?" he asked. "Was he tardy again?"

"Uh, no, actually. He's been on time ever since then." *Wow.* Maison was really impressed.

Surprise flashed across Matthew's features. "Well, that's good to hear. What is it that you want to talk to me about then?"

"It's about our trip to London. We're still going, right?"

"Of course. I've been practicing my speech."

"Okay, but what are we going to do about Hutch?"

By Matthew's expression, she could tell that she hadn't been the only one to forget about him. "Shit," he muttered. "I didn't think of that."

"Should we let him stay here?"

Matthew brought his hand to his chin as he contemplated an answer. "No," he finally said. "He'll come with us."

Maison felt her stomach bottom out. *"What?"* Come with us? She hadn't exactly been expecting that answer. "But-but—"

"Oh, come on. It'll be fine. Hutch is a good traveler and

he can help you with anything you need done. I know you're up to your head in work. That's why I brought him here. Ask him to help you and maybe after this trip you can finally take a vacation."

But I don't want to take a vacation, Maison thought. Matthew had always urged her to take time off but she never listened. She much preferred staying busy than moseying around doing nothing. But before she could say that, Matthew turned around and opened the door. *"Wait!"*

But Matthew either didn't hear her or he was purposely ignoring her. He moved briskly to the elevators, stopping only briefly to wave to someone before he was gone.

Maison stood there, feeling the weight of Hutch's gaze on her. Damn, hopefully he hadn't heard all that.

When she turned around, it was to find him already standing behind her. A look of concern marred his beautiful face. "Is everything okay?"

Maison forced herself to nod. "Y-yes. Everything is fine."

Hutch didn't seem to believe her. *But it would be fine*, she told herself. *It had to be.*

She forced herself to look at him and realized that she had to crane her head *way* up. Damn, why did he have to be so damn tall? It made her feel so small, and in turn, it ratcheted up her anxiety even more.

"S-so I asked your dad about the trip . . ."

"Really? What did he say?"

"He told me to bring you along."

Hutch blinked. "Really?"

"Yes," she breathed. Which meant that she would be spending *more* time with him. She really hoped her heart could take it. It was already pumping hard, trying to beat out of her chest!

"Wow, I wasn't expecting that."

"Yes, well, I guess that means you'll need to prepare. We'll only be staying there for a couple of days. Is that okay with you?"

"Of course."

Dammit, she'd hoped that maybe he didn't want to go. But then she immediately felt bad for thinking that. What was so wrong with having him come along? It was like Matthew had said, he could help her and make things go a lot smoother.

Nevertheless, anxiety had her in a stronghold and her distress continued to escalate as she thought about what traveling to London with him would be like.

"Maison?" Hutch leaned into her and his spearmint and eucalyptus scent engulfed her. "Are you okay?"

She blinked. "What? Oh yes. I'm fine." She smiled at him but it came out forced. "I should get back to work. I have a lot of stuff still left to do before we leave."

"Don't you want to have lunch?"

Was he asking her to go out with him again or was this just a general question? She shook her head. It didn't matter. She still had to stick to her diet.

"No. I'll just eat at my desk if I get hungry." Her stomach was too tied up in knots to eat now.

Hutch nodded. "Okay, but don't work yourself too hard. It's still early in the day."

"Okay." This time, her smile was genuine but it didn't completely eliminate her fear. If she was going to make it through this trip, she had to be strong.

She'd been so confident that everything was going to go great before Hutch was set to come with them. Why then was she so nervous now?

It's because you're going to be with him.

Maison did her best to shake it off. She was working with

him now and as long as Hutch planned to work here, she'd have to learn how to deal with his presence. Besides, he wasn't unpleasant. He was just the opposite in fact.

And that was why Maison had to watch herself. If she wasn't careful with her heart, she just might end up falling in love with the guy.

ELEVEN

O N THE DAY THEY WERE SET TO LEAVE, MAISON couldn't contain her nervousness. Usually she was excited for these trips; it was one of the perks of her job that she loved. However, this time she knew that the cause for her anxiety was Hutch.

She'd met both him and Matthew at the airport and was surprised to see them in casual wear. While she'd seen Hutch in sweats before, she'd forgotten how good he'd looked in them.

The sneakers on his feet were free of dirt and scratches and, for a moment, she wondered if he took care of them or if they were brand new. The gray sweatpants he wore hung lose over his thighs, but whenever he turned around, she was blessed with the sight of his great ass.

"Dammit," he muttered before he suddenly stopped before her. "I think I may have left my wallet in the cab."

"Better go quick before the taxi leaves," Matthew said.

On quick feet, Hutch sprinted back to the taxi, bending so that he could speak to the driver. *Oh my.* She'd nearly swooned out loud. Who said men were the only people who could appreciate a good booty? Maison watched on as Hutch opened the back passenger door and went to retrieve his wallet from inside.

"Maison? *Maison!*" Matthew barked, pulling her out of her trance. "Are you sure you didn't forget anything?" By his tone, that hadn't been his first time calling her. Maison blushed furiously and glanced back at Hutch.

"Uh, no. I think I'm good."

"Okay then, let's go check our bags."

"Okay." Bending to retrieve her bags, she turned to find Hutch running back towards them. "Did you get it?"

He flashed her a smile under the brim of his baseball hat. "Got it."

Good. That'd been close. The driver had nearly left.

"Come on," he said grabbing a hold of her bags. "Let's go."

"It's okay. I've got it." She'd always been a light packer and two bags were more than enough for the couple of days they'd be there.

"Maison, it's okay. Let me help."

"Oh." She immediately let go as his hands clasped over hers. "O-okay."

By the time they checked in and boarded the plane, some of her anxiety had disappeared. Despite her earlier nerves, Maison wasn't a nervous flier so maybe she could finally relax during the eleven-hour flight. She felt a spike of unease when she realized that she was going to be spending those long hours sitting beside Hutch and Matthew!

"Maison, are you feeling all right?" Matthew asked.

"Huh? Oh yes, I'm fine. Why?"

"I don't know. You're unusually silent today. Did you get enough sleep last night?"

"Not really." But she wasn't going to admit that the cause of her worry was his son.

"Well then give me your bag. I'll put it away and you can get some rest."

"Thanks, but that's not necessary. I can—*Hey!*"

Matthew had taken a hold of her hand and was already walking towards Hutch. She hurried after him. "It's okay. I've got it."

Matthew handed her bag to Hutch who then looked down at her. "Is everything okay?"

Matthew answered for her. "Maison's tired. Put her stuff away for her, will you?"

"Oh, sure thing." He flashed her a smile and Maison felt her insides turn to goo.

Dammit! She felt perfectly fine. Matthew turned back to her and guided her to her seat. "Shh," he said when she started to protest. "Hutch will handle it. Just sit down and rest."

As soon as her bottom hit the chair, she realized just how tired she was. Since she'd been nervous all night, she hadn't gotten the sleep she needed. And with the busy days ahead of them, she'd better get some sleep while she could. "Okay, fine," she muttered when Matthew sat down beside her. Why was he so concerned about her anyway? Usually he kept to himself and she was the one who was fussing over *him*.

Whatever. Her eyelids grew heavy so she allowed her head to fall back against the headrest and let herself drift off into a peaceful slumber.

* * *

When Maison woke, it took her a moment to remember where she was. She was squished between two very handsome men. However, the one on her right held her interest the longest.

Now a few hours into their flight, Maison was surprised to learn that she'd fallen asleep during takeoff. Now everyone else seemed to be enjoying the flight by either watching some movies or taking a nap. Hutch was one of them.

She should probably feel guilty for watching him while he slept but this was the first time she could stare at him without interruption. Plus, she was no longer nervous.

Despite the fact that Hutch still wore his baseball hat, she could still see his features nicely. She was immediately envious of his dark, thick lashes and his smooth, blemish-free skin. He also had the most delicious-looking lips she'd ever seen. Plump and perfectly formed, Hutch had the lips that many Hollywood celebrities paid a lot of money for. How was this male gifted with so much perfection? It was so unfair.

What was it like to be physically superior to everyone else? She would obviously never know. Maison had never been blessed with a pretty face or a slim figure. And no matter how many times she went to the gym, she enjoyed chocolate too much for it to make any difference. She already knew Hutch Happa-Hewitt was simply out of her league. She was just having trouble accepting it.

Biting her lip, Maison fantasized about what it would be like to be Hutch's girlfriend. If only she could find the courage to walk up to him and pull him into her arms. Maybe if she was feeling a little bolder, she'd run her hands over his arms and chest, feeling every bit of golden skin beneath her fingertips. She'd wrap her arms around his neck and kiss him ruthlessly. No more holding back, no more fearing what might come. She was just going to enjoy him and let herself go.

Once he was breathing heavily, she'd climb his body and wrap her legs around his waist, squeezing tightly until her core clenched. She'd kiss him until he was panting for her, begging. And then maybe she'd start by taking off his clothes.

As each delicious muscle was revealed, she'd lick a path to his lips. And once again, she'd take her time kissing that beautiful mouth of his.

Tongues would be involved, of course. How could they not be? Especially when she made her way down his body and started to undo his pants.

Maison let out a moan.

Oh God, she realized with a start. She was getting turned on! And Hutch was right beside her! Hopefully he hadn't heard her.

She chanced a peek at him from the corner of her eye and was relieved to find that he was still fast asleep. *Phew! That'd been a close one!* But she'd have to hit the pause button on the sexy scene playing out in her mind. She didn't want to risk accidentally waking Hutch up. Or worse, his father!

Once they landed, she'd just have to fix the problem in her hotel room.

Pronto.

The eleven-hour flight went by pretty smoothly. Turned out, Maison was a pretty good flier. She seemed completely at ease, except for the one time when he'd just woken up and she was looking at him funny.

He wasn't exactly sure but he got the feeling that she'd been watching him while he'd slept and that made him really happy. Maybe now she was starting to notice him.

They quickly retrieved their bags and were about to grab a taxi to their hotel when Maison came up to him. "Thanks, but I can carry my own bags." She moved to take the bags from him but Hutch pulled away.

"It's okay. I've got it." He'd been surprised to see that she'd packed light. Most women he knew would've taken their entire wardrobe with them. But he really shouldn't be surprised. Maison wasn't a fussy girl and he really liked that about her. She'd always been ready and willing to use what was available.

"No, really. It's fine. I can—"

"Maison, just let him," Matthew drawled. "It's only a bag."

"Precisely. Which is why I can carry it myself." She reached for it again, but instead of pulling away this time, Hutch grabbed a hold of her hand.

He felt like an electric shock went through him. Maison must've felt it too because she gasped audibly. "Sorry," he said when he let go. "But don't worry. I've got it covered."

"The taxi is here," Matthew announced and moved to greet the driver. He turned back to them. "Where's the hotel again?"

As she rattled off the address, Hutch took that opportunity to put their bags in the trunk.

Sliding into the back seat with her, Maison glanced over at him. "Thanks," she said with a smile.

He grinned back. "No problem." One day, she'd get used to having him around.

* * *

When they get to the hotel, Hutch had to take a moment to process everything. While he knew they were going to be attending a big conference, he didn't think it was going to be this big.

The lobby was packed with men in business suits. For a moment, he wondered if there was something else going on until some people caught sight of his father and rushed over to them.

"Mr. Hewitt, Mr. Hewitt!" one of them called. "Can I get a picture?"

A picture? Hutch balked at the man. *What the hell? Had they mistaken his father for a celebrity?*

But then he remembered, in the business world, Matthew Hewitt was a legendary name. He just didn't think his father would have actual *fans*.

"Move quickly!" Maison urged as she took Matthew's arm

and steered him away from the fawning fans. To his surprise, she also grabbed his arm. "Let's move!"

Hutch had no choice but to follow. "Wait, the bags—"

"It's fine," a young man called out. "I've got them."

"Thank goodness."

They quickly moved to the front desk, but then Maison suddenly froze. "What is it?" his father asked.

"Maison, are you all right?" he asked.

"Oh my God," she breathed. Pain was etched onto her features.

He immediately grabbed onto her. "Maison! What's wrong?"

"I can't believe it!"

"What is it?" Matthew demanded.

She turned to him. "*The rooms!* I forgot to get another one for you!"

"What?"

Maison dropped her head in her hands. "I can't believe I forgot."

He and his father looked at each other. Why was she so upset about this? "Maison, it's fine." Matthew began soothing her. "Maybe they have another one available."

"Yeah." He didn't need one close by. It didn't even need to be on the same floor. As long as it was someplace in the hotel, he'd be fine.

Maison looked up as Matthew went to the front desk and spoke with the man there.

"I'm sorry, sir. Because of the conference, all rooms have been booked."

"Oh no!" Maison wailed. She turned to him. "I'm so sorry!"

He put his hands on her shoulders. "Maison, it's fine. Don't worry about me."

"Of course I have to! It was my responsibility to book everything! I can't believe I forgot to check the hotel."

"It's fine. You've had a lot on your plate."

His father returned to his side and shook his head. "They said there's nothing left."

"That's fine. I'll find another hotel nearby or something."

"What? *No!*"

"Shh, Maison. It'll be fine." Matthew turned to him. "And that won't be necessary. You can just room with me."

Hutch couldn't hide his horror at the idea. *"What? I'm not staying with you!"*

"Well, you're not sleeping with Maison."

He stiffened. Dammit, now that that thought was in his head it would be all he thought about. He glanced down at Maison to find her turning red. Was she thinking about it too now?

Never mind. He had to get that thought out of his head. "Why can't I just find another hotel?" He *really* didn't want to share a room with his father.

"Don't be ridiculous," his father said. "We're already here. Come on." He turned for the elevators.

Hutch gritted his teeth in frustration. There he was again, making decisions for him and trying to control him. He really hated when he did that.

Maison turned to him. "I'm *really* sorry, Hutch. Are you sure it's okay?"

He forced his anger back. "It's fine," he gritted. "Let's go up to the rooms."

It turned out that the room Maison had booked for them was pretty big. He probably wouldn't need to worry about his father as long as he left him alone. However, he was still seething when Maison left to go to her room next door.

He spun on his father. "I don't know why you do that!"

Matthew paused in unbuttoning his shirt. "I don't know what you're talking about."

"You! Controlling me! Do you get off on it?" As the CEO of Gleam Enterprises, his word was law. Was that why he thought he could also do the same with his children?

"I'm not controlling."

"Yes, you are. You're a control freak! You're always deciding things for others without even asking what they want."

Matthew turned to him. "What do you want then?"

Hutch shook his head. "It's too late for that now."

"No, tell me. Did you really want to waste your time finding another hotel room when you could've stayed here? There's more than enough space here to fit both of us."

"Yeah, but you didn't even ask me!"

"I was trying to solve the problem as quickly as possible. Besides, it's only for a couple of nights. We'll be out of here before you know it."

"That's not the point and you know it."

"Maybe not. But I've made it easier on all of us."

"How does this make things easier?" They've been alone for five minutes and they were already fighting!

"Do you know what the schedule is tomorrow?" Before he could answer, his father continued, "Do you even know where things are going to be held? Let me answer that for you. No, you don't. And do you know how I know that? It's because I don't either. Only Maison does. But for whatever reason, she's more tired than she usually is and is having a tough time. So instead of you finding another hotel room and making her have to go pick you up, I've made it so that she can get a little more rest before tomorrow. So you tell me, was it wrong of me to do that?"

Hutch snapped his mouth shut. *Shit. He hadn't been*

thinking about Maison when his father had decided that.

"You're always looking for something to be mad at me about when all I've done is looked out for you."

Hutch gritted his teeth. "I don't need you to look after me."

"Too bad. You're my son. That won't ever change just because you're older now. Deal with it."

With a sneer, Hutch headed for the door. He wasn't going to stick around and listen to him talk. He needed to blow off some steam. Thankfully, his father didn't follow him.

Did he really look for the bad in his father? He didn't think so, but then again, he also didn't consider Maison when his father had told him to room with him. He'd been too alarmed with the fact that he'd be alone with Matthew that Maison had been pushed from his mind.

· *Maison.*

Why was she so tired lately? It wasn't like her to forget things. Especially with that planner she had. Was that why she'd been acting differently lately?

Hutch found the bar and quickly got comfortable. Now that he and his father had argued, he'd likely be spending more of the evening here until it was late enough to go back to the room. He really didn't want to face his father again.

After ordering himself some hard liquor, he thought about the last time he'd drank.

God, that'd been terrible too. He'd been all over Maison. He wouldn't be surprised if she'd told him that he'd drooled on her too. But whatever feelings he'd had stored inside of him had simply boiled over when he saw her. And those feelings only seemed to have amplified since he'd started working with her.

He loved seeing her focus and determination every day. Although many saw her as shy, Maison was a force to be reckoned with. He grinned, thinking about that time she'd gotten upset with him.

Yeah, he thought. She had fire.

"Hutch? Are you all right?" He turned to find the woman of his thoughts before him.

"Maison? What are you doing here?"

"Your dad told me you stormed off so I came to look for you."

Dammit, why the hell had he done that? He'd already said that Maison needed some rest. "I'm fine. You should go back to your room."

Maison shook her head. "Not unless you come back too."

Hutch gritted his teeth. *No, he didn't want to face his father just yet.*

The bartender appeared then. "Are you staying? Did you want a drink?"

Maison took one glance at him and sat back. "No alcohol for me," she told the man. "I've got an early morning tomorrow."

Guilt consumed him. He probably shouldn't be drinking either.

"So what did you two fight about?" Maison asked.

He was surprised by her question. He'd thought that his father would've told her already. But he really didn't feel like rehashing it with her.

"I'm really sorry about the rooms," she said instead. "I can't believe I forgot."

"Hey, don't be so hard on yourself. You've had a lot on your plate. And it's fine. I don't mind staying with Dad."

The look she shot him had him laughing out loud. "Okay, maybe I do. But it's only for a couple of nights. I'll survive."

He was surprised when she smiled at him. And then she surprised him when she said, "I'm glad you're here, you know."

"Really?"

Maison nodded. "I was a little bit nervous about it all but having you around has made things easier for me."

Wow. He never expected to hear those words from her.

That was when he realized that she wasn't stuttering anymore. Did that mean she was comfortable with him now?

Hutch raised his glass in the air. *I'll drink to that.*

TWELVE

THE WEATHER IN LONDON WAS A COMPLETE ONE-eighty to what Maison was used to in Moonrise Beach. While she'd come prepared and brought warmer clothes, she hadn't expected it to be *this* cold. The wind made everything worse, and now she wished she'd brought a hat or even some mittens.

Figuring she could warm up with a hot cup of coffee, Maison sipped her fresh brew while going over Matthew's schedule for the day. His first appearance was in an hour, and after spending hours poring over this in preparation, she knew everything was going to be perfect.

Twenty minutes before the event, she already had Matthew situated by the stage, already micced up and ready to go. "Are you okay?" she asked him. She knew he'd practiced his speech numerous times already but she just wanted to make sure.

"I'm fine, Maison."

"Okay." She took a breath and smiled for him. "Good luck."

To her surprise, Matthew reached out and cupped her face with his large hand. "Thank you for being here."

"O-of course." She wouldn't have it any other way.

"But since I'm already here and everything looks to be all set, why don't you and Hutch go grab a coffee or something?"

Maison looked at Hutch, who was standing behind her. "But I wanted to watch you speak."

Matthew shook his head. "Not necessary. You know exactly what I'm going to say anyway. And if something goes wrong, one of the people here can help me. You've done enough. Why don't you go and enjoy yourself?"

"Are you sure?" She was more than happy to stay.

"Yes, I'm sure. I noticed you didn't have anything to eat this morning. Go and grab something before you keel over."

"Okay." She turned to Hutch and he looked just as surprised as she was. "What's up with him?" she asked on a whisper.

Hutch shrugged. "No idea. But he's unusually nice today."

"Do you think it was because of the fight you had yesterday?"

"I don't think so. He still hasn't talked to me."

Maybe it was her then. Had she done something wrong? Was that why he didn't want her around to see him speak in front of everyone?

As panic rose, Hutch grabbed her arm. "Come on. I haven't eaten either and I'm starved." He dragged her to the nearest coffee shop. Walking in the cold weather made it feel a mile away. Maison's eyes were already tearing up and her ears hurt so much that she had to put her hands over them to protect them from the chilling cold.

She was going to start rubbing her hands together when something fell over her face and wrapped around her neck. Suddenly the biting pain lessened and she looked up into the dark orbs of Hutch's eyes.

He'd given her his scarf and it was now warming her up better than a hot cup of coffee. "Wha—" she began but Hutch simply shrugged.

"You looked cold." Then he reached for the coffee shop's door and held it open for her. "Ladies first."

Maison felt herself blush. She hadn't expected that from him.

As they entered the coffee shop and stood in line, Maison

couldn't help but notice the way Hutch's scarf smelled like him. Spearmint and eucalyptus wafted all around her and she wanted nothing more than to drown in the freshness.

Wow, this place was nice. Maison was used to the big franchise coffee houses like Starbucks back home, but there was something really nice about coming to a local family-owned coffee house too. The atmosphere was different, definitely a lot cozier, and she loved all the smiling faces of the staff and its customers.

When she walked up to the cashier and was about to order, Hutch gently pushed her behind him. "I've got this one."

She began to protest but then her mouth snapped shut as Hutch began to speak.

"She'll have a caramel Frappuccino."

Maison felt her mouth drop open. How the hell did he know what she was going to order? She was still balking as he paid and they moved to the side to wait for their drinks. When he caught her staring at him, he grinned. "What's wrong? Why are you staring at me like that?"

Maison immediately averted her eyes and blushed. "Sorry. I didn't mean to be rude."

"No, it's fine," he said. A smile curled his lips. "I kind of like you staring at me."

Maison glanced back at him to find that his smile had turned into a full-blown grin and she blushed even further. "Relax, Maison. Everything is fine. Dad can handle things on his own."

But that wasn't what she was thinking about. She wasn't worried about Matthew at all. Now her thoughts were consumed with Hutch and of their great time they'd had last night.

Despite drinking, Hutch seemed steady today. A lot

steadier than he'd been when she'd found him in his father's house that one night.

She was glad to notice that he wasn't like that anymore. Maybe Matthew had been right and working at Gleam was good for him. Whatever it was that was making him happy, she was glad for its presence.

In working with him, she'd also started to notice more about the guy. While she'd known him for years, they'd kept a respectable distance, and never went beyond friendship. Now, Maison felt bad for not paying more attention to him like he did with her.

While he could likely list out her favorite foods without hesitation, Maison realized that she wanted to know more about him. About his interests and his goals. And about what he liked to read and what he liked to do on the weekends. The problem was, she was too shy to ask, and so, she'd just have to go on wondering.

Hutch grabbed both of their drinks and they found a table to sit down at.

She took her first sip of coffee and moaned. It was so good. Possibly even better than what she usually had at home and back at the hotel. "Good, huh?" Hutch smiled.

She nodded. "It's amazing."

"Don't you want to have some of your croissant?"

"Oh yes." She broke off a piece and brought it to her mouth. On her tongue, the sweet taste made her moan again. "Do you want some?"

"No, thanks." He held up his bagel. "I'm good." Now that they were seated, Maison became increasingly aware of the fact that they were away from everyone else in a private corner. She suddenly felt nervous again. "You okay?" Hutch asked after taking a sip of his coffee.

Maison nodded. "Wasn't it nice of Matthew to let us get breakfast?"

"Yeah, I guess."

"Are you still angry with him?"

When Hutch didn't answer, Maison went back to fidgeting with her food. Hutch reached out and grabbed a hold of her hand. "I'm sorry. Am I making you nervous again?"

Maison felt her face go hot. "I should be the one apologizing. I shouldn't have brought him up."

"I don't mind. You're not nervous when it comes to my father."

She wasn't sure how to answer. "You're right. But Matthew is different. He's . . ."

"Older?"

"Yes, but—" Her cheeks flushed hot and she suddenly wished that she wasn't wearing his scarf any more. She shook her head. "Never mind." She didn't want to say that *all* the Happa-Hewitts were special to her. "Anyways, is this your first time in London?"

"No, I've been here once. But it was a long time ago."

"Oh." Somehow he'd managed to pin the weather down better than she had and she'd been here many times before. Guess he was better at packing than she was.

"Have you traveled a lot?"

She'd been born and raised in Moonrise Beach and had never traveled often as a child. Only with her work was she able to go to the places she'd always dreamed about visiting.

"Not much, to be honest," Hutch said, taking another sip of his coffee. "At least not as much as the rest of my family apart from the tours I've been on."

Oh right. While others traveled to exotic locations for fun, he'd done it for his country. Not only that, but he also hadn't been able to come back whole.

Maison suddenly regretted asking the question. In her effort to try and get to know him better, she had reminded him of what he'd lost.

She bit into her croissant, trying to muster up the right words to apologize when Hutch asked, "What about you? Did you travel a lot as a kid?"

Maison stiffened. "Ah, no. I didn't." She didn't expand or elaborate but she could see that Hutch was expecting her to, but unfortunately, that wasn't a topic she wanted to discuss with him.

"You don't have any siblings, right?"

"No, it's just me." And thank goodness for that. She couldn't imagine her parents having another child. Her parents did a little bit of traveling, but it was rarely overseas like this. They were only willing to travel to neighboring states for work functions and the like.

"Where are your parents now anyway? You haven't mentioned them much."

Maison hesitated. "Ah, well." She wasn't comfortable talking about her parents. But she also didn't want to come across as rude. It wasn't his fault that he didn't know that she wasn't on good terms with her parents. She rarely talked about them.

Just then, her cell phone rang and when she glanced down at the name on the screen, she felt herself frown. "What is it?" Hutch asked.

"It's your dad." She immediately hit Answer. "Hello? Matthew? Is everything okay?"

To her surprise, Matthew sounded apologetic. "Maison, sorry to bother you, but do you think you can come back?"

Maison was already on her feet. "Of course. What's wrong?"

"It's my fault. I've spilled some coffee on my shirt and I'm on in five minutes. I'm really sorry. My nerves just—"

"No need to apologize, sir. I'll be right there." She snatched up her drink and called for Hutch.

He immediately appeared beside her. "What happened?"

"Matthew's on in five minutes and he accidentally spilled coffee on himself."

Hutch laughed. "Wow, I would've liked to see that."

"Come on, we have to hurry." It'd taken them maybe ten minutes to walk here. They'd have to try and be back in two to be able to reach Matthew in time. Grinning, Maison said, "Last one there will have to wash out the stain!" Before Hutch could even respond, she had bolted down the street, smiling as she heard Hutch cursing behind her.

They'd made it. With one minute to spare, Maison had somehow produced a fresh shirt for Matthew to change into. He smiled down at Maison. "Thank you. I can always count on you."

Maison beamed at the praise. "No problem, sir."

"Where'd you even get a shirt in the first place?" he asked.

"From my purse. I always carry one around just in case."

"Really? Always?" That seemed a bit extreme, but he wouldn't deny that it'd come in handy.

"Thanks for coming back so quickly," Matthew said. "I really hated to bother you."

"I told you, it's absolutely fine so stop feeling bad. You've got a speech coming up!" She gave him a mega-watt smile and a thumbs-up.

Matthew grinned at her. Then he reached for his coffee again. As he brought the cup up to his lips, Maison snatched it out of his hand. "Let's not chance it, okay?" Before his father could even protest, she dumped the cup into the nearest trash bin.

Hutch stifled a laugh at his father's expression.

To his surprise, Matthew was fighting his own grin. They hadn't talked at all since their argument the night before, but he was glad that his father was smiling at him again.

When his name was called, Matthew moved towards the stage. A roaring applause shook the venue as he walked onto the stage. Hutch felt his eyes widen as the cheers continued. *Wow, all these people were cheering for his father?*

As the CEO of one of the biggest companies in the world, he guessed he shouldn't be so surprised that so many people looked up to him. Hutch just didn't expect the response to be this overwhelming. The whole stint with the admirers when they'd first arrived at the hotel was nothing in comparison. This was admiration on a whole other level.

Maison grabbed a hold of his arm. He didn't want to make such a big deal of it, but this was the second time she'd touch him so casually. Did that mean she was getting used to him?

She quickly dragged him towards the mass of people all sitting together as they watched his father up on the stage. To his surprise, a few people recognized him and greeted him also.

When he could finally sit down and watch his father, Matthew was already well into his speech. Not surprisingly, he spoke with great elegance and authority. Hutch could see that some people were even taking notes as he spoke while others settled for filming him instead.

Beside him, Maison laughed and clapped as his father recited a joke. It wasn't particularly original. In fact, it was a little on the cheesy side, but Hutch found himself chuckling along anyway. Soon, he was applauding with the rest of them.

He was proud to see his father up there, speaking in front

of thousands of people talking about his growing company and business ethics. If all these people here looked up to Matthew, maybe he should do the same.

Hutch would be the first to admit that he took a lot of things for granted. Take his leg for example. Only with its loss did he learn to miss and appreciate it.

He thought about what his father had said to him the night before. Did he really look for things to hate him for? A lot of their fights were over stupid things. What if he tried respecting his father more? Would that help their relationship?

It was just like his adjustment now. He never thought he'd be able to find something he might enjoy in Moonrise Beach simply because he was too focused on what he'd loss with the Army. But thankfully Sam had shown him that he could find enjoyment here too.

If he could learn to see his father the way all these other people did, maybe he wouldn't hate him so much and they could get over their strained relationship. The notion was so simple yet he knew it would take a while for that to change.

After his father's speech, they'd celebrated with drinks. This time he took it easy with his choice and opted for a beer instead.

Hutch wasn't sure if it was because his father was in a good mood after doing his presentation or if his change in thinking had really helped him, but they all chatted for the next several hours before returning to their rooms.

Hutch had just gotten out of the shower when his father walked over to him. "Could you do me a favor?"

"Sure."

"Drop these over to Maison's room for me. I'm beat and would like to shower too."

"Okay." He rose, taking the files from his father and moved

for the door.

Maison was situated just next door, so he really didn't mind doing this for his dad. Besides, he really wanted to see Maison again.

When she opened the door for him, he was surprised to see her already in her pajamas. Apologies quickly spilled from his mouth. "I didn't realize how late it was."

"I'm really tired."

"Then I'll let you get some sleep." He handed her the files. "My dad asked me to give these to you."

"Thank you."

For a moment, Hutch felt stupid for standing there and staring at her, but he couldn't look away. Maison's hair was wet from her shower and her long, blonde locks rested at her shoulders.

The pajamas she wore were pale pink and cozy-looking, likely to combat the evening chill, but what amused him the most was the fact that they had little white snowflakes all over them. "I know it's cold, but it's not *that* cold," he teased. When Maison frowned, he pointed at her pajamas.

"Oh!" Her cheeks flushed instantly. "I, um." He could've sworn that she got even redder as he stared at her. "Well, I don't have any reason other than that they're warm."

He couldn't help but laugh. "They're cute. It suits you."

Maison flushed even further.

"All right then, Snowflake. Get some rest."

He turned away before she would say anything to the playful nickname he'd given her. *His little Snowflake could be too cute sometimes.*

Hutch went to bed, thinking about Maison and her cute snowflake-covered pajamas.

THIRTEEN

O N DAY TWO OF THE CONFERENCE, MATTHEW WAS scheduled for an intimate Q&A with some of his "fans." Maison chuckled to herself as she thought about Matthew's reaction if he heard her calling them that. Although they certainly adored him like any other Hollywood celebrity, Matthew still kept things very professional. She wouldn't be surprised if he scolded her calling them that again.

At least things between Matthew and Hutch were improving. She hated seeing them argue. At the bar last night, they'd been talking to each other again and it gave her so much pleasure to simply sit between them and enjoy each other's company.

Today, however, she was feeling even more tired than the day before. "Oh no," she muttered as she wondered if she'd somehow caught a cold. Her body ached in various places and she was feeling sluggish. The only thing missing was a headache.

Maison blearily stumbled out of bed and instantly regretted it as twin points of pain lanced through her temples. *Dammit, why the hell had she stayed up so late?*

Although she'd already been dressed for bed at nine, after Hutch had dropped off the files from Matthew, she'd spent some time going over them. Before she knew it, several hours had passed and she realized that she'd have to get up in another four hours.

She'd stumbled into bed in the early morning but she knew

the day ahead of her was going to be tough. She could barely stand up without wanting to keel over.

Nevertheless, she pushed through her fatigue. She was thankful that she had the foresight to shower the night before. Now all she had to do was put her clothes on.

Finally dressed, she texted Hutch that she was going to go grab some breakfast before meeting them. Some food and coffee would definitely enliven her.

By the time she was done eating, she felt marginally better. Her headache was gone but that feeling of grogginess remained. A second cup of coffee would definitely be required in her near future.

When Matthew and Hutch finally arrived, they both sported twin looks of concern. "Are you all right?" Hutch asked immediately.

God, did she really look that bad? "I'm fine. Just a little tired."

"Didn't sleep well?"

"More like, I didn't sleep at all."

"Don't tell me you went over the files again instead of sleeping," Matthew said.

Maison felt herself blush.

"Maison," he scolded. "You didn't need to do that. You could've done that when we got back to Moonrise."

"I know. I was just curious and wanted to double-check that everything is where it's supposed to be."

Hutch grinned at her. "You're such a perfectionist."

Matthew shook his head. "No, she's crazy. Next time I won't be giving you anything until we get back."

"But—"

"Come on, let's go. We don't want to be late."

Because she didn't want to be late either, Maison allowed

Matthew to lead the way. She was surprised that he knew where he was going. Maybe he didn't need her after all.

"So what's on the agenda today?" Hutch asked. "Just the Q&A?"

"Yup. And then we're free to do whatever we want."

"Not anything. We do have to fly back tomorrow," Matthew gently reminded her.

"Don't worry. I wasn't planning on getting drunk," Hutch replied.

As Matthew got prepared for his big moment, he asked, "Do you guys want to grab some breakfast or something?"

Maison shot him a look. "Considering how that went yesterday, I think I'm going to say no."

Her boss grinned at her. "I think I'm capable of keeping my shirt clean for ten minutes, Maison."

"We'll see about that. Besides, I already had breakfast." She looked to Hutch.

"I did too," he added.

"Good. So we'll just go out front and find a couple of seats there, okay?"

Matthew nodded. "Okay. Thank you, Maison."

"No problem."

Together, she and Hutch moved to the front to find seats. The crowd today was much smaller, but there was still a little raised podium that Matthew would be on while he answered questions. They settled for a spot closer to one of the walls, leaving the best seats in the house for his fans.

As soon as she sat down, Maison let out a long sigh. Man, she must be really tired. Hutch glanced down at her. "Are you okay?"

"I'm fine. I'm just a little tired."

"Well, good thing all we have to do now is just sit here for an hour. You can take a nap if you want."

"I'm not going to sleep!" She wasn't that tired and it would look terrible if Matthew Hewitt's assistant was caught sleeping during one of his Q&As. Hutch flashed her a sexy smile.

"Don't worry, I'll cover for you, Snowflake."

"I don't need you to cover for me. And what's with you calling me Snowflake? Stop, it's annoying."

"I find it amusing." His sexy smile widened as she let out a growl.

Instead of arguing with him though, Maison ignored his sexy smirk and focused back on Matthew. He'd just stepped up to the podium and introduced himself. As expected, cheers and applause erupted. *How the hell did Hutch think she could sleep through all that?*

As the Q&A began, her head started to feel heavier and heavier. Maison did her best to push past it but it was already dark in the room and her eyelids kept drooping down.

For a moment, she allowed herself to close her eyes. Man, she wished she had a pillow to rest her head on but she wasn't lucky enough to have one on hand.

Whatever. In a second she would open her eyes again.

She just wanted another moment to rest.

Hutch had been surprised when he looked over to see Maison with her eyes closed. He was even more shocked when her head started to dip sideways. He fought the urge to laugh. He couldn't believe Maison Lane had actually fallen asleep!

Instead of laughing out loud like he wanted to, Hutch stayed still as her head found a spot on his shoulder. He had to scoot down a little more in his seat so that she could comfortably lean on him, but he wasn't going to complain.

From this position, he could smell her scent. Light yet

intoxicating, Hutch got lost in thought as he imagined what it would be like to share a bed with this wonderful woman. He thought it'd been adorable when she'd worn her snowflake pajamas and now he couldn't stop himself from imagining her in anything else.

When Maison's soft snores sounded in his ear, he had to stifle his laugh or fear waking her. She was more tired than she'd let on. A part of him even felt angry that she wasn't taking better care of herself. Maison was always doing something for others when she should be worrying about herself more.

He let her sleep through the entire Q&A. Although there were a lot of people around them, no one seemed to notice her snoring away.

He found it funny that she was currently using him as a pillow. Did that mean she was getting used to him? Maybe even feeling comfortable with him?

He looked down at his shoulder and took in her beauty. He knew Maison was self-conscious about her looks, but had she always been that way? He didn't see anything wrong with her appearance and he wondered if there was something else playing a part in her insecurities. He didn't believe Maison's misconstrued body image was a result of her own thinking.

Suddenly, her eyes fluttered open and her head lifted. "Wha—" She looked adorably confused for a second before realization hit her. *"Oh my God! Did I fall asleep?"*

Hutch grinned at her. "It's okay, Snowflake. You dozed off a little but no one noticed."

As expected, her cheeks flushed. "I can't believe I just did that!"

"Relax. It's fine. I was watching over you." His hand came over her leg to offer more reassurance but she let out a little squeak.

"Sorry," she mumbled.

Hutch smiled again. "It's okay. No need to beat yourself up over it. We're all a little tired this morning."

"I didn't sleep on you, did I?" Horror masked her features. *"Oh God, I did, didn't I?"*

He could only grin in response. "I make a good pillow."

Groaning, Maison got to her feet and he did the same, following her over to where Matthew was. Now that he was done, they had the rest of the day off.

He could hear Maison's voice above all the chatter. "Great job! You were perfect." *Funny, how would she know that if she'd been sleeping through the whole thing?*

He stifled a laugh. "Yeah, you were great," he agreed.

"Thank you." To his surprise, Matthew patted him on the shoulder.

As Hutch tried recovering from his surprise, a man he was fairly certain he knew walked up to them. "Matthew, hey. I just wanted to congratulate you. You've done an amazing job these past few days."

His father looked surprised by the newcomer, but a second later, his professionalism was back in place. He shook the man's extended hand. "Brian, it's good to see you here. Maison, you remember Mr. Melwood, right?"

Maison stepped forward. "Yes. Hello, sir." As they exchanged pleasantries, Hutch went over what he remembered about this guy.

From what he could recall, Brian Melwood also worked for Gleam Enterprises. However, his focus was on the international side of things. His father's partner, Clive Davenport, had brought him in in an effort to expand their business overseas. But he knew there had always been a subtle thread of tension between his father and Mr. Melwood.

When Brian's gaze landed on him, surprise flashed over his features. "Hutch? Is that you?"

He stepped forward. "Yes, sir." His father may not like the man but Hutch would always be cordial to everyone he met.

"Well, I'll be damned. I didn't know you were going to be here. I heard you were working for Gleam but I didn't expect you to tag along on the trips as well."

Tag along. Like he was a little lost puppy. Hutch gritted his teeth. "My father was kind enough to invite me."

"Well, good. I hope you're enjoying your time in London."

"I am. It's been fantastic. But I am looking forward to returning to the warmer weather."

"Ah, too chilly for you here?" Brian laughed. "Me too. I can't want to return to Moonrise. Hey, will you be attending the charity event when we return?"

Charity event? No one had mentioned anything about a charity event.

His expression must've revealed his confusion because Maison said, "It's for the American Cancer Society. Gleam Enterprises has done it every year since your mother passed."

Oh right, he knew all about that. What he didn't realize was that it was happening so soon.

"You're free to come," she said. "I just wasn't sure if you wanted to."

"Will you be there?"

"Of course." While the idea of dressing up made him want to strangle himself, he'd loved the chance to see Maison in a dress again.

"Maison, do you have a date?" Brian asked.

Beside him, Maison flushed. "Ah. No. I don't usually go with anyone since it's a work thing."

"Don't be ridiculous. Everyone needs a date. What about

you, Hutch?"

"Considering that I didn't know it was happening until just a moment ago, no. I don't."

"No girlfriend?"

Hutch glanced at Maison who was still flushing. "Unfortunately, no."

"Well then, since you two don't have dates, why don't you go with each other?" Brian suggested.

"Ah, I'm not sure that's really necess—"

"That's a great idea," Matthew said.

Both he and Maison turned to him in surprise. "*What?*"

"Oh come on, it'll be great. Hunter and Owen will be there too. I just need to convince Dacey now."

Hutch laughed. "Yeah. Good luck with that." Dacey was the most hardheaded out of all of them.

"Wonderful," Brian chimed. "I guess I'll see you then."

Hutch nodded. "See you then."

After he left, he turned to Maison. "What the hell was that all about?" she wailed.

"Don't mind him. He's just a little chatty."

"No, I mean about the charity thing!"

He stiffened. "You don't want to go with me?"

"*No!* I mean, yes, I do. But I just think it would be better if—"

"Maison, if you don't want to go with me, you don't have to. I won't force you. But I am going to be there." He'd do it for his mother. *And*, he thought, *for his father too*. It'd be nice to be able to go and support him again.

"Are you sure you want to go with me? I mean, you can bring someone else—"

"I *want* to go with you." He smiled down at her. "In fact, there's no one else I would rather go with."

As his words sunk in, Maison's cheeks reddened adorably. "O-okay. In that case, I'll go with you."

"Great. I'll pick you up."

"It's fine. I can get there myself."

"Maison, let me pick you up." He couldn't stand the thought of her standing there alone, waiting for him. "Please."

She rolled her eyes at him. "Oh fine. We'll talk about it more when we get back to Moonrise Beach."

He smiled. "Perfect."

Now all he had to do was find something to wear.

FOURTEEN

THE RETURN TRIP WAS PLEASANT AND QUICK, MOSTLY because Hutch loved spending uninterrupted time by Maison's side. Although he was tired, he wouldn't allow his fatigue to make him miss a single moment.

Now that they were back in Moonrise Beach, however, he would have to wait to see her again. It was a good thing that she'd agreed to go with him to tonight's charity event.

Although the rest of his family was going to be there, his sister, Dacey, had declined the invitation. She'd told him earlier that she wasn't interested in seeing her old co-workers. Given that her ex worked at Gleam too, that was understandable. After ditching her in India while she was suffering from typhoid fever, their engagement had ended badly and returning to Moonrise had caused a lot of new changes in his sister's life. Now, she had her own booming business to look after.

Still, Hutch didn't realize what a hardship finding nice clothes to wear would be. Thankfully, Dacey had shown up at the house a half hour ago and was trying to help him put together something to wear. Greyson, her boyfriend, had also come with her but he and Buddha, Dacey's French bulldog, were watching an old episode of America's Next Top Model instead of helping him out. "Will you turn that garbage off and help me?" he called out. If he didn't find something soon, he would be screwed.

Both Greyson and Buddha glanced in his direction, but neither of them looked interested in what was happening. "But this is the good part," Greyson whined as he gestured at the TV.

Beside him, Dacey rolled her eyes. "Don't mind him. I'll get you situated." She held up a suit he had in his closet. "What about this one?"

Hutch frowned. "Are you sure?" He hadn't worn it in years and he wasn't even sure if it fit him anymore.

"Try it on and let's see how it fits you. You've gotten a little bit bigger but I think it'll still look good."

That didn't give him much confidence. He wanted to look good for Maison and not in a way to just impressed her. He wanted her to be happy to be his date for the night.

When he went to the bathroom and tried it on, he realized that Dacey had been right. It still fit, but it was a little snugger than he was used to. It did, however, outline his broad frame nicely.

Hutch examined himself closely in the mirror. What would Maison think of him when she saw him wearing this? Would she think he looked silly? Or would she actually like what she saw?

If only he could be a man worthy of her attentions.

Dacey banged on the bathroom door, startling him from his thoughts. "Hey, come out and let's see what it looks like!"

"Hold on." It had been a long time since he'd seen himself in something other than a band T-shirt and jeans. He still wasn't used to seeing himself this way. While working at Gleam meant that he was dressing better, he still had a ways to go if he wanted to look like his father.

As soon as he stepped out of the bathroom, Dacey let out a whoop of excitement. "Wow, look at you! You look great!"

From the bed, Greyson let out a wolf whistle. "Lookin' sharp, my man!"

"You think so?" He still wasn't sure. A button-down shirt

he could handle, but this felt like too much.

"You'll definitely catch some lady's attention wearing that," Greyson said.

"I'm really only interested in impressing one girl."

"Oh really, who? Are you bringing a date to this thing?"

"Yes, I am," he replied smugly.

"Who?" Dacey suddenly seemed *very* interested.

"Maison."

"Maison? As in Maison, like *our* Maison?"

"Yes, *our* Maison." And he was still over the moon about it.

"Did you force her to go with you or something?"

"Hey! That's not very nice. And no, I didn't. I asked her and she said yes."

Dacey snorted. "Yeah, right. Why would Maison lower herself to *you*?"

Greyson chuckled and rose from the bed to join them.

"Does Dad know?" Dacey asked.

"Yeah, he was there when I asked her."

"You know, I kind of like it," Greyson stated and that earned him a horrified look from his girlfriend.

"How can you say that? He's going to corrupt Maison!"

"I'm not going to corrupt anyone!" He liked how Maison was just fine. "Relax, okay? We're just going to this thing together. It's not even a date." *Why were they making such a big deal about this?*

"But do you *want* to date her?" Greyson asked.

"You can't!" Dacey cried. "I'm not losing her as a friend after you're done with her!"

"Who said anything about doing that?" He didn't intend on ever hurting Maison.

Dacey pinned him with a look. "I know you, Hutch. We all know how you are with women, and I'm not going to let you do it to Maison!"

Their yelling brought Owen to his door and Hunter poked his head in. "What's going on here?"

"Did you know that Hutch is going with Maison to the charity event tomorrow?"

Hunter looked momentarily confused and then he said, "Oh, you are? That's cool. So what's the problem here?"

"*Thank you*," he breathed. At least *someone* had his back.

"That doesn't bother you?" Dacey asked.

"Why would it bother me? Maison can take care of herself."

"Maison is going to get her heart broken!"

"Maison is a big girl," Hunter retorted. "And I'm sure she can decide on her own who she wants to go out with."

"I can't believe you guys. You're all such *men!*" Dacey said the last word as if it was an insult.

Greyson came to stand between them. "Okay, okay. That's enough. Hunter is right. Maison is more than capable of handling herself." Hutch was about to thank him for having his back when the guy turned on him and said, "But don't be reckless with her. I have a feeling underneath those big, blue eyes she's got some bite."

Hutch nodded. "Noted."

"Fine." Dacey stomped out of the room and Buddha and Owen followed after her.

Hunter let out a low whistle. "She was really upset about that." He turned to Greyson and grinned. "Good luck with that."

Greyson groaned. "I want you happy, man, but you know I won't hear the end of it if you mess shit up with her."

Hutch gave him his best winning smile. "I won't."

"Good." And with that, Greyson left after his girlfriend. Hutch never expected to rekindle his friendship with his childhood friend, but he was definitely glad for Greyson's presence now.

Alone with his brother, Hunter didn't say anything to him, which only made him feel uneasy. They'd never had much to talk about, especially now that they were older. But if his older brother had any advice to give, he didn't share it now. Instead, Hunter just walked out of the room.

On a sigh, Hutch turned to face the mirror again and adjusted his suit. "No breaking Maison's heart," he muttered to himself. That would be easy enough. He had no intentions of ever hurting her. And while he had experience with a lot of women in the past, he had a feeling that none of that would work with her.

No, what he really wanted was to *win* Maison's heart.

FIFTEEN

MAISON WAS A BALL OF ANXIETY BUT NO AMOUNT of deep breathing was going to get her to calm down. With the charity event tonight for the American Cancer Society, she was running amok, trying to get everything done.

Normally, an event like this wouldn't be enough to put her into a panic, but ringing in the back of her head was the reminder that she wasn't going to be going alone this time.

For the first time since she started working for Gleam Enterprises, Maison actually had a date to go with. And it wasn't just any date either! She was going with Hutch Happa-Hewitt! Hutch could easily have any woman in the world but he'd asked her. Why? She still couldn't believe it as she gazed at herself in the mirror.

Her hair was still damp from her shower and she'd actually written a reminder down in her planner to shave her legs too. The extra primping was needed if she wanted to look good tonight.

While she would really love to look like a Victoria's Secret model, she only had herself to blame. With the stress from work and traveling, she had completely disregarded her diet and had recently gained a few pounds. Unfortunately, she didn't know any instant weight loss system that worked.

Whatever. She had to remind herself that this was a work function and not a date. As thrilled as she was about tonight, she couldn't expect it to actually mean anything.

Maison took her time applying her mascara. Two coats would do. Or would a third coat make her blue eyes really pop? While she normally didn't wear much makeup, she wanted her eyes to look sexy and sultry for a change.

When she was satisfied with her makeup, she went over to her closet to change. She'd picked out her favorite dress earlier but then noticed something she hadn't before. *What was Hutch's scarf doing on her bed?* She realized with surprise that she'd totally forgotten to return it to him when they'd come back from their trip. She would have no use for it now since the weather in Moonrise was warm. Still, a part of her was reluctant to return it.

Picking it up, she brought the scarf to her nose and took a sniff. It still smelled strongly of Hutch and a shiver went through her. If she hadn't already been thinking of him before, she was now. That's when her anxiety hit her.

Was the dress she picked out too safe? Black normally worked for all occasions and disguised any unwanted lumps and bumps she had, but Maison was tired of wearing dark clothing and blending into the crowd.

She had no doubt that people would be watching her tonight, especially since she was going to be arriving with Hutch. She hadn't considered this before saying yes to him, but now that she had, what would people think about her? Would they laugh and wonder how a girl like her could think she could run with the likes of the Happa-Hewitts? Hutch's entire family was superstar quality. They were all so good-looking and successful. Maison would look stupid beside him.

"I guess I just need to put my best foot forward." How embarrassing would it be if she showed up looking like she'd just trekked through the sewers? No, she was going to look nice tonight! While she would never be on the same level as any of the Happa-Hewitts, she at least wanted to look like she could be a part of them.

Maison returned her plain black dress and pulled out a siren red one. She'd bought it but never worn it before. It was supposed to be a motivational tool for her weight loss. She'd hoped to one day lose enough weight to wear it but that day hadn't come.

Until now.

While she hadn't reached her ideal weight yet, she was hoping she could pull it off. The color was stunning and she thought it would look nice with her blonde hair and blue eyes. If only she had the confidence to match.

Whatever. It was the best she had and after slipping on the dress, she realized that she didn't look too bad in it. The straps of her bra were showing but maybe if she tucked it in a little bit, it wouldn't be as visible.

Dammit. Why was she overthinking everything? It was just a stupid dress!

She switched out her bra for a strapless one and immediately regretted it. Her boobs just didn't have enough support. She felt like she would spill out of the cups at any moment. She was already uncomfortable and she didn't need any more to worry about. Deciding that she didn't want to risk a wardrobe malfunction, she changed into a black one with straps. At least if the straps showed it wouldn't clash too much with the rest of her outfit.

As a finishing touch, she then applied a matching red lipstick. "Wow," she murmured as she examined herself in the mirror. She'd never seen herself like this before! While she wasn't used to exposing this much skin, she had to admit, she did look pretty good!

Her curled hair softly accentuated her facial features and

she liked that the bright lip matched her dress. Although she'd
been worried that the color might be too shocking, it had the
right amount of statement without being too loud.

Damn, she looked good!

But just as quickly as she'd built herself up, her anxiety
took her down a notch.

In the previous years, she'd normally drive over to the
Hewitt house and they would all go together, but this time
Hutch had insisted that he come and pick her up.

Now with nothing left to do but wait, her anxiety tripled.
She still couldn't believe she was going to be going with Hutch!
She really hoped she didn't say anything stupid or make a fool
of herself in front of everyone. Then she'd really regret saying
yes to him!

Checking the clock, Maison realized that she had a few
minutes to spare, so she went into the kitchen and made a cup
of chamomile tea. It would help in calming down her nerves a
little. Her palms were already getting sweaty. Damn, she really
hoped her deodorant held up through the night.

When the doorbell rang, Maison swallowed past the lump
in her throat. "Okay, here we go. Just have fun," she reminded
herself as she opened the door.

She felt her heart lurch in her chest as she took Hutch in.
Wow.

Are you kidding me? She thought seeing him in his dress
shirts and slacks at work were hot but Hutch all dressed up in a
tux was going to kill her! *Holy shit! He looked amazing!*

Dressed in a black suit, Hutch looked hotter than a jala-
peño. His hair was slicked back, revealing his warm eyes and
sharp cheekbones. He'd even shaved and the neat look only
added to the editorial look he was going for. Not even movie
stars could compete with him tonight. At this rate, it was likely

that he was going to give her a nosebleed!

"Hey, Maison." Hutch's warm eyes crinkled before running down the length of her. His jaw dropped. "Wow, you look amazing!" Maison felt herself flush. *Not as good as you look.* But she was glad she'd put in the extra effort. "That dress is stunning on you."

"Thanks." She blushed even more. *God, at this rate, she was going to flare up before they even got to the charity event.*

"So are you ready to go?" Hutch asked her.

She just hoped that she wouldn't regret this night.

"Maison, are you okay?"

"Um, yeah." She was just overthinking things. There was nothing to worry about, and she deserved something special every once in a while. For one night, she was just going to enjoy herself and not care what other people thought of her.

Maison forced herself to smile, hoping it looked convincing. "Come on. Let's go." In a bold move, she took Hutch's hand. "I don't want to be late."

* * *

To her surprise, the night progressed smoothly. No one batted an eye at her arriving with Hutch, and Matthew didn't even seem weirded out to see them sitting together. After the charity work was done and Matthew had said his speech, the rest of the night was devoted to food and dancing. Normally at this point, Maison would say her goodbyes and head home, but with Hutch here with her, she didn't think that would be appropriate.

He'd been glued to her side all night and, surprisingly, Maison was growing more used to his presence. Her anxiety had long disappeared and she was happy to finally be able to enjoy her night. She was quickly realizing that despite Hutch's rebel reputation, he was a really nice guy. He held up her champagne glass. "Do you want another refill?" When she nodded, he rose to refill it.

Her gaze followed him all the way to the refreshments and that was when she caught the gaze of Michael Davenport. Michael, or Mickey as he was better known as, was Clive's son and she hated him more than any other person she'd ever met in her entire life.

Mickey was a slob and that was a nice way of saying it. As the CEO's son, Mickey indulged in his father's money often, using it more than a kid had the right to. And at twenty-nine years old, that was not an attractive quality in a man.

Catching her gaze, he smiled at her. "Oh God," she muttered. "Here we go."

"Maison, it's good to see you again. You look amazing."

Maison pasted on a fake smile. As much as she hated the guy, she couldn't be rude to him. "Mickey, nice to see you too."

"So I heard this year you came with a date. Is he your boyfriend?"

"No," she said immediately. She didn't want to start any false rumors about her and Hutch.

"Ah, but do you *want* him to be your boyfriend?" The mischievous sparkle in his eyes made her want to throttle him. This guy just didn't understand the meaning of space.

Ugh.

Hutch finally returned with their drinks and Maison wanted to clutch him like a lifeline. "Here you go."

She settled for smiling at him. "Thank you."

"So, Hutch," Mickey started now that he'd returned. "Why are you working at Gleam Enterprises?"

Beside her, Hutch shifted in his seat. He obviously wasn't

affected by his questions as she was. "Well, I started working here because I needed something to do."

Mickey snorted. "What? Can't find any friends?" He laughed but no one else at the table joined him.

Hutch glanced at her. "I have friends, but my father stressed that having a job was important."

Once again, Mickey snorted. "Yeah, my old man is the same. I don't know why though. I mean, they earn enough money as it is. Why can't they continue to support their own children? It's way better than handing it over to stupid charities like this."

Maison frowned, not liking where this conversation was going.

"I think donating is admirable," Hutch said.

Mickey rolled his eyes. "Nah, it's a waste of time and money."

Not surprisingly, their conversation had gained other people's attention and Maison found herself growing embarrassed. Mickey, however, seemed oblivious to it.

She had a mind to put him back in his place, but doing so could open up even more problems for them.

"If you think charity work is a waste of time, then you're clearly fortunate to have everything go perfectly in your life. However, my mother's death could have been avoided if we had the resources to treat her," Hutch growled. "And I'm sorry to say, but not even money can buy life. If there is something that we can do to help aid research for cancer patients, then I'm all for it."

Maison sat there, completely shocked by Hutch's words. They were diplomatic but still managed to shut Mickey's mouth in the process. She glanced over at their audience, seeing their frowns turn into smiles.

She was smiling herself and in an effort to comfort and thank Hutch all at once, she wrapped a hand around his. Hutch turned to her, surprise flashing over his features before he asked, "Want to dance?"

Maison flushed immediately. "Oh, I'm not good at dancing."

"Don't worry, just follow my lead." As he dragged her to her feet, she felt her heart start to pound wildly. From the corner of her eye, she caught Mickey's gaze and flushed. He was glaring at them, obviously not pleased by Hutch's words. Hutch chuckled in her ear. "Relax, Maison. It's just dancing."

As they reached the dance floor, one hand reached out to grab hers while the other went around her waist. Hutch then pulled her closer until there was nothing but a slither of air between them. "That's it," Hutch whispered as they began to sway to the music. *Oh God! She couldn't believe she was doing this!* She looked up and their eyes met before the corners of his mouth twisted up in a sly grin. "What are you thinking about?"

"I'm concentrating on not stepping on your toes."

His chuckle ran through her. "Don't worry. You're so tiny I doubt I'd feel it."

"But I'm wearing heels."

"And they look wicked good on you. I've never seen legs so long before."

Her cheeks heated at the compliment but instead of focusing on that, she said, "Thanks for saving me back there."

Hutch scowled. "I don't know what his problem is."

"I don't either but he's always been a little bit of a jerk. Don't know how that's possible since Clive is such a nice guy."

"Maybe he's adopted."

As they laughed together, Hutch brought them closer.

"I probably shouldn't say this but—" He broke off without finishing.

"But what?"

"Mickey likes you."

Maison groaned. "*Ugh.* I know." But she *definitely* didn't return the sentiment.

A smile twisted Hutch's lips and it made him look so handsome that her heart skipped a beat. "What? Don't return the feelings?"

"You're joking, right? It's been a long time since I've been kissed but even then, I'm not *that* desperate."

"Really? I mean, you look absolutely gorgeous. Who wouldn't want to kiss you?

She shrugged, feeling her cheeks heat again. "I guess I'm too shy."

"I think I know of a way to fix that." Before she could do anything, Hutch dropped his lips to hers.

Maison could do nothing but gasp, which only gave him an opportunity to dip his tongue inside her mouth. To her utter embarrassment, she let out a moan, feeling both thrilled and scared with everything that was happening.

Oh God! What the hell was she doing? Was she kissing him back? As the shock of his lips on hers disappeared, arousal flared in its place. And when Hutch's arms tightened around her that was when she really lost it.

Maison snapped her eyes shut, allowing herself to just let go. As her mouth fell open, Hutch's tongue darted inside, brushing against hers. Instantly, her body grew wet and needy. *Wow.* She hadn't known his kisses would be that drugging.

Then again, maybe she did. And maybe that was why she closed herself off from him so much. But she could only resist him for so long. Now that she knew just what Hutch

Happa-Hewitt was capable of, she would always want him. And that scared her more than anything else.

No. *No.*

Seizing back control, Maison pushed him away and ran for her life.

Hutch couldn't even get a word out before Maison was gone. One minute she'd been in his arms, kissing him back fiercely, and in the second, she was gone.

He could see her rushing for the doors while everyone else around them turned to glance back at him. *What the hell? What had he done?* "Maison, wait!"

"What happened?" Hunter asked as he rushed to his side.

"I don't know!" They both started to run after her. "Did you see which way she went?"

"This way." Hunter pointed towards the ladies' room and Hutch darted for it.

He knocked once on the door but heard no response. "Maison!" he called out. "Can we talk?" *Had he pushed her too hard? Had he hurt her in some way? Fuck, it was killing him not knowing what he'd done wrong!*

The door opened and Hutch stepped back, but it wasn't Maison's beautiful blue eyes staring back at him. It was an older woman, beautiful and svelte in her own way, but she didn't hold a candle to his Snowflake.

"I'm sorry," she said, "but whoever you're looking for isn't in there. No one is in there actually. It's just me."

Hutch cursed. "Are you sure?"

"Yes, I checked myself."

Disappointment flooded him. "Okay. Thank you."

With a sad smile, the woman left, leaving Hutch feeling more forlorn than ever. Everything had been going perfect until she ran away from him. What did he do wrong?

Dammit. Had the kiss scared her off? It'd been the best damn kiss of his entire life, so why the hell had she run off?

Despite what the woman had said to him, he darted inside the washroom, checking the stalls for Maison. He needed to apologize. But just as the woman had said, all of them were empty. If she wasn't here, then where the hell had she gone?

He headed for the front entrance, scanning the crowd for her. "Did you find her?" he asked Hunter when he reappeared by his side.

"No. I think she's gone."

No. He couldn't accept that she'd just run away like that.

His father appeared a second later. "What the hell happened in there?" he asked.

"Maison's gone. Have you seen her?"

"No. I just saw her run out here."

Shit. What had he done? Neither his father nor his brother said anything as he hunched over and dropped his head into his hands. *Had he ruined everything between them?*

SIXTEEN

AFTER RETURNING FROM THE CHARITY EVENT, THEY all arrived home with uneasiness still rolling through them. Hunter still wasn't sure what exactly had happened with Maison and his brother, but Hutch was still clearly upset about it. He'd gone straight to his room without a word and slammed the door behind him.

Hunter wanted to go to him and ask him what happened but figured it'd be better to give him some time to settle down first. Besides, Owen's babysitter was still downstairs. Returning to the first floor, he paid Cybil and showed her out. When she was gone, he turned back to find Owen already fast asleep on the couch. Turning off the cartoons, he scooped him up in his arms and carried him back to bed.

His heart warmed as he gazed down at his son. Things obviously hadn't gone well tonight but he still felt grateful that his kid was healthy and happy. Hopefully, the rest would fall into place soon.

Closing the door to his bedroom as quietly as he could after tucking him in, he returned downstairs to grab a glass of water. As he quenched his thirst, he loosened the tie at his throat and let out a long sigh. Man, he hated dressing up. It was always such an annoyance, but every year Gleam Enterprises held this event in honor of his mother, so Hunter would endure the dress-up game for her.

He thought he was the only one downstairs when there was a rustle and then his father called his name. Hunter froze.

Was his father still trying to work? Even after coming home late from the party?

He made his way to his office and peered inside his office. "What is it?"

Matthew sat behind the big desk in the center of the room. Behind him, the curtains of the window were pulled back, allowing the moonlight to come in. "Sit down. There's something I want to ask you . . ."

Oh no. Hunter hated going in his father's office. Not only did it bring back bad memories of when he was being scolded as a kid, but he could also guess what his father wanted to talk to him about. Hesitantly, he walked inside and sat down in one of the chairs before his father. "How's Hutch?" Matthew asked.

"He's upstairs and he's still upset."

Matthew nodded. "I don't know what went wrong tonight but I've already tried calling Maison."

"What did she say?"

"She didn't answer, so I left her a message and asked her to call me back."

Now it was his turn to nod. Hopefully she was okay and tonight was just a simple misunderstanding. "In that case, I think I'll go to bed." He started to stand.

"Not so fast." Matthew motioned him to sit back down. "There's something else I have to ask . . ."

Hunter's stomach tightened. *Shit. He was going to ask him again, wasn't he?*

Matthew leaned forward and gazed at his face. "When are you going to take over Gleam?"

Shit. There it was. The question he hated hearing.

It was a question that his father had asked him many times over the years, and each time, he'd always given him the answer he didn't like. This time, however, instead of asking him *if* he could take over Gleam, he'd asked *when*.

As if time would change his mind.

It wouldn't.

Hunter replied with a cool smile. "Are we really going to do this again?"

"Yes, we are." He folded his hands together. "You'll find I'm a very patient man."

At that, Hunter snorted. "*You?* Patient? You're kidding me." His father didn't have a patient bone in his body.

"Maybe patient isn't the right word. But I am determined. So, let me ask you again, when are you going to take over Gleam?"

"I told you already, I'm not going to do it." The CEO thing had never fit his personality. He'd been born an athlete and when his injury had happened and forced him to pick another career path, he'd been happy working at the coffee shop. He couldn't even wear a tie for more than a few hours tonight. How could his father expect him to wear suits to work *every day?* No. Taking over Gleam was never going to happen.

"I'm getting older," Matthew said. "I should be retired already but I'm still working."

"If you hate it so much, then you should retire." Money wasn't an issue for them and his father should be able to retire very comfortably.

"I want to know the company is in safe hands before I do."

"You have Clive for that." His best friend and business partner had been there for him since the beginning.

Matthew shook his head. "The position is meant for you."

Hunter rose to his feet. He was really getting tired of this conversation. "But I don't want it so stop trying to force me into it."

Matthew stood as well. "What do you plan to do then? Since your divorce you haven't been doing much."

"Having been doing much? I've been raising Owen all on my own!"

"Then I suggest you reconsider my offer. After all, you're going to need to support Owen somehow."

His hands formed a fist and Hunter gritted his teeth. His father could be such an asshole sometimes. No, scratch that. He was *always* an asshole. There was never any leniency or second chances. Matthew always expected perfection from himself and everyone around him. He was so sick of it!

"I'm not working for Gleam, okay? So you can stop asking me." Before Matthew could argue with him, he walked out and quickly climbed the stairs. He was so done with having this conversation.

Only when he was in the safety of his bedroom did Hunter allow himself to relax. Man, that conversation had really riled him up. He thought by now his father would give up this dream of having him take over his place in the company, but apparently not. He was still as pushy as ever.

Tonight he'd stepped over the line when he brought Owen into it though. Didn't he realize he'd just gotten out of a divorce a few months ago? Things were still shifting beneath his feet and until he found his footing again, Hunter planned on taking it slow. That didn't mean he wasn't providing for his son. He was doing his very best with his time and efforts, but apparently, his father didn't think it was enough.

Would becoming the CEO of Gleam Enterprises really solve all his current problems? Hunter highly doubted it. Which was why he continued to turn down his father.

And he would continue to do so because although he was closest in temperament to his father, he was never, ever going to follow into his footsteps and become the cold bastard his father was.

Since her return from London, Maison realized that she hadn't yet seen Rissa, so after making a quick call to her to see what she was up to, she learned that her Little Sister had a school project due soon. And since she felt bad for not checking in sooner, Maison offered to help.

That was how Maison and Rissa spent their Sunday afternoon. It thrilled her that Rissa was really opening up to her more and she felt like things were finally progressing well with them.

The teen's latest art project involved creating a model of her ideal house, complete with mini tables and mini chairs and mini windows. Maison remembered a time when she had to do something similar in high school, but unlike her, Rissa was an overachiever and the plans she had made seemed elaborate and complex. She had no idea how they would be able to bring them to life, but they were going to try.

Luckily, Rissa's talent was art. She could paint, draw, *and* design, making her a lethal threat and quite the artist. But despite her natural-born talents, Rissa's mother had always discouraged her daughter from pursuing any kind of career in that field. She said it was because it didn't bring in any money and that saddened Maison.

It bothered her that her mother couldn't support her just because she thought it wouldn't pay the bills, and it especially bothered her that the only contact she had in her daughter's life was when she was scolding her for something. Every time she did that, it dimmed Rissa's sparkle and the girl didn't need anything more weighing down her life.

That was also why she'd agreed to help her. Rissa had

brought over all the materials and tools she'd need to create her model home. *Oh boy.* As Maison stared down at the cardboard, foam, fake moss, and wire, she suddenly felt overwhelmed. *How the hell were they going to do this?*

Lucky for her, Rissa seemed to know what she was doing and took the lead. As they started measuring out how big they wanted the model, Maison moved to make the four walls and the roof. "How was your trip?" Rissa asked, breaking the silence.

"It was great. Matthew did a wonderful job."

"I've never been to London before."

"Oh, it's beautiful." It was then that she recalled the conversation she'd had with Hutch and sadness consumed her.

"What's wrong?" Rissa asked.

"Huh? Nothing's wrong." She didn't want to talk about what had happened at the charity event. The memory still stung. "Come on," she pushed. "Tell me."

But Maison simply shook her head. After measuring out the pieces, she started on cutting the cardboard. When she was finished, Rissa proceeded to glue the pieces together.

Despite the good process they were making, Maison felt bad about not answering earlier and she couldn't help but notice how quiet Rissa was. "So how are things at school?" Maison asked, trying to make peace with her.

"It's okay." *Uh oh, were they back to two-word answers? Or was she mad at her for not sharing more information?*

"What happened with that guy you like?"

"You mean Boone?"

"Yes. Boone. What's going on with him?"

The younger girl shrugged. "Nothing really. I actually haven't talked to him recently."

That made Maison frown. "Really? How come? The last

time we talked about him, it seemed that he was interested in you."

"I don't know actually. We were talking every day and then one day he just . . . stopped."

Her frown deepened. "That's weird, don't you think?"

"Yes!" Rissa exclaimed. It was the first real emotion she'd seen from her today. "I don't know what happened. He's even started talking to another girl!"

Uh oh. That didn't sound good. While she didn't personally know this Boone character, a girl had to be careful if a guy could swap between girls so easily like that. Too smooth guys were often too much trouble.

Kind of like another guy you know, she thought.

Maison shook her head, trying to dispel thoughts of Hutch from her mind. She didn't want to think about him.

"So is this new girl his girlfriend now or something?" she asked. "Or is she just a friend?"

"I don't know." Rissa's expression turned dejected and the usual spark in her eyes faded. Maison was well acquainted with that look. She'd seen it just this morning in the mirror.

"You know what?" she drawled, hoping to elevate the mood. "Forget about Boone."

To her surprise, a smile curled Rissa's lips. "You sound mad."

"Mad? Why would I be mad?"

"I don't know. Something tells me you're not thinking about Boone anymore. Want to talk about it?"

Crap, was she really that transparent? When she'd woken up this morning, she'd been faced with her regret of last night. What she'd done to Hutch was completely, totally unforgivable and she hated herself for her loss of control. What the hell had happened? One moment she was happy to be by his side and then, suddenly, she was running away from him. Had his kiss really freaked her out that much?

When Rissa simply stared at her, Maison sighed. "Okay, so maybe something did happen last night . . ." But talking about it would be difficult. She was already embarrassed and it would only bring her awareness back on her anxiety.

"Well, don't leave me hanging!" Rissa exclaimed.

Maison shook her head. "I'm sorry, I just don't think this is appropriate. I shouldn't even really be talking about this with you."

Rissa latched onto her. "Oh, come on, Maison! You know I won't tell anyone! Besides, you're the only one I can talk to about these things."

A surge of sympathy hit her as she thought of the lack of people in Rissa's life. "Where is your mother anyway?" Rissa hadn't mentioned her at all lately.

Rissa's expression turned shuttered. "I don't know."

"She hasn't checked in on you?"

When Rissa shook her head, Maison's frown deepened. What kind of mother didn't even check in with her own child?

"Hey, don't try to change the subject! I want to know what happened."

With a roll of her eyes, Maison sighed. "Fine, I'll tell you but this is just between you and me, okay?" When the teen nodded, Maison filled her in on the trip to London and the charity event. The same set of emotions she'd felt the night before returned in a rush.

God, she'd acted so terribly! What had she been thinking? Did she really believe that a man like Hutch would actually want a girl like her? She'd allowed herself to believe that she could actually have all that, to have people look at her like she was some special beauty all dressed up with a red dress and fancy shoes. But inside, she was still the same shy, plain Maison Lane who blushed at every word.

And when Hutch had pulled her onto the dance floor, she remembered all the confused gazes on her. No one obviously expected her to be in his arms, let alone be on the dance floor with him. Then, Hutch had kissed her and she hadn't known how to react.

She was so stupid! Why had she run? Too many emotions had been swirling around in her head and she didn't know how to deal with them.

God, she was so stupid!

When she'd first started working as an assistant to Matthew, people had asked her why she'd bothered putting up with him. Everyone knew Matthew to be harsh and demanding, and not worth the effort. Some had even thought it was because she wanted a way into their family, as if being Matthew's assistant had elevated her status somehow and she could go on pretending like she lived a different life.

But her life was still the same as ever. And until recently, she'd managed to keep work and her personal life separate.

Oh, Hutch.

Her heart squeezed again at the thought of him. She hated how she'd run from him, but realization had hit her when he started to kiss her. All these emotions she'd felt while around him, all those times she'd been nervous, it was because she'd done what she'd said she'd never do.

She told herself that she wasn't going to get involved, that she would keep a professional distance from him, but all the trip to London had done was make her fall in love with him even more!

God, what the hell? She'd known the guy for years, and although she'd noticed his good looks and killer charm, she'd been smart enough to realize that he was out of her league then. So why the hell was she acting so stupid now?

"Wow," Rissa said when she finished. "That really does suck."

Maison dropped her head in her hands. "I know!" she cried. And worst of all, she would have to face him tomorrow at work. "I'm so stupid! I don't know what came over me!"

Rissa reached for her. "Hey, it's okay. I get the feeling that you don't lose control often. You just panicked, that's all."

"I just don't know how I'm going to face him again now. He's my boss's son! I should've known better than to go with him!"

"You did it because you like him, and there's nothing wrong with that. So maybe it didn't work out the first time but not all risks are bad, Maison. Sometimes they are worth it in the end."

Maison blinked, blindsided by the teen's words. They were so wise for her age.

Except it wouldn't be that easy for her. For all her life, she'd been raised to believe that risk-taking was dangerous. It'd always resulted in disastrous consequences for her. And so far, following her mind, not her heart, had worked out in her favor.

And the one night she'd actually allowed herself to enjoy had blown up in her face. Maybe she was better off sticking to her boring, safe life.

Maison straightened and did her best to recompose herself. She had to stop acting like a whiny baby. She was the adult and she shouldn't be wallowing like a teenage over the mistakes she'd made with some guy.

After compartmentalizing her worries, she refocused on their task. "Okay. Let's get back to work."

She ignored Rissa's protests and resumed cutting out the

cardboard pieces they needed.

Hutch wasn't sure what to expect when he arrived at work on Monday. Would Maison be in? Would she ignore him again? The other night had ended so badly that he wasn't sure what to expect now. Not only that, but he wondered what other people were saying about her abrupt departure.

His anxiety eased when he caught sight of her at her desk, already hard at work. Despite the roiling emotions he was feeling, a small smile quirked his lips. It was just like her to come to work and pretend like nothing had happened.

Maison, ever the professional.

She was talking to someone else but she did shoot him a small smile as he walked by. That was good, right? That meant she wasn't mad at him. Hutch waited patiently until the person left. "Hey. Can we talk?"

For the briefest moment, her mouth dipped down in a frown but then she nodded. "Let's find a quiet spot."

Good idea. There were people who were staring already. He followed her to an area away from the rest of the office.

Already his heart was beating in his chest and his palms grew clammy but he wasn't going to back out now. He opened his mouth to speak first, but she beat him to it. "I'm so sorry about the other night. I don't know what came over me."

He blinked. "*Wait, what?* I'm the one who should be apologizing. I'm so sorry, Maison! I didn't mean to scare you off like that. Do you want to tell me what happened?" He'd been so worried that he hadn't slept at all that night.

"I just had a lapse in judgment that's all."

Hutch stiffened at her cool tone. He didn't believe that. How could the epic, soul-burning kiss on the dance floor have been a simple "lapse in judgment" for her? He felt like it had changed his life.

Stepping forward, he tried to get her to look at him. When she did, he searched her eyes for that sparkle he'd seen the other night. To his disappointment, her beautiful eyes were devoid of it. "Come on, Maison. What happened between us was magical." Maybe if he could get her to admit that she wanted him too, they could salvage what was between them.

But to his disappointment Maison turned away. He could see the flush crawling up her chest and cheeks and he relished the sight. Despite how cold she was being, he could still affect her.

Hutch drew his finger up and gently turned her head so that she was facing him again. "We have chemistry, Maison. The explosive, soul-burning kind. Please don't throw it away." He wasn't sure that he'd be able to survive it.

He also knew he was pushing her, but he'd continue to do it if that was what she needed to admit her feelings for him.

Hutch held her gaze, hoping, praying that what he was saying would get through to her. However, it looked like Maison had already made her decision.

Dammit!

"Hutch, what's wrong?"

He realized with a start that he was shaking. For a moment, he thought it was due to his devastation, but then he realized it wasn't. No, he was shaking because he was angry. He drew in a breath. "You're making a mistake, Snowflake. You don't always have to be lonely."

"Who said I was lonely?" Maison shot back.

"I can see it in your eyes. You want this. So why are you fighting it? Why don't you ever let yourself have some fun?"

Instead of answering this question, she countered with, "You're trouble, you know that?"

A wide grin spread over his face. Was she cracking? Could he actually convince her to go out with him again? "I'm no trouble at all," he said with all the innocence he could muster. "The only trouble you'll have is if you try to ditch me, 'cause I'll keep pestering you until you agree to go out with me again."

"I haven't gone out with you."

He grabbed her wrists and brought them to his chest. "Then let's do it. Give me a chance. Come on, Snowflake. One drink, that's all I'm asking."

"One drink? Really?" She looked adorably skeptical.

"Yes. Just one. If you're really sorry about what happened, you'll have a drink with me."

He could see her debating with herself. *Please just give me a chance.* He really wanted to make things up to her. After a long debate with herself, she said, "Okay, fine."

"Yeah? You'll have drinks with me?" He couldn't hide his surprise.

Maison rolled her eyes. "Yes! Do I have to repeat myself?"

"Great, we'll head to my favorite place after work."

"Wait, you mean *today*? But it's Monday."

"Yeah, what's wrong with that?" *Hadn't she heard of happy hour?*

Maison shook her head, but her lips were tilted up in an amused smirk. "You're going to get me into trouble."

He gave her a knowing smirk. "Ah, yes. But trouble worth your time."

SEVENTEEN

W HAT HAD SHE DONE? MAISON HAD NO IDEA WHY she had agreed to go with Hutch for drinks! Hadn't she learned from her first mistake already that she couldn't be around him? She didn't fit into his life and pretending like she did would only make her seem more desperate than she really was.

Still, there was no doubt that she was addicted to his smile and dark eyes. He was like double-chocolate cake; she knew he was bad for her, but she still couldn't stop herself from having a taste.

Like a gentleman, Hutch held the door open for her. She really wished he didn't fuss over her like that. If he were a jerk then maybe it'd be easier for her to get over him. But no, he had to be all considerate and shit.

After he'd pulled out a chair for her to sit on, he asked her what she wanted to drink. "Don't worry," he said with a chuckle, "why don't I just get you a beer?"

Maison nodded, feeling a flush wash over her face. *God, what the hell was she doing in a bar? She didn't even drink!* She contemplated leaving when Hutch returned again with two beers. "Why are you looking at me like that?" she asked when he just sat there and stared at her.

"Sorry. I guess I'm just happy that you're here with me." He had to stop being so sweet to her. "So," he said as he settled back into his chair and grinned. "Why don't you tell me more about yourself?"

Maison shook her head. "You already know everything about me." Besides, there was nothing exciting about her. She was just a normal woman.

"I'm pretty sure there are things about yourself that even I don't know."

"I don't have any dirty secrets if that's what you're digging for."

His eyes brightened. "Dirty secrets, that's exactly what I want to hear!"

Despite her resistance, Maison found herself smiling. "Sorry, but I'm not sharing. What about you?"

"Where do you want me to start?" Hutch drawled and her grin widened.

She loved his easy-going attitude and the fact that he wasn't really pressuring her. It was easier to let her guard down around him. "You know, you haven't ever told me what happened to you while you were gone."

Just like that, Hutch's smile vanished. *Uh oh. Had she done the wrong thing again?* Although it'd been a while since Hutch had returned, no one really talked about what had happened to him and she'd always been curious but too afraid to ask. "I haven't told anyone what really happened actually."

"Hey, if you don't want to talk about it, then that's fine." She respected him too much to invade his privacy.

"No, I don't mind. It's about time I talked to someone about it anyway." Hutch let out a long sigh before speaking. "I was actually meant to come home a week before the ambush occurred," he revealed. "But insurgents fired machine guns and threw grenades down at us. Unfortunately, one fell down the open hatch of our Stryker vehicle and exploded."

Oh my God. She was sure her shock showed in her expression. Inside, she was shaking.

"I remember the blast," he continued quietly. "My entire side was blanketed in shrapnel and a major artery was cut in the blast. Worst of all, my leg had to be removed." His voice dropped an octave. "That was the hardest for me, spending months in the hospital alone."

"Why didn't you call your family?" She was sure they'd come to see him if they knew.

"I asked the doctors not to. Our family was never that close and we drew even further apart after Mom died. It would've felt strange if they were there. What if they didn't even care?"

"Hutch! You can't believe that! They're your family! Of course they would care!"

"Maybe now they would. But back then, years would pass without us speaking to one another. I'm just glad Sam was there. She has helped me through it."

Sam? Who was this Sam person and why was this the first time she'd heard about her?

Maison's heart felt heavy in her chest. All she could think of was Hutch writhing with pain in a hospital bed with no one to help him but the nurses and doctors. How could he have thought that his family wouldn't care that he'd gotten hurt?

"This might sound strange but I had the time of my life while I was there," he mused. "Everything about it just fit me completely and I never felt out of place or alone. Every day I worked towards my goals and, really, being in the Army gave me a sense of purpose in my life.

"As much as I'm struggling with losing my leg," he continued, "I wouldn't change a thing. I'd still want to be there when the grenade blew up." As Maison sat there speechless at the admission, the corner of his lips tipped up in a parody of a smile. "How's that for a dirty secret?"

Oh God. Her heart hurt too much. She knew he'd suffered

but she hadn't known the extent of it. After learning the truth, Maison wanted to weep for him. She wanted to hold him and comfort him to make up for those moments when no one else did. She wanted to tell him that it was okay, because even with his leg missing, he was more of a man than all of the men she knew.

Hutch Happa-Hewitt was a hero in every sense of the word, but despite that title, a part of her knew that he'd rather be seen as a solider than a decorated hero slash amputee. Tears wetted her eyes but she wiped them away before he could see them. "So you're saying that you want to go back . . ."

Hutch gave her a stern nod. "But I have to be able to perform to the same standards as all others serving in combat." Her eyes grew wide at the picture he painted. She knew how challenging and rigorous their training was. She couldn't imagine how someone without a leg could do it all. In his expression, she could see how much it was hurting him that he couldn't do what he loved.

"For what it's worth," she whispered, "I think you can do it."

"Thanks, but they already said no."

"*What?*" She couldn't hide her shock.

"Yeah, I didn't make the cut." He tapped his leg under the table. "Mobility is harder now and I can't move as fast as I used to."

When had he done it? And how could they have said no? Then she remembered the time when Matthew and Hutch had argued. It'd been the same night Dacey and Matthew had argued too, right before he disappeared for a few days. Was that why he'd been so upset? "You must be devastated."

Hutch nodded again. "I am. But I think my father is relieved. He'd probably take my other leg off if it meant me staying with him."

Despite the morbid topic, Maison laughed. That actually sounded like something Matthew would do.

Hutch grinned at her. "What about your parents? Are they as crazy as Matthew?"

Her smile disappeared. She never brought up her parents much. They were both doctors and experts in their fields. They often strived for excellence, which normally wouldn't be a cause for concern except that her parents took it to the extreme. They expected perfection in everything. In their marriage, in their workplace, and especially in their daughter. Maison hadn't talked to them in over a year.

"Believe it or not, my parents make Matthew look like a saint."

Hutch's eyes went wide. "No way. That's impossible."

"Seriously. When I was in high school, they expected me to get straight A's in everything. If I got a B, they wouldn't sign the assignment. Instead they'd write a note telling the teacher it wasn't good enough."

"What! That's insane!"

"Yeah," she said softly. But at the time, she hadn't known any better. She'd thought that all parents were like that and that she was just dumber than all the other kids her age. In an effort to please her parents, she'd forced herself to study harder. Luckily, it'd paid off and she got the straight A's she'd wanted, but of course, she couldn't be perfect all the time.

It wasn't until she was older that she realized that her mother had been verbally abusing her. Her constant picking at her wasn't normal and growing up in that environment had impacted her life greatly. In her teenage years, she grew quiet, shy. And her own self-esteem had plummeted to the ground under her mother's care.

Now, Maison wondered what her mother would think if she saw her sitting here in this bar, having drinks with Hutch. She'd probably have an aneurysm. The thought made her grin. "You okay?" Hutch asked her as he leaned into the table. "Want another drink?"

"Sure, but let's do shots this time."

One of his dark brows rose. "Are you sure that's a good idea?"

She nodded. "Absolutely." She was already here. She might as well enjoy herself.

"Okay, but don't have too many. We still have work tomorrow."

"Don't worry. I'll be fine."

When the shots arrived, Hutch handed one to her and held his up in the air. "To dirty secrets," he toasted.

"And crazy parents," Maison chimed. Holding Hutch's gaze, she threw the shot back and wished her mother could see her now. Laughing, drinking, and for once, having fun.

Hutch checked his watch. Normally, he wouldn't care about hanging out late at a bar, but they still had work bright and early in the morning and Maison looked like she'd had enough to drink.

The alcohol had loosened her up and they'd ended up talking for hours, laughing and spilling secrets. As much as he loved it, it was probably best to head back home. There was no doubt Maison had drunk more than she was used to and he worried that her hangover would be a bad one if he didn't get her home now.

He quickly paid for their drinks and gently guided her into his car.

"I had fun tonight," Maison said as she buckled in. "Best

night I had in a while actually."

"Glad to hear that." He'd enjoyed himself too. After to-night, he felt like he knew her better now. After making sure her seatbelt was on securely, he closed the door and jogged to the driver's side. "Are you okay?" he asked once he was settled. Maison nodded, her glassy eyes focused on the area before her. "Worth the trouble?" he teased.

Her gorgeous light eyes flashed with mirth. "You're not really trouble, you know."

"I'm not?" He started the car and pulled onto the road.

"No, I just said that to convince myself that you're not the man for me. But you've never actually done anything to me that's bad."

"Not even when I tried to kiss you in front of all our co-workers?"

Maison laughed. "No. Not even then."

Good. He'd hate if she'd regretted their first kiss.

For a few minutes, they sat together in simple silence, enjoying the ride and each other's company. But then Maison turned to him, her gaze expectant. "How many girls have you kissed?"

The question was so unexpected he felt completely off guard. "Uh. Quite a few," Hutch answered honestly. He glanced over at her to gage her expression. He hoped that that wouldn't upset her.

Her brows knitted together but she didn't seem too angry about it. When they finally reached her house, Hutch walked her to the door. "You sure you're going to be okay?" he asked once they stood at the steps.

"Yes. I'll be fine."

As he smiled down at her, he couldn't help but think about kissing her. But he fought off the urge to do so. "I'll see you tomorrow," he said instead. Grabbing a hold of her hand, he brought it to his lips.

He wasn't trying to tease or torture her; he just wanted to make sure she didn't have another one of those freak-out moments when he kissed her again.

The next time he kissed her, Hutch was going to make sure she loved it. And so with a simple goodnight, he slid into his car and forced himself to drive home.

EIGHTEEN

WHY DOES MY HEAD FEEL LIKE SOMEONE USED IT TO *smash a walnut?*

As the world slowly came into focus around her, Maison's second thought was of Hutch. Normally thinking of the sexy man was enough to get her all riled up, but instead of feeling better, she felt *worse*.

"Oh God, what happened last night?" Groaning, she realized she was still dressed in her clothes from the night before. A few buttons of her blouse were undone but thankfully her pants were still on. She was glad that the drinks she'd had hadn't suddenly turned her into a hussy and made her jump Hutch on her front porch. God, she wasn't sure what she'd do to herself if she had drunk sex with him.

But usually kisses preluded the action down below and as the night came back to her in pieces, she recalled the way Hutch pulled back from her. Why hadn't he wanted to kiss her? Was he afraid she'd make a run for it again if he tried?

God, she was really regretting having all those shots now. But the night had been so fun for her that she really would do it all over again if given the chance. Groaning, Maison pushed herself up into a sitting position.

"*Shit!*" One look at the clock and she realized that she was already late for work! Why hadn't she heard her alarm? And then she remembered it was because she'd forgotten to set her alarm in the first place! Fumbling for her phone, she called Matthew to let him know she would be running late this morning.

"Good morning, Maison," Matthew drawled when he picked up. "How are you feeling?"

Maison paused. He was unusually cheery this morning. "I'm sorry, but I'm running a little late today."

"Don't worry. Take your time. I'll see you when you get in."

"Okay." He hung up without another word. *What the hell? Why was Matthew in such a good mood?*

Whatever. She had to get a move on and haul ass if she wanted to make it in before it was lunch. But that proved more difficult than she anticipated. Her movements were sluggish as she grabbed her towel and a change of clothes for her shower. It also didn't help that her head was pounding ruthlessly at her temples. *Hmm. What were the chances that someone would find her in her home if she passed out in the shower?*

Grumbling, Maison started the water, turning it all the way until it was freezing. A cold shower was just what she needed to wake herself up.

She started with washing her hair before reaching for the bar of soap. It slipped out of her hands before she could get a good grip on it and it fell to the ground. "Goddammit." Bending down to retrieve it, she promptly lost her balance as her foot slipped out from underneath her. Her head slapped hard enough on the ground that her teeth clattered.

Ugh! This was why she didn't drink. It stopped her from being productive and she didn't like having to make excuses for herself. "I'm never drinking again," she vowed. Even if that meant saying no to Hutch.

Hutch spent the morning in his father's office. When

Maison didn't show up in the morning, he had explained to his father that he'd apologized to Maison last night and took her out for a few drinks. He expected a lecture from his father on how to treat women more delicately, but instead he surprised him by shooting him a cocked grin. "It's about time she let herself have some fun."

Hutch blinked. "Wait a minute. You're not mad?"

"I was upset at first," he admitted. "But I realize that if you don't push Maison out of her comfort zone a little bit, she'll happily stay within her shell forever."

Yeah, the drinks last night had definitely brought her out some more. "I think she may be regretting it now though."

"Why? How much did she have to drink?"

"About the same amount as me."

Matthew's eyes went wide. *"Hutch!"*

"Yeah," he agreed with sympathy. He hoped she wouldn't hate him all over again.

"Let's hope she's brought some aspirin with her when she gets here."

"I brought some for her." He'd actually gone and made his own homemade hangover cure. Hopefully it would ease her a little bit.

A half hour later, Maison finally arrived at the office. For someone who was suffering from a hangover, she sure looked beautiful.

Her hair was still a little bit damp and was pinned back away from her face in a high ponytail. She also didn't have a stitch of makeup on. She'd chosen a flowy blouse in a sweet blush color and a tight beige pencil skirt that showed off her curvaceous figure. While he presumed she'd gotten ready in a rush, she still looked as polished as ever.

"I'm here, I'm here," she called out as she reached her

desk. She had her purse in one hand and her planner in the other.

"Get in here," Matthew called out.

"I'm so sorry, sir—" she started but his father lifted his hand up, effectively silencing her.

"How are you feeling?" he asked her.

Surprise seemed to hit her like a brick because Maison stood there, adorably confused. He moved forward, offering the hot cup of coffee he'd gotten for her.

She frowned at him. "What is it?"

"It's coffee. You know what coffee is, right?"

Matthew gave a chuckle behind his desk.

"Yeah, I know what coffee is," she growled irritably but she did take the mug from him. Hutch suppressed a snicker. Yup, she was definitely hung over.

"Drink it all. It'll help. Trust me." In his other hand, he held out a bottle of aspirin. "This will help too."

"Go on, take it," Matthew encouraged. "I need you functioning for our meeting later."

Hutch groaned. "Why do we need to have another meeting?" It seemed like every day they had one.

"We have some important stuff we need to discuss."

"Really?" Because in all the meetings he'd been to so far, the majority of the time people were staring down at their phones or their laptop screens. The only person talking was Matthew, with the occasional pitches from Clive or someone else.

His father pinned him with a look. "Yes, really. And I expect the both of you to be present for it, understand?"

Hutch scowled. "Fine. Come on," he said to Maison. "You need some food."

"But I just—"

Matthew spoke over her. "Go with him," he said. "I doubt you had breakfast yet, am I right?"

She nodded.

"Then I'm sure your work can wait a few more minutes while you get some food into you."

Wow, even Hutch seemed surprised by his father's kindness. "Come on, let's go." He couldn't help but smile when she slipped her hand into his and followed him out the door.

NINETEEN

TOGETHER, THEY WENT DOWN AND WALKED ACROSS the street to the breakfast place that a lot of their co-workers frequented. But instead of letting Maison choose what she wanted, Hutch ordered for her. He knew she'd likely choose something small because of her diet, and after the night they had together, she needed something a little more substantial than toast or yogurt.

"Is it just me or has your dad been acting weird lately?" she asked as they settled at a table.

"Weird?" he echoed.

"Yeah, he's in a good mood."

"Yeah." He'd noticed that too. "I don't know what's changed for him but he does seem less angry."

"How are things at home?"

"Good actually, now that you mention it. We haven't been fighting much."

"Wow, that's great."

"Yeah," he agreed.

Maison shot him a small smile. "Hey, I'm sorry about last night."

"What do you have to be sorry for?" *Did she regret it again?*

"I'm sorry for the way I acted. I don't really drink that much."

"Yeah, I noticed," he said with a sly grin. "But you don't need to apologize. I had a great time last night." He leaned in, brushing his fingers across her cheek. "Besides, I liked taking care of you."

That beautiful blush returned. "You were really nice."

"Nice." He gave a laugh and sat back in his chair. "I don't get called *nice* very often."

"You are. Not many men would've walked away when you did."

He arched a brow at her. "So you're glad I didn't kiss you?"

"I don't know. At first I was disappointed," she admitted. "But at the same time, I think I like it more that you didn't."

"And why is that?"

"It shows you care about me." A small smile accompanied her words. Fuck, she was cute when she blushed like that.

"I do." He brushed his thumb against her cheek again. "I care a hell of a lot."

When she flushed even more, Hutch chuckled and pulled away.

That was when their food arrived and Hutch watched happily as Maison dug in. "Ugh. I can't eat anymore," she said when she'd finished half her meal. "I'm already way off my diet restrictions."

"I still don't understand why you're on a diet. There's absolutely nothing wrong with your body."

"You're just saying that to be nice."

"I'm not. I promise you. From what I've seen of your body, I love it. So finish that plate up."

Grinning, Maison stabbed a hash brown with her fork and brought it to her mouth. "You're cute when you're bossy like that."

He grinned right back. "After finishing that, I want you to drink this bottle of water. It'll help rehydrate."

Her lips curled into a smile. "Sounds like you've had a lot of experience with hangovers."

"Oh yeah. *Lots.*"

"I wish I could go home," she admitted. "Lying in bed sounds good right about now." Immediately, images of Maison lying on white sheets flashed through his mind and Hutch grew painfully hard.

"Why don't you just take the day off?"

Maison shook her head. "I can't. We have the meeting later on, remember?"

"Screw the meeting! We're all just going to be packed into the room like sardines, listening to Matthew talk. When was the last time you took a sick day anyway?"

"I haven't."

"Ever?"

"Nope," she said with pride. "Not once since I started working for the company."

"That's insane! How does Matthew expect you to work those kind of hours?"

"Actually, he's always telling me to take some days off. But I decline."

"Why?"

She shrugged her shoulders. "I don't really have any places I want to go and I know no one would go with me anyway. I hate traveling alone. Trust me, it's not worth it. So I just continue to work."

Hutch remembered what his father had said to him earlier about Maison. *If you don't push Maison out of her comfort zone a little bit, she'll happily stay within her shell forever.*

"You know what I think you need?"

"What?"

"You need an adventure."

"An adventure?"

"Yes, you just need to take off and do something spontaneous."

"Like what?"

"Anything. Go hiking or take a road trip."

Maison scrunched her face together. "That doesn't scream 'fun' to me."

"Okay, then. I have something else in mind. Let's go."

"Wait! I have to pay for my meal."

"Already got you covered." He'd paid for them both while ordering.

"Hutch!"

"Don't worry about it, you can get the next one."

"There's going to be a next one?"

"Oh yeah." Hutch took her hand. "Come on, let's go."

Maison had absolutely no idea where Hutch was taking her, but she had to admit, she was enjoying his spontaneity. She wasn't much for going with the flow so already she could feel her heart racing in her chest.

He'd quickly led her to his car, instructing her to get in. As Maison put on her seatbelt, she couldn't help but wonder what Hutch was thinking. "So where are we going?"

Reversing from the parking lot, Hutch let the roof down, allowing the sun to pour in and the wind to blow tendrils of her hair free from its ponytail. She didn't have her sunglasses because they were still in her purse, so Hutch offered to let her use an extra pair he kept in his glove compartment. "They look good on you," he said when she examined herself in the side mirror.

"You think?" She hardly recognized the woman staring back at her. Her hair was frizzy and flapping in the wind. And although she was still a little hung over, she'd never seen herself happier.

It wasn't long before Hutch started slowing down. He stopped behind a truck surrounded by kids. "We're getting ice cream?"

"What, you don't like ice cream?"

Oh, she did. It was one of the reasons why she had to go on a diet in the first place. "I do but I don't think I should have some."

Ignoring her, Hutch opened her door and led her towards the truck. "Which one do you want? I think I'm going for the Choco Taco."

"The Choco Taco?"

"You've never had a Choco Taco?"

She shook her head. "It looks like a taco but it's actually made of waffle cone, vanilla ice cream, peanuts, fudge, and chocolate."

Wow. Her mouth was watering at his description. "Sounds delicious."

"It is. Do you want that one too?"

Oh, why the hell not? She'd already fallen off the tracks with her diet with that breakfast. Might as well make today a cheat day. "Yes, please."

"Good. Wait here." The smile he shot her made it seem like she'd agreed to another date with him.

She watched as Hutch walked up to the truck. Surrounded by kids, his height made him tower over them and she chuckled to herself as one kid tugged on his pants and held out his hand. For a beat, Hutch stared down at the kid in confusion before the kid said, "Don't leave me hanging!"

"Oh!" He gave the kid a high five and Maison laughed again.

When he returned, Hutch was grinning from ear to ear, looking just as excited for the ice cream as all the children surrounding them were. "Come on, let's go back to the car."

As they settled back into the car, Maison thought they were going to eat there, but Hutch turned on the engine. "Too many kids," he said by way of explanation.

A minute later, they stopped on a smaller road away from traffic and people. "What is this place?" she asked.

Hutch grinned and waggled his brows at her. "It's my secret spot."

It was beautiful, and despite living here for years, Maison had never encountered a place like this. Trees surrounded them, giving them some privacy, but they actually weren't so far away from everyone else because she could hear the kids shouting and playing.

"Hey, don't forget about your ice cream," Hutch said. "It'll melt."

"Oh yeah." After peeling the packaging off, she took her first bite and groaned as the sweetness touched her tongue. It had been a long time since she allowed herself a treat like this. Similarly, she *never* allowed this much freedom in her life before either. If it weren't for Hutch, she'd never find herself in this position.

"It's good, right?" Hutch said around a mouthful of ice cream.

Maison licked her lips. "Delicious."

They polished off their ice cream in minutes. And then, just because she felt like it, she allowed herself to sit in the car and take in the scenery.

"You got something on your face."

Maison swiped at her chin.

"It's still there." Hutch leaned over. He was so close she

could see the gold in his warm eyes. "There," he said as he brushed her cheek softly. "It's gone now."

But it wasn't. The spark between them had always been there; Maison just didn't allow herself to see it until now. And this close, it was impossible to ignore.

She realized with a start that she wanted him to kiss her. She wanted him to take her away from this world and show her what pleasure felt like. She'd denied herself for so long that all she wanted now was just another taste. Another kiss.

Hutch slowly removed the sunglasses from her face and leaned in further. "You're beautiful, you know that?" he whispered. "No. You're more than that. You're extraordinary." She certainly felt like it in that moment. Especially with the way he was staring at her. "Can I kiss you now?"

The words set her on fire and she could only manage to nod before Hutch's mouth descended on hers. This time, she was ready for it and she fell wholeheartedly into the kiss. God, she missed this. Missed him. Nothing was better than being in Hutch Happa-Hewitt's arms. He made the world simply disappear and made it feel like she was the only girl in the world.

On a groan, she pulled him closer, until the both of them were straining towards each other. She liked how he felt against her, all hard and warm and it all made her want to torture him more. "Let's go to the back seat."

Hutch broke away. "What?"

"I want to go to the back seat," she said again.

"Okay." She loved that he wasn't balking at her boldness. It was bad enough already that she'd basically ordered him to do as she pleased.

As she slid into the back seat, Hutch jumped on her, making her giggle. "Hutch!" she exclaimed, right before he took her mouth.

As tongues clashed, Maison felt herself start to burn. Her body grew hot and she pulled at her top, trying to loosen it. "Dammit."

Hutch pulled back, but only enough to undo the top buttons of her blouse. He cursed when her bra was revealed. Although she had big boobs, they weren't perky and that made her self-conscious.

"Hey, what are you doing?" Hutch gently removed her hands. "You're covering exactly where I want to be."

"No. My boobs are ugly."

"I'll be the judge of that," he murmured before his mouth captured a nipple.

"Oh my God," she gasped as pleasure sang through her body.

Hutch chuckled. "I see you have a thing for sexy lingerie." His finger passed over the lace detail on her bra. "But what are you wearing below?"

Scooting back, Hutch's hands grazed her thighs. With the tight skirt she had on, she couldn't spread her legs wide enough, but it was just enough for Hutch to see a glimpse of her silky panties. "Fuck me," he breathed. "Do you wear lingerie every day at work?"

"Not the same one, obviously. But yes, I do wear lingerie underneath all my clothing."

Hutch cursed again before rising up to kiss her. "I'm looking forward to seeing them every day then."

Maison felt herself go molten as he continued to kiss her. When his hand found its way between her legs again, she gasped. "Do you like that?" he asked, gaze burning as he stared down at her.

Maison nodded. *God, what the hell was she doing?*

Hutch applied more pressure and she bit her bottom lip in response. More pleasure shot through her body. *More. She needed more.* She started to grind her lower body against his palm, feeling the pulsing pleasure surge through her. The moan she let out was desperate.

"I'll make it better," Hutch growled before claiming her mouth again. All the while, he worked her below, moving his hand in circles until she was squirming against him. "Look at that blush."

Her eyes flew open to find Hutch so close that she could see her reflection in his beautiful dark eyes.

Wow.

Her orgasm blindsided her and she cried out, gasping. Hutch moved quicker, drawing her orgasm out as he sucked on her nipples. *Holy shit!* Her eyes had definitely rolled back on that one! It'd been so long since she'd come that hard and that had only been his hand. How much more would it be with Hutch's hard cock pounding into her over and over again?

Hutch pulled back, lounging on the opposite side of the car as he caught his breath. "Fuck, that was hot." A wicked smile curled his lips. "You've made me so hard, I could probably drill through rock."

At the words, Maison's gaze dropped to his crotch. "Do you want me to . . ." She pointed at the loaded gun in his pants.

Hutch chuckled, reaching over to kiss her again. "If I ever get those lips wrapped around my cock, I'd be a goner. You'll have to hide my body here and drive my car back."

She laughed. "Stop it, it probably won't take long," she said as she reached for his zipper.

"Careful, you'll deflate my ego with comments like that."

Ignoring his teasing, she wrapped a hand around his girth and reveled in his strangled groan. She couldn't quite get her fingers to meet around him but she'd managed. "It's just like licking ice cream," she purred as she licked a path up his length.

Hutch's gaze intensified. "God, woman, you're really going to kill me."

Maison licked at the pre-come at the tip before swallowing him whole again. This time, she didn't gag and kept up a pace she knew that would drive Hutch over the edge.

His cock seemed to pulse in her hand and she leaned over to tongue the thick vein before she jacked him off in short, tight motions. "Shit." Hutch's belly clenched and his thighs firmed up. *"Shit, I'm coming!"* Maison wrapped her mouth around him, continuing to milk him through his orgasm. "Wow," he breathed. "That was fucking amazing." The kiss he gave her next made her needy all over again. "Sorry," he said when he saw the desire swirling in her eyes. "But we need to get back."

"Oh, right." She'd almost forgotten! She'd gotten so caught up in her passion and desire that she'd neglected all her other duties. This was so unlike her!

Kissing her one last time, Hutch helped her back into the front seat and they drove back to the office in comfortable silence. Throughout the ride, Hutch's hand stayed wrapped around hers and Maison caught herself smiling in the side mirror. God, what a day she'd had so far and she had a feeling things would only get crazier from here.

But she was glad she'd taken this leap of faith with him. She hadn't realized what she was missing until this moment.

When they returned, they each went back to their own desks. Maison pulled up the files she needed to prepare for the meeting and glanced over her screen. There, her gaze collided with Hutch's.

She hadn't realized it before but he'd been staring at her the whole time and his heated gaze left no question to what he was thinking about. *Dammit,* she thought as her cheeks flushed bright red. *How the hell did she think she was going to get anything done now?*

TWENTY

To make up for her tardiness the day before, Maison came to work a half hour early to get a head start on her work. Despite her efforts, it seemed that no matter how many hours she spent here, it wouldn't be enough time to go through the pile of work that had accumulated on her desk. Her to-do list in her planner was a mile long and she knew she would no doubt have to stick around while everyone else went home to catch up.

Despite all that, she was still in a good mood and didn't regret any of what happened yesterday. She still couldn't believe they'd done all that stuff outside and in Hutch's car! It was a position she never thought she would be in, but she shouldn't have underestimated him. Hutch was the only one who was able to bring her out of her shell.

Maison knew the moment he arrived because she could feel his hot gaze on her. She didn't dare lift her head up to greet him or she'd completely lose track of what she was doing. But she was quickly discovering that it was impossible to ignore him. She would always be aware of him.

When she looked up, he was already at his desk, a coffee cup in hand, sporting the biggest smile she'd ever seen. A hot flash went through her. She realized then that Hutch Happa-Hewitt was an expert at eye flirting. Although he was doing nothing by sitting there, his gaze expressed everything that was on his mind. "Good morning, Snowflake."

A bolt of lust shot through her. Dammit, all he had to do

was smile at her and she melted into a pile of goo for him! "Good morning," she returned, hoping she didn't sound as breathless as she felt.

"You're here early. How long have you been here?"

"Only since seven thirty."

"Ouch." Hutch winced before waggling his brows at her. "Does that mean a break is in order?"

"No." She had a lot to catch up on. "No breaks today."

She tried not to notice how good his lips looked when he pouted like that. "Fine, I'll let you work," he said as he turned back to his computer. Disappointment flitted through her as she realized he was giving up. Wait, did that mean she *wanted* him to bother her?

Her phone rang suddenly and Maison moved to answer it. "Hey, boss."

For the second time in a row, Matthew sounded pleasant as he greeted her. "Maison, can you come in for a second? I have some questions to ask."

"Sure." Quickly locking her computer, she headed into Matthew's office. "What do you need help with?" she asked once inside.

Matthew offered her a brief smile. "Why don't you sit down?"

"Uh. Okay. Is something wrong, sir?"

"No, there's nothing wrong. I just want you to tell me about Hutch." *Hutch?* Wait, why was he asking about—*Oh God!* Had he somehow found out what they'd done yesterday?

As panic riddled her body, he asked, "Has he been doing a good job?"

Maison forced herself to swallow past the lump in her throat. "Yes, he's doing well. He's been working hard and he's very efficient." *Yes. Very efficient in taking my clothes off!*

"Really?" Matthew's brow quirked. "You're not lying to me just to save his hide, are you?"

"No, sir. Not at all." Hutch really was a great worker, and despite the fact that she knew this job wasn't what he wanted for himself, he was getting on really well.

"Good. I was hoping a job like this would put him on a better path. From what I've seen, he seems to be getting better."

She'd noticed that too. For a while, everyone worried that Hutch was suffering from PTSD, but now that she knew the reason behind his actions, she could understand him a lot better.

Not many people would understand his desire to return. Most would think he'd already sacrificed so much, but Hutch wasn't bred to work at Gleam Enterprises like his father. She wasn't foolish enough to think that this would sustain him for long. As scary as it was to accept it, Hutch was bred for war and combat. One day he would eventually grow restless and want to move on. Did that mean he'd move on from her too?

"Keep looking out for my boy," Matthew said to her. "He's suffered a lot, but he's strong. I just wished he opened up to me more."

"Well, he's only just starting to open up to me."

"Good. At least he has someone to talk to." His voice had softened. "Sometimes I wish I were more nurturing like Camilla." Maison gasped at the mention of his now deceased wife. "She would know how to get him to talk to her. But I can see that you've had better luck at getting him to trust you." Matthew leaned back, a small smile playing over his lips. "You two make a good couple."

Wait. What? Maison felt her face flare with embarrassment. "But, sir, we're not—"

"It's all right. No need to be shy. If you like him, I don't see what's the matter with—"

"But I don't like him," she blurted quickly.

"You don't?" *Shit!* Why had she said that? She knew she did. Hell, she was pretty sure she was half in love with the guy already, so why the hell was she sitting here denying it?

Her heart was starting to pound and she really wished she'd kept her mouth shut. God, why the hell was she panicking again?

Maison just never expected herself to be one of those people who mixed business and pleasure. So far she'd done a great job of keeping the two separate, but Hutch had walked into her life and was making her reconsider herself. She just had no idea how to handle it all.

Taking a deep breath, she released it. "I'm sorry. I don't know what I'm saying." She sighed again. "I'm just . . . confused."

Matthew's smile grew. Over the years they'd become a really good duo. Not only was Matthew a great boss to her, but he was also a wonderful friend. She realized too late that she wasn't talking to her boss at the moment, but a concerned friend instead. "It's okay," he whispered. "I know how it feels. Love is . . . confusing at times. But it'll get better."

Love? Maison shook her head. She could admit that she felt lust for Hutch but not love. No, she wasn't sure if she should allow herself to get too attached like that, especially with someone like Hutch. Maison swallowed past the lump in her throat. "Is there anything else you'd like to talk about?"

"No, that's all."

"Okay, I'll go now." She rose and headed for the door, pausing only when Matthew called out for her.

"He's actually not a bad guy," he said to her surprise. No, she didn't believe Hutch to be a bad guy at all. But if that was true, then why was she still so torn?

When the door opened and Maison stepped out, Hutch wondered what his father had been talking to her about. While most would assume it was about work, her pinched expression made him wonder if something else was the topic of their discussion. Had they been talking about him? The way she avoided him as she made her way back to her desk made him believe they'd been. What had his father said to her? Did he warn her off him? Did he tell her to save herself the trouble of dealing with a bad boy like him?

Or was he asking her about his behavior as it pertained to work? About his progress or whether or not he was helping her out or simply making a bigger mess of things?

Dammit, he wanted to know. He wanted to know what she thought of him!

When his buddy Boyce, the security guard, walked past him, Hutch grinned behind his desk. The mail courier was with him, the same one who seemed to be harboring feelings for Maison, and with him, he carried a bouquet of red roses.

Normally when another man walked up to his girl with flowers, he'd throttle the guy, but Hutch stayed rooted in his seat. He wasn't surprised to see the mailman's eyes light up. Maison, however, frowned upon seeing him. "What's all this?"

"This is for you." He placed the bouquet of red roses on her desk for her. Maison's eyes grew wide.

"For me? Oh my God." She glanced around as the other people in the office stared at her. A blush was creeping up her neck and cheeks, the beautiful shade making her look lovely and alive. After signing the form, the mailman left, leaving her alone with the roses.

He watched as Maison plucked the card from the bouquet and read it. A brilliant smile spread across her face as her hand came up to her mouth.

On the note, he'd written:

Hey, Snowflake,

Wanna go on a date?

He'd signed it with a simple H, knowing that his first initial wasn't very popular. So she'd know exactly who was sending it to her.

Once again, her blush deepened. When her gaze lifted and collided with his, her smile was broad and unrestrained.

He knew romancing Maison Lane was a gamble. She was a strong, independent woman whose sights were set on her career, but he was hoping that he could somehow worm his way into her life.

Setting the card aside, Maison turned back to her computer. "Wait, what?" Hutch muttered. That was it? She wasn't going to say anything to him?

But then, a moment later, an email popped into his inbox. His heart started a fast thrumming when he saw that there was nothing in the subject line.

Only one word was in the body of the email:

Yes.

Hutch felt himself grin. When he looked back over at her, it was to find her already staring at him. She'd plucked a rose from the bouquet and was holding it up to her nose. A shy, sinful smile curled her lips.

Damn, she was beautiful, so beautiful she made his chest hurt.

There was no way anyone looking at her couldn't tell who the flowers had come from now with the way she was looking at him.

Trying not to show how much she was getting to him, he shot her a wink and turned back to his computer. There was no way he could focus on work though.

As he stared at the blank screen, Hutch thought about where he wanted to take Maison next.

Maison had to admit, the roses were a really sweet gesture. She never expected this from Hutch. But now she was feeling even more conflicted. How could she go from deciding against him in one moment and then falling head over heels in love with him in another? She was going to give herself whiplash with her constant indecision!

No one had ever sent her flowers before. *No one.* So when she'd read the note, a wash of excitement had flushed through her. She wanted to cross the distance between them and crush her mouth to his, but with everyone already looking at her, she settled for teasing him with an email instead.

Despite the excitement of the day, she still had a lot of work to do and she appreciated that Hutch wasn't nagging her so she could do it all. Finishing one project, she decided to print it out. However, an error popped up as she tried to. Apparently, someone had forgotten to add more paper. *Ugh. What a pain!* Now she'd have to go to the other side of the offices to get a replacement.

Whatever. The walk would be good exercise for her.

Smiling as she passed her colleagues, she headed for one of the boardrooms located at the far end of the building. The company had mistakenly ordered too many office supplies last month and because they wouldn't fit anywhere else, they'd just packed it all in here. No one had bothered to organize it since then and now the boxes were piled up on top of each other.

She scanned the boardroom, trying to find an open box when big hands seized her and pulled her back. She slammed into a hard body and gasped.

Hutch's husky laughter sounded in her ear. "Easy,

Snowflake." He ran his hands up the length of her arms, eliciting a full-body shiver. "I didn't mean to startle you."

Maison spun around in his arms. "You didn't just startle me. You scared the shit out of me!"

She followed that with a smack in his chest, but instead of punishing him, it elicited a grin. "I just wanted to know when you can go on that date with me."

Hutch! *That's why he'd followed her?*

"Shh! Someone will know we're in here!"

Maison lowered her voice. "You can't be in here!" What if someone saw them together?

"Why not? I'll just pretend I'm also looking for printer paper too. You look gorgeous, by the way. It's a distraction."

"Oh, I'm sorry," she drawled in a mocking tone. He was acting like she was asking for this.

"You should be sorry," Hutch said as he leaned in. "I can't get any work done." His mouth dropped over hers and, suddenly, Maison was kissing him. *Oh* God, what was it about this guy that made her melt like butter? She just couldn't resist him! Wrapping her arms around his neck, Maison drew up on her toes so that she could reach him better.

His kisses were drugging, making her drowsy by the second. Soon she was swaying on her feet and wetness grew between her legs. When she pulled away, she was gasping. "Thank you for the flowers," she whispered. "They're beautiful." She still couldn't believe he'd done that for her!

"You're welcome." Hutch's hands went to her hips, a little rough and a little bit sloppy as they roamed over her curves. She tried to look back at him, but he held her in place. "W-what are you doing?"

His low voice sent shivers down her spine. "Shh. We're taking a break from work."

Her eyes went wide. "Hutch, you don't mean—" But when she turned around, she could already see that he was rolling a condom on. *"Hutch!"* The door to the meeting room was open! Anyone could walk by!

He reached for her. "Don't worry. No one is going to see us."

Maison shook her head. "I don't think I can do this." It was so reckless!

The words had Hutch freezing in place. He glanced at the door. The hallway was empty. "Fine," he breathed. "Should I take the condom off?"

Maison's heart was beating frantically, and despite her concern, she was still majorly turned on. What if she did go through with this and had sex with Hutch in this boardroom? Would someone see? Would they care?

While a part of her seized at the thought of it, another part of her wanted to dance on the dark side. If she returned to her desk now, she wouldn't stop thinking about it and she'd no doubt spend the rest of the day horny as hell. Might as well scratch the itch now when Hutch was willing and ready.

"Hold on," she said just as Hutch was going to remove the condom. Maison walked to the door and instead of walking out, she closed it, securing it with the lock. Then she walked back to Hutch. "Okay, let's do it."

Hutch arched a dark brow at her. "Are you sure? I don't want to force you."

"Check my panties. They're soaked through."

Hutch cursed. "Okay." He shot her a wicked grin. "Turn around and bend over the table." Just like that, her body heated again.

Maison lifted her skirt and did as asked. A bolt of excitement hit her. She couldn't believe she was really going to do this! Behind her, Hutch grabbed a handful of her ass and cursed. "Garters?" he moaned. "You wear garters, too?"

Maison smiled even though he couldn't see it. She'd put them on today with him in mind, but she never thought he'd get a chance to see it.

"Last chance," Hutch said as he positioned his cock at her wet entrance. "You can still back out."

Heat poured off her and Maison glanced back at the door she'd locked. She was so wired up, she didn't care if anyone saw them now. "Fuck me now," she demanded, wiggling her ass in the air.

On a curse, Hutch joined them together. Maison sucked in a breath as the sensation singed through her body. There was a long moment when she felt impossibly full. Although she wasn't a virgin, it had been a long time since she'd last slept with someone. And she'd never been with anyone this big before.

Hutch leaned over her, the heat of his body cloaking her all at once. "Don't think about them," he murmured in her ear. "There is no one else right now. Only us."

Hutch swirled his hips and Maison let out a low groan. She clutched the table beneath her, using it to push back on him and delighting in his low, guttural growl. He started slow and then Hutch picked up the pace. She cried out with the force of it. The sounds of their bodies slapping together echoed loudly in the room.

She didn't care if anyone heard her now. She was just too consumed in this boiling pleasure. This was what Hutch made her do; he made her reckless and bold; made her forget her fears and simply *feel*.

She'd never felt so alive before.

With that, Maison let her fantasies fly. What would it be like for Hutch to fuck her face? Or maybe he'd like to put his hard cock between her breasts?

The images in her head only seemed to push her towards a quick release. Before she knew it, she was hit with a climax so hard that she had no warning as she came wildly around him. Hutch thrust his hips faster, sending her spiraling out of control. "Oh my God!" she cried as another release hit her hard.

More. She wanted more.

She was an addict and Hutch was her drug. Reaching back, she slipped a finger beneath her garters and gave Hutch a smoky look. Instantly, his body drew up and he was spilling inside of her, his face morphing into a mask of pleasure. It was the most beautiful thing she'd ever seen.

Hutch's voice was still ragged and breathy when he said, "That was amazing. I can't believe we just did that."

She chuckled softly. "I can't believe it either." But that was what Hutch did to her. He made her fearless and bold.

Hutch kissed her before letting her go. "You might want to go to the bathroom and clean up," he suggested.

Straightening her skirt, she nodded as she watched Hutch get rid of the condom. When he returned, he brushed his lips across hers. "Do you regret it?" he asked softly.

Maison smiled. "No, not at all. That was easily the best sex I've ever had."

"Good. Me too." He captured her mouth again and the kiss was enough to make her grow needy again. "Come on. We better get back before someone notices we're both missing."

She grinned. "Good idea."

Taking her hand, he led her back to the door but then paused abruptly. "What is it?" Had someone come by?

"You still didn't tell me about when you wanted to go out on that date."

Her jaw dropped. "We just had sex in a boardroom and

you still want a date?"

Hutch's grin was shameless. "Of course. So when are you free?"

This man was insatiable! "What about Friday? I now know better than to go out with you on a weekday."

Hutch laughed. "Okay. Friday it is. I'll pick you up around seven for dinner. How does that sound?"

Maison beamed. "That sounds perfect."

TWENTY-ONE

WHEN FRIDAY NIGHT CAME, HUTCH FELT LIKE A kid going to Disney World for the first time. His excitement level had never been so high and he'd spent the entire night imagining how their date would go.

He knew that she wouldn't mind which place he picked—Maison was easily pleased like that—but Hutch had thought long and hard about making sure he picked someplace she'd like so she didn't have to fake it. After hours of deliberation, he finally settled on the perfect place.

When they arrived at the lavish restaurant, Maison's eyes grew wide. "Hutch, are you serious? We're eating here?"

"You don't like it?" He would happily turn the car around and find someplace else she preferred.

"No, no. That's not what I mean. I love it. I just didn't realize we were going somewhere so fancy."

Phew! He was glad to hear that. And of course he would go all out for her. He suspected she rarely treated herself. "So you recognize this place?"

They'd been here before for his mother's birthday. Maison had only been working for Gleam for a couple of weeks then but his mother had liked her enough that she wanted her to be there. Since that moment, Maison had been a constant presence in their lives. It wasn't until now, however, that they'd grown close.

"Of course I do. I miss this place," she admitted. "It's been a while since we've been here, huh?" There was a touch of sadness in her tone and he had no doubt that she was thinking of his mother.

He nodded. "Yeah, it has been."

Sotto Sotto was full of memories, but instead of reminding him of his loss, he hoped to be able to make new memories with Maison tonight.

When they were seated, Maison gazed around the dining area, her pretty blue eyes lingering at the other patron's dishes. Excellent. She'd brought her appetite tonight. He hoped that she indulged. Maison pointed to one of the dishes their neighbors were digging into. "Can I order that?" she asked.

Hutch smiled in delight. "You can have anything you want, Snowflake."

"Okay, I'll have the pasta and some wine to go with it."

"You got it." He loved that she wasn't trying to restrict herself anymore.

Hutch quickly rattled off what they wanted to the waitress. "So what do you think of this place so far?" he asked once they were alone again. "Is it as good as you remembered?"

"It's even better." A smile curled her lips. "To be honest, I don't get around much. I usually go back and forth from work and home."

"A workaholic."

Maison nodded. "Yup, that's me."

Hutch took a sip of his wine, allowing his gaze to hold hers above the glass. She looked so beautiful in the dim lighting of the restaurant. The dress she'd decided to wear tonight showed off her shoulders and Hutch wanted nothing more than to lean forward and sink his teeth into her creamy skin.

When a man walked by and caught her gaze, Maison flushed and looked away. But the man's gaze still lingered despite the fact that he was right in front of her. Hutch's possessive side reared its ugly head and a growl formed low in his throat. He tried to disguise it but it was too late. The man glanced in his direction, widened his eyes in fear and scuttled away.

Damn, when the hell had he become so possessive?

Technically, now that he was working at Gleam Enterprises, he could move out at any time. He'd held up his end of the deal with his father but Hutch actually found that he was in no hurry to leave all of a sudden. Now that he wasn't so angry and he and his father seemed to be getting along for the moment, there was no hurry. Hutch also believed that a key motivator in getting him to stay was Maison.

"You know, you haven't really told me about the stuff you do when you aren't working. You do get some downtime, right?"

"I'm not *always* working," she said. "But I do work a lot. I like keeping myself busy and I don't see what the problem is when I love my job so much. There are worse things to be than a workaholic."

A touch of strain edged her voice and he wondered if people in the past had given her a hard time over it. He would never. He loved Maison's drive and persistence.

She answered his smile with one of her own. "I bet you wouldn't believe that I'm a part of a Big Sister Little Sister program."

"Really?" He didn't know that. But when he thought about it, it fit her perfectly. Maison had that nurturing, motherly quality to her, not to mention that she was responsible as hell. She would be a wonderful role model for a young girl. "How is it? Can you tell me about her?"

"Well, Rissa is fifteen years old. She's half African-American and Hispanic. She came into the program when her father first went to prison. She still has her mother, but she's not around very much. Her grandmother is the one that raises her." Maison smiled. "Despite all that, Rissa is a good kid."

Damn. It saddened Hutch to know that a teenage girl had to deal with all that. But with the way Maison spoke of her, he could tell that she really cared about her.

Hutch thought back to his own childhood. Compared to Rissa's, his was a walk in the park. He guessed he should be more appreciative of what he had and stop taking the people in his life for granted.

Across the table, Maison had a troubled look on her face. "What's wrong?" he asked. Although she tried to keep her negative emotions within, Hutch became very good at recognizing cues. Something was definitely bothering her.

"I'm just worried about Rissa, that's all."

"Why?"

"She has this dance coming up and she thought a boy was going to ask her. But it looks like his interests have fallen on someone else."

Ah, teenage heartbreak. It was the worst. "Who is this guy anyway?"

"I don't know much about him other than his name and that he's a major heartthrob at school."

"Do you need me to knock some sense into him?"

Maison laughed. "I'm probably overacting but I know Rissa is feeling down about it."

Hutch reached over and clasped Maison's hand. "I'm sure he'll come to his senses. Men can be slow sometimes." He leaned back, grinning broadly. "And if he doesn't, I'll go with her."

"W-what?" He'd never met Rissa, but what he could tell from Maison, she was a great person. A sweetheart like that should never have to spend a dance alone. "You can't go with her."

Hutch smiled as she frowned. "If it's because of the age difference, I can assure you—"

"No, it's not that. It's because you're taken."

His eyes widened with surprise before his lips curled into a sly smirk. "Am I?"

"Yes, you're mine." Her voice was soft, but there was no mistaking the possessiveness.

Hutch groaned so loud that the people around them stopped to glance at them. "That was hot! Say it again."

"Hutch!" She was flushing now, that beautiful blush making her go a stunning shade of pink.

Hutch chuckled and he picked up his fork again. "All right, that's enough. I fear that if you get any redder, the chefs will think you're a tomato and throw you into one of their soups." That earned him a kick under the table. *"Ow!"*

"Behave," Maison scolded and Hutch grinned again.

"Yes, ma'am."

* * *

Hutch's first date with Maison was a great success. Throughout dinner they'd laughed and chatted and flirted some more. Despite Maison's shy personality, he could really see her coming out of her shell. And it thrilled him to know that she was learning to trust him.

He'd liked what she'd said about him belonging to her. It was sexy and possessive, and before tonight, he'd never seen Maison Lane take so strongly to another person.

Still, he wanted to take it slow. Maison deserved a man who wooed and spoiled her, and Hutch had plans to do all that.

He drove her home and was entirely surprised when she asked him to come inside. She chuckled when his eyes widened.

"Don't look so surprised there, buddy. I had a good time tonight, and I don't want it to end."

"I don't either."

"Well, good. Let's go inside then."

He hadn't been inside Maison's house for quite some time and a lot of things had changed since then. "Wow, it looks amazing in here," he said as he took in the rooms.

The cream walls were made less stark by beautiful watercolor paintings and he also loved the authentic wooden furniture dotted throughout the first floor.

"Thanks. I finally got it the way I want it. It did take a long time on my own but I think it came out great."

"It's more than great. It's extraordinary." Just like the woman who lived in it.

"Do you want something to drink?"

"Sure."

"Let me see what I have in the kitchen. Go ahead and make yourself at home."

Hutch nodded, heading for the living room. As he heard Maison rumbling in the kitchen, he started to look around. Not surprisingly, everything was perfectly polished and in its rightful place. He should've known that Maison would have her home perfectly organized as well.

He paused by a picture frame sitting on the coffee table. Sitting down on the couch, he picked it up and examined it more closely.

It was of Maison and his entire family at her thirtieth surprise birthday. He loved that she'd kept it and decided to frame it. He remembered that day clearly. It'd been the same day he'd returned home after spending a few days with Sam. His family had been so worried about him, thinking the worst. But he really just needed to spend some time with a friend who knew exactly what he was going through.

Thinking back on it now, he realized he probably should've told someone where he was so they wouldn't worry, but his family hadn't been on his mind then. He'd been selfish, thinking about himself only when he'd left in a hurry.

Placing the frame back down where he'd found it, he searched the room for more photos but didn't find any. As he frowned, Maison appeared then with two glasses of wine. "Here you go. I hope this will do."

He took the glass from her. "Thank you. Hey, how come you don't have pictures of your family?"

Maison shook her head. "I don't like to keep them out."

"Why?"

When Maison dropped onto the couch, Hutch settled down beside her. "I didn't particularly like my childhood," she admitted. "So seeing pictures of that time doesn't bring on good memories for me."

He recalled what she'd said about her parents the other night. Were they really that bad? Had they really pushed her to be so perfect that anything less than their opinion of excellence wasn't acceptable?

Wow. And he thought his father was a hard-ass.

Suddenly, he was glad she didn't have pictures of them up. Despite the fact that they were her parents, her family hadn't provided her with the support and reassurance every daughter deserved. Instead they had drilled that perfectionist mentality into her mind until she'd been brainwashed into thinking that nothing she did was ever good enough. A thought occurred to him. Was that why she was always so worried about her weight? Or why Maison always worked herself to the bone? Was she still trying to prove herself to her parents?

Hutch reached out and took her face into her hands,

kissing her desperately. Once again, he'd caught her by surprise, and when she gasped, he took that as an opportunity to
stroke his tongue against hers.

He heard her moan before her body melted into him. He
loved the way her body molded to his. He drew her closer until
his back hit the couch.

For a long while, they just kissed. There was no urgency.
No rush. Hutch loved foreplay and quickly realized that they
could enjoy each other's company all night if they wanted to.

When he finally pulled away, he was breathing hard. "What
do you want to do?"

"More of that if we could."

He barked a laugh at her eagerness. But instead of kissing
her again, he reared back. "Want to watch some TV?"

"Sure." She didn't sound too disappointed in the change of
plans so he reached for the remote and turned on the big flat
screen TV. To his horror, a set of oiled-up six-pack abs flashed
onto the screen. *What the fuck?*"

"Oh! Magic Mike!" Maison squealed. "I forgot I was
watching it before!"

Hutch glanced back at the screen, horrified to see more
hips and more skin. "Is this the movie about . . ."

"Strippers, yes." She giggled. "Oh, look! This is the good
part!"

"The good part" involved a lot of gyrating and hip thrusting. As Maison cheered, Hutch dropped his head in his hand.
He could *not* have his woman cheering on another guy as he
took his clothes off. His ego wouldn't have it.

Suddenly, he stood and Maison glanced at him. "Hutch,
are you okay?"

"Sit back," he ordered. "You're going to get a show."

She frowned in confusion. "A . . . show?"

He started with his hips, knowing that would heat things up quick. Maison's laughter bubbled up immediately. "Oh my God! I can't believe you're doing this!"

He had to bite down on his lip to keep from laughing himself as he spun around and swayed his ass back and forth. He knew he looked ridiculous, but nothing mattered more to him than seeing Maison smile.

Thrusting his hips forward, he started his slow striptease, smile widening as Maison let out a whoop of encouragement. "Oh my God!" she cried as he whipped off his shirt and flexed his muscles for her. She was brighter than a tomato but she was also having the time of her life. "Lose the pants!" she called out.

His grin widened. *Damn, where was this side of Maison coming from?* He'd never seen her so excited.

"You mean these?" He hooked his thumbs into the top of his pants, drawing them down but not completely off. Again, Maison hollered more encouragements.

He was at her side in the next moment, grinding up on her as she tried to tug down his pants. He was sure the wine was to blame because they were both laughing, both fumbling around as he tried to keep up his act.

But when Maison popped off the buttons of his jeans and started to pull them down, he knew he wouldn't last.

"Nuh uh." He wagged a finger at her as she reached for his boxers. "Not yet." He was already hard from their making out and seeing Maison's greedy eyes only served in making him hotter.

"Oh, come on!" Maison pouted playfully, pretending to be upset with him. "You're actually pretty good at this," she admitted.

"Of course I am." Hutch swooped in and claimed her mouth, letting his tongue lick a seam across her lips before pulling back.

"So what color are they this time?" he drawled as he lowered himself between her legs. Pushing her legs apart slowly, he froze when he caught sight of her silky panties.

Red. They were red. The color of passion. The color of love.

Looking at Maison in lingerie had him moaning in pleasure. He pushed her dress up, lowering his face so that his scruff grazed the sensitive inside of her thighs.

Maison gripped his hair and pulled his head up so his eyes met hers. "Stop teasing me." Desire swirled in her irises and Hutch grinned wolfishly.

"Isn't that what this is about?"

In answer, Maison snapped her legs shut. God, he loved when she was like this, all smiling and playful. His cock grew painfully hard as he pried her legs open.

With a smile, Maison widened them even more as he drew her red panties down her legs.

She was beautiful, all pink and perfect. His mouth was watering just thinking about tasting her. As he sucked on her clit, Maison let out a cry.

Okay, fuck the striptease! He wasn't going to last!

Rising up, he removed his boxers and slipped on a condom. Maison grinned at his hurried actions as she removed the rest of her clothes.

When her body was revealed to him, Hutch took a moment to take it all in.

He had no idea why she kept trying to change her body. As far as he was concerned, every bit of it was perfect. Maison always worried, pushing for something more when she was already beautiful the way she was. Hutch hoped one day she would realize that. Until then however, he was going to show her just how beautiful she was.

Gripping the back of her legs, he laid her out and positioned himself. He let out a long groan as he slowly penetrated her. "Fuck, you're tight."

Maison hummed her approval as he angled himself deeper. "Oh God, Hutch." Each thrust sent him spiraling towards climax and her breathy moans helped him in reaching it quicker.

He reached out and grabbed a fistful of her breasts. *Oh yeah. They were beautiful. How could she ever think they were ugly?*

He plucked the hardened nipples between his fingers and soothed the sting with his tongue. He could feel his seed shoot up the length of his cock. Any moment now and he was going to lose control.

Maison let out a cry as she came first, tightening around him until he couldn't breathe. Sweat poured down his body as Hutch clenched his eyes tight and came deep inside her.

"Oh my God . . . *Hutch*."

Breath ragged and body spent, Hutch rolled onto his back and removed the condom. After disposing it, he lay out on the couch, trying to catch his breath. Maison was spread out beside him, her head resting against his chest. "That was a pretty good show you performed there. Don't suppose you've got a cop uniform lying around," she drawled.

"What? What are you talking about?"

Her smile grew. "It's in the movie."

Oh my God, was she still going on about that?

"Sorry, I don't have a cop uniform, but I've got my ACUs." His Army Combat Uniform would be just as recognizable and respected as any cop uniform.

Maison grinned as mischief glinted in her eyes. "That's even better."

TWENTY-TWO

"HEY, LADY, WATCH WHERE YOU'RE GOING!"

"*Sorry!*" Rissa giggled beside her. "I don't know what his problem is," Maison muttered as they walked away from the grumpy man. *He* was the one who had bumped into *her*. Whatever. She was more preoccupied with making this day a good one for Rissa.

When the teen had called her earlier asking for a ride to the mall, Maison wondered if this was going to be their new thing. Today just wasn't any old trip to the mall though.

Rissa was even more excited than usual because there was something that she needed to pick up. Apparently, Rissa's mother had pulled through and bought her a new dress for her upcoming dance. Maison knew that Rissa had been worried that she'd have to wear one of her old ones, but she was thrilled to learn that her mother had been putting aside some money for her just for the occasion.

This was the first time she'd done something truly nice for her daughter and Maison wondered if this would be the start of something new. Either way, she was thrilled for Rissa.

"It's so beautiful," the teen mused when asked about her new dress. "I can't wait for you to see it."

"I can't wait either."

They made the quick drive to the mall and Rissa wasted no time as she made a beeline for the store. Maison had never seen her so excited before and it almost made up for the fact that she wasn't going to the dance with anyone.

With beauty and intelligence like hers, Rissa would easily be the belle of the ball. But she knew her family's constant moving affected her friendships.

When Rissa came out of the dressing room with her dress on, Maison lost her breath. "Wow." The dress was absolutely stunning on her! It was pink, of course, because that was Rissa's favorite color. "You look incredible!"

"I know!" Rissa wailed, just as excited. "I don't normally look this pretty."

"You're *always* beautiful." The girl just had to remember that. "So what happened with Boone?" Had the kid finally come to his senses and asked her to the dance?

Rissa's expression fell and she shook her head. "No, he asked that other girl."

"Oh, Rissa, I'm so so—"

"No, it's okay. I'm not upset about it anymore. I'm not going to change who I am just because of a boy."

A smile spread over Maison's lips as pride filled her. That had been the message she'd been trying to instill into Rissa from the moment they'd met. Like her, Rissa suffered from self-esteem issues, but hers centered more on how she measured up with other people in society while Maison struggled with trying to live up to her parents' expectations.

"C'mere." She pulled Rissa into a hug, trying to mask the onslaught of tears. She felt like a mother hen, clucking her excitement about her baby. "Okay, let's go pay for it."

As Rissa went back in to change, Maison dabbed at her eyes. After they paid for the dress, Maison offered to hold it for her. The tailors had slipped it into one of those sleeves that would protect it from getting wrinkled or dirty and Maison took extra care as she laid it out in the back seat of the car. Rissa shot her a smile to show her appreciation. "Are you ready to go?"

"Yup!"

As they slid into the front seats, Maison checked to see that Rissa had her seatbelt on. Only when she was sure that they were safely secured did she pull onto the road. Her protective instincts were rising up again, but that was only because she felt like Rissa was growing up so fast.

This time, she allowed Rissa to pick the music and they both sang along as a popular song started to play.

Maison was starting to like this new version of herself. She hadn't changed. Not really. And not in the ways that still made her her. But she was just allowing herself to let go a little more. To become a little less rigid and more adventurous. So far, it was paying off greatly. She was no longer concerned about what others thought about her and she'd also stopped comparing herself physically to others. If Hutch found her attractive, then what else was she worried for?

Maison frowned as something before her caught her attention. She squinted as she learned forward. "What is that?" At first, she thought it might be something happening on the road before her, but when she realized that the smoke was coming out from the hood of her car, she quickly pulled onto the side of the road.

"What's going on?" Rissa asked, understandably confused.

"Don't worry, I'll take a look at it. Stay in the car."

Dammit. It was just her luck to have some car trouble while she was with Rissa. When she popped the hood, smoke billowed out.

Oh no! Now what was she going to do? She had no idea how to fix this! She immediately pulled out her cell phone. But instead of calling for help, she called Hutch.

He picked up on the first ring. "Hey, Snowflake. What's up?"

"Hutch, I need your help."

Hutch immediately dropped into solider mode. "What's wrong?"

As she told him where she was and what had happened, Hutch said, "Okay, I'll call someone about the car. But I'm coming to pick you guys up personally. I'll be there in a few, okay?"

"Okay." After hanging up, Maison checked on Rissa. "Are you okay?"

"I'm fine. What happened to the car?"

"I don't know," she said honestly. "But I'm guessing the engine overheated."

"Oh." The teen's expression fell.

"Don't worry. I have a friend who is going to come pick us up. I'll still get you home safely."

"Okay." She smiled.

It didn't take long for Hutch to arrive. While he spoke to the guy who was going to take her car away, she and Rissa sat inside his car. They had nothing to worry about now. Hutch was here. But Rissa was still clutching her dress towards her chest and Maison felt a little pang of guilt as she realized that she'd ruined this special day for her.

Hutch returned to the car with a grin on his face. "Okay, we're all set. They're going to take it to the garage and fix it. Where were you guys headed? I can drop you there."

"We were on our way to my house," Rissa answered.

Hutch turned his gaze towards the teenager and grinned. "You must be Rissa. Maison has told me a lot about you." Maison would've thought that the girl had instantly fallen in love with him with the way she smiled at him. "I'm Hutch. I'm . . ." Hutch glanced at her, unsure what to call himself in front of the younger girl.

Maison chuckled. "He's my boyfriend."

"Boyfriend," Hutch agreed. "Do you guys want me to take you home or do you guys feel like having some fun?"

Oh no. Maison knew that look. Hutch was no doubt looking to turn things up after seeing Rissa sulking. Normally, she would put a stop to all this before it even began, but then she remembered the look in Rissa's eyes earlier. "What do you have in mind?" she heard herself ask.

Rissa looked suddenly intrigued too.

"Well, I was thinking we could have a bonfire on the beach. What do you think?" he asked Rissa.

"That sounds awesome!"

"Cool, but we should probably ask permission first." The last thing they should be doing was carousing around Moonrise Beach with a teenager and have people worry about her. "Let's call your grandma and see if she'll let you go."

"Okay." Rissa took her phone from her and dialed her home number. As she spoke, there was clear respect in her voice and it sounded like the answer would be a yes at least until Rissa handed the phone to her.

"What is it?"

"She wants to speak to you."

"Oh, okay." She took the phone back. "Aba?"

But it wasn't Rissa's grandmother like she expected. It was Rissa's mother. "Who is this?" the unfamiliar voice asked. She wasn't rude about it, just concerned.

Maison muttered an apology. "I didn't realize it was you. I thought you were Aba."

"No, I'm her mother. This is Maison, I take it?"

"Yes."

"Rissa is asking if she can go to a bonfire with you."

"Yes, but if you're not okay with it, I can bring her home right away." She wasn't going to get in the way of their family.

But when the woman said, "No, it's okay. I trust you." No one was more surprised than Maison at hearing the words. "You've looked out for Rissa when I haven't and I'm forever thankful for your kindness. I bought her a dress, hoping it would make up for my mistakes, but I know it'll take time for her to trust me like she does with you. I appreciate you going with her today to pick up the dress."

For a long moment, Maison remained silent. *Wow. She hadn't been expecting that!* "N-no problem. I love hanging out with Rissa. She's a really good kid."

"She's very fond of you as well. She can stay with you but I'd like her home before ten if that's okay."

"Of course."

"Thank you again, Maison. For everything."

Maison wanted to say more, to tell the woman that she was doing the right thing for making an effort for her daughter, but she didn't. She couldn't do that with Rissa around, so instead she said her goodbyes.

"So what did she say?" Rissa asked, on the edge of anticipation. "Can I go with you?"

Maison grinned. "Yes, you can. Should we pick up some stuff for s'mores along the way?"

Rissa's excited squeals told her yes and Maison was convinced that they might actually end up having a good day after all.

They ended up stopping for more than just s'mores. Hutch had called ahead and asked his sister if he could stop by with a couple of friends. Of course Dacey was game and she even suggested that they pick up a few other items for snacks. So their quick run to the grocery store ended up far more costly than they first anticipated. It didn't matter though; all the junk food they'd consumed would be worth the company they'd have together.

Hutch glanced over at Maison beside him who was bobbing her head and singly softly to the song playing over the radio. He glanced in the rearview mirror and saw Rissa's bright, round eyes. She'd obviously never been in this area before and was taking in the sights. Hutch was thrilled to see that she was enjoying herself.

When they arrived at Dacey's beachfront home, Greyson already had the bonfire going. They even had some soft music playing from a boombox set on the beach.

"*Wow!*" Rissa cried as she took in the ocean. "It's so beautiful!" Hutch had to agree. He'd always thought the view to be stunning as a kid. But it'd been a long time since he'd really spent some quality time with the sand and the ocean.

Dacey came over and checked the bags in his arms. "What did you guys buy?" She made a face at him when she finished rummaging through the bags. "Wait. You didn't get me my green juice?"

"God, no. We're not drinking green juice at this bonfire!" Beside him, Greyson chuckled.

"Oh fine!" She then stomped back to her seat beside Maison. While the girls chatted, Hutch went to stand by Greyson by the fire. Man, he couldn't recall the last time he and his family had done something like this and he almost felt guilty about not inviting Hunter, Owen, and his father.

"Should I call the others?" he offered.

Greyson took a swig of his beer. "Sure, why not? We've got enough food to feed a village."

Hutch pulled out his cell phone and was surprised when

his older brother answered on the first ring. "What do you want, *nerd?*" Hunter said by way of greeting.

"Hey, who you callin' a nerd?"

"You, dumbass. I thought nerds were smart."

Hutch rolled his eyes. For being the eldest of his siblings, Hunter sure knew how to act immature. "I'm not getting into this with you." If he did, a full-on fight would occur.

"Fine," Hunter said. "Is there a reason why you called me?"

Well, at least Hunter's mood had lifted since the last time he'd seen him.

"I called to say that I'm at Dacey's and we're having this epic bonfire party. But I've changed my mind. You guys can't come."

"Screw you," his brother snarled. "Owen and I are heading over."

"What about Dad?"

"I don't think bonfires are his thing. But I can ask." Hmm. Guess he was right. Hutch tried to imagine his father with them all, singing and laughing with the glow of the fire on his face but he couldn't see it happening. His father was too serious, too stern of a man.

"Did something happen between you and Dad?" he asked. Although Hunter had been teasing him just a few minutes ago, Hutch noticed that his brother had been keeping to himself a lot recently.

"No. We're good," Hunter replied. But Hutch wondered if he was lying.

"Bring him," he said, surprisingly himself. "He deserves a little outing every now and again."

"Okay."

About a half hour later, Hunter, Owen, and his father arrived. Dacey jumped to her feet as she saw them walking down the beach before pulling them into her arms. Maison stood then, walking over to him. "This bonfire has become quite the party. Are you enjoying yourself?"

Hutch patted the spot beside him and Maison lowered herself until she was curled against him. "I am. What about you?"

"I love it. Thanks so much for doing this for Rissa."

Hutch glanced at the kid. Rissa was still on the opposite side of the fire, now playing with Owen. She had a big grin on her face and it made him happy to see her enjoying herself so much.

A few minutes later, Hunter came over to greet everyone. His gaze intensified as they landed on him and Maison holding hands, but he didn't comment on it. The last thing he needed was his big brother hassling him over having a girlfriend. Even Matthew looked unbothered by their PDA.

Hutch stood, going over to the icebox to pull out a beer. He ripped the cap off and brought it over to his father. "Here you go."

Matthew looked surprised. "Thank you," he said as he took the bottle from him.

"Want some food? There's plenty to go around."

His father nodded. "Thanks, I'll go get some myself."

That was enough, Hutch thought. If the man was hungry, he was more than capable of getting his own food.

For a moment, Hutch wondered if Matthew ever got lonely or if he ever thought of his mother. Since Camilla's death, he'd never taken a day off work or tried socializing with others. Was he using a busy schedule as an excuse to cover up his grief? It shamed him that he didn't know. In fact, Hutch didn't know what was going on with his father because he'd never bothered to stop and ask how he was doing. He'd been too caught up in his own grief to notice that other people were hurting around him too.

Hutch turned around and sat back down beside Maison. As everyone else ate and danced to the music, Hutch simply sat back and enjoyed the soft curves pressed against him.

Never in a million years did he ever think he'd be happy at Moonrise Beach, but he was starting to see why so many flocked here. It wasn't just because of the hot beaches or the small-town feel. It was because of the people.

Moonrise Beach was filled with captivating individuals, and right now, Hutch felt like he was surrounded by some of the best of them.

Used to be, he wanted to get out of this place. Now Hutch was wondering how he could ever leave.

TWENTY-THREE

MAISON WAS PLEASED TO NOTE THAT THEY'D gotten Rissa back home safe and sound before her mother's designated curfew. The girl didn't have to express how much fun she'd had; it was written on her entire face.

She could only hope that Rissa never stopped smiling like that. The girl had a big heart and she was smart; she could go far if she wanted to. Maison was just glad that her mother was finally taking notice of that too. "She's great, isn't she?" Hutch mused as he pulled out of the teen's parking lot.

Maison beamed. "Yes, she is."

"Girl's smart too. Just like someone else I know . . ." As he trailed off, Hutch's gaze slid to hers, a teasing smirk curling those luscious lips.

Maison felt her face go red. God, she would never get used to Hutch's compliments or his flirty remarks, and she hoped it would always be that way. "Where do you want to go now?" she asked him.

"I thought you might want to go home, but we don't have to if you don't want to." No, she wasn't ready for the night to end. She'd had a wonderful time with Hutch's family. But she didn't really know where she wanted to go either. When she told him that, Hutch said, "That's cool. We can head back to my place for a little bit if you want."

That sounded like the perfect idea. Soon they were both sitting in Hutch's bedroom, watching Netflix. "There's nothing good on," Hutch groused as he flipped through the movie selection.

"There must be something you like in there."

"I've watched everything already."

"Really?"

"Screw it!" Hutch dropped the remote and turned to her, planting his mouth over hers. "I'd rather be making out with you instead."

He'd acted so quickly that she'd been caught completely off guard. Her mouth opened in a gasp and Hutch took that as an opportunity to thrust his tongue in her mouth. He groaned. "You feel amazing."

No, he did. She'd never get enough of his big, hard body on top of her. It almost felt like a wall against the world where she could pretend it was just the two of them.

When Hutch kissed her again, she groaned out loud. "Shh," he said. "We have to be quiet."

Dammit! It hit her then that they weren't alone. Hunter and Owen were probably already sleeping and his father—*her boss!*—was working downstairs. "Oh my God. We can't do this in here!"

Hutch gave her a mischievous smirk. "It'll be okay."

"*Okay?* Hutch Happa-Hewitt, you are a bad influence!"

"Bad?" Hutch lowered himself until he was draped over her again. "I'll show you bad." He took her mouth in a scorching kiss. "Take your top off."

With a smile, Maison slipped out of her blouse, letting it fall to the ground before Hutch mounted her again. He was so big, and so muscular, that all she wanted to do was run her hands all over his body. Maybe if he was lucky, she'd follow that with her lips and tongue . . .

"What are you thinking about?" Hutch asked as he painted

imaginary circles with his finger around her navel.

Frowning, Maison caught a hold of his finger. "What are you doing?" Her stomach had always been a part of her body that she wasn't comfortable with. She didn't have the flat tummy or the six-pack abs that a lot of the other girls on Moonrise Beach had. So she didn't like that he was focusing on it now.

Hutch seemed oblivious to her anxiety as he drew up the length of her body and began to kiss her breasts. She liked that he liked them, but that didn't entirely erase the anxiety she felt when he focused so much on them.

Hutch abruptly pulled back and stared down at her. "Okay, stop. I can tell you're not into this, so why don't you tell me what's bothering you? Is it because of my family? Do you want to go somewhere else?"

Maison shook her head. "No, it's not that. I'm just wondering what we're doing."

Hutch arched a brow at her. "Isn't it obvious?"

"What I mean is, why are you doing it with *me?* You're gorgeous. You can have any woman you want. Why are you here with me?"

"You've got it all wrong, Snowflake. Why do you still think you're unattractive? Haven't you noticed the way men gawk at you at work? I promise you every one of those men would love to be in my place right now."

His smooth words were doing a good job of making her feel better about herself because she managed a small smile. "You think so?"

"God, yes. Just look at you! You're a wet dream come to life. I'm getting hard just looking at you." Her gaze dropped to his crotch and she realized that he wasn't lying. Hutch was practically bulging out of his pants.

Maison crawled over to him, swatting his hands away

when he tried to reach for her. "No, let me do this."

She wanted to apologize for interrupting what he'd started, but instead of using words, she had a better way of doing it. "What are you doing?"

"I'm trying to fix the problem." She reached for his zipper, easing it down slowly. And then she wrapped her hand around his length, squeezing tightly as her hand went up and down.

Hutch let out a whine.

When her mouth engulfed the bulbous head, Hutch growled. She loved the sounds he made and he looked absolutely gorgeous spread out before her, staring down at her with dark, obsidian eyes. When he couldn't take it any longer, Hutch pushed her away before reaching for a condom.

As he slid it on, Maison removed the rest of her clothes. Hutch raised himself over her. "Ready?"

She nodded, widening her legs until he was between them. Maison gasped as he slowly entered her and then groaned as he started to move.

As Hutch rocked into her body, his hands gripped her hips. She knew she was fleshy there, but he didn't seem to mind as he lifted her up, further impaling her on his cock. She wrapped her arms around him, wanting to have him as close as possible to her heart.

Hutch chuckled in her ear. "You're so beautiful."

Suddenly, all her insecurities were gone. All she could think of was how good Hutch was making her feel. As he continued to rock her body on his cock, Maison closed her eyes, allowing herself to get lost in the sensation.

Soon she was clamping her hand over her mouth to try and muffle her cries. The pleasure had built to a sharp point, pain and pleasure mixing together until she felt like she couldn't breathe.

She moved faster against him, chasing the pleasure until she burst into flames. As wave after wave of bliss bombarded her from all sides, Hutch gripped her harder. *"Oh God!"*

She melted against him, feeling boneless as he laid her out on the bed. *Wow.* That had been different to all their previous lovemaking. In the past it had been about exploration and chasing pleasure. This time, it felt a lot more like devotion. Hutch had worshipped her body and, now, she felt spent.

The only problem was Hutch was still hard as he jerked himself off with his hand. An idea popped into her head. "Come here," she said as she pressed her breasts together. Because of their size, she knew it wouldn't be hard for him to understand what she wanted.

His eyes lit up. "Are you sure?"

"Yes." She had fantasies of doing this but never had the confidence to actually carry it out. Having Hutch here, however, was making her want to do everything.

Slowly, Hutch straddled her, pushing his hard cock between her breasts. Maison held them together, watching as the wet tip appeared and disappeared between her breasts. He'd taken the condom off and she loved the feeling of skin on skin.

The long groan he let out made him sound like he was dying and Maison tried to hide the satisfied smile on her face.

When his thrusts got shorter, Maison knew that he was close and so she urged him on, saying dirty things she never thought she knew until this moment.

Hutch's body seized up and his thrusts grew more uncontrolled. *"Ahh!"* His seed spurted over her breasts and stomach. *"Fucking hell,"* he breathed, forcing her to look at him. His dark eyes seemed to glimmer with gold as he stared down at her and tried to catch his breath. In that moment, Maison felt like the prettiest girl in the world.

They both got up to clean off before falling back onto the bed in a tangle of limbs. With Hutch lying on his back, Maison rested her hair against his chest, feeling the soft rise and fall of his breathing and the steady thumping of his heart.

She loved this man, she realized. Despite how she had initially felt about him, Maison was quickly realizing that no one else had made her feel this way. No one else had made her feel beautiful and desired like Hutch did. And her world felt so much better for it now.

They dozed off together, both blissfully happy and sated. Only the shrill sound of Maison's phone ringing in the early morning woke them up.

On a tired groan, Maison forced herself up. *What the hell?* The screen showed that someone from her house was calling. How could that be possible? She lived alone. Who could be calling her cell phone from her house?

"What's wrong?" Hutch asked.

"It's my house," she explained. *"Someone is calling from my house!"*

Hutch frowned. "Answer it."

Maison hit the Accept button. "Hello?"

"Maison?"

Her stomach plummeted as she recognized the voice immediately. *"Mom?"*

"Where are you?" her mother said. "For heaven's sake, we were waiting outside for you for so long! Why aren't you at home?"

What the hell? "What are you doing at my house?" When she'd first moved in, she'd given them a spare key to use in case of emergencies but they'd never used it before now.

The voice on the other end of the line sounded annoyed. "I'm your mother. You act like I can't come visit my daughter."

But it'd been so long since she'd last seen them. Why would they show up out of the blue?

Her parents had always been like that. They didn't care about what was best for her. They only cared about what other people thought. Her repressed anger at them returned in a flood. "That doesn't mean you can just come into my house whenever you want!"

"I can come whenever I want," her mother snapped. "And show some damn respect for your parents, Maison! Or have you lost that too since I last saw you?" Maison gritted her teeth, trying hard not to snap back. She couldn't believe this was happening right now. "I expect you to return immediately. Your father and I want to talk to you."

The words caused her stomach to churn, tightening into knots. "Why? What's going on?" But her mother had already hung up. "*Ugh!*" Maison threw her phone away and flopped down on the bed.

Hutch was by her side in the next instant. "What's going on?"

"It's my parents." She got up and started to get dressed. "They're here."

"*Here?* What are they doing here?"

"They're at my house. Waiting for me."

"But I thought—

"Wait for me," Hutch said as he shifted off the bed. "I'll drive you over."

"It's okay. I've got—" That was when she remembered that her car was still at the garage.

Dammit! She'd totally forgotten all about it! She forced herself to slow down and take a breath. "Okay. Thanks. That would really help." She really needed to calm down. Just because her parents were in town that didn't automatically mean that something bad was going to happen.

Hutch came over and kissed her forehead. "Don't worry, Snowflake. Whatever happens, we'll deal with it together."

She smiled at him but it didn't quite reach her eyes. She loved that he was willing to be there for her. But he didn't know her parents. Didn't know how toxic they could be.

All she knew was that whatever slice of heaven she had made for herself here with Hutch was quickly going to come to an end.

* * *

On the outside, her house looked the same as always. But Maison knew the moment she stepped into it, it'd be a whole different matter. After taking a deep breath, she started to walk towards her front door when Hutch caught a hold of her wrist.

"Do you want me to come in with you?" He looked so worried about her that it melted her heart. Maison offered him a smile, but she knew it came out strained.

"Thanks, but no. It's probably best if I face them alone." She still had no idea why her parents were here so she wanted to be sure before she involved Hutch.

"Okay. Will you call me later?"

This time, her smile was genuine. "Of course." She loved that he wasn't pushing her on this. The last thing she needed was to have an argument with him in front of her house where her parents could see. Maison stood up on her toes and kissed him.

When she turned around, however, she realized that they were no longer alone. Her mother stood in the doorway, a look of disapproval on her face. She kept glancing between them, as if what she was seeing was a mirage or something.

"Uh oh," Hutch whispered against her lips.

"I better go," she said before she turned away and started walking towards her mother.

"Where the hell have you been?" her mother scolded as she approached. "Were you with that guy all night?"

Maison ignored her as she passed her. She had neighbors and she didn't want to wake them up with their yelling.

"*Well?*" her mother prompted when she closed the door behind them. "Aren't you going to explain yourself?"

Maison calmly turned to her. "What is there to explain, Mom? I'm thirty years old! I can spend my time with anyone I want!"

"But that's just not anyone, Maison. He's your boss's *son*." Maison stiffened. *How in the hell did her mother knew who Hutch was?* "Did you even think about what you were doing before you went off with him?"

Rolling her eyes, she headed for her kitchen, finding her father sitting at the table enjoying a cup of coffee—*her coffee!*— and reading the morning paper. How long had they been here anyway? It annoyed her how quickly they'd made themselves feel at home. And instead of answering her mother's question, she posed her own. "What are you guys doing here?"

In answer, her father set the paper down. His sharp eyes assessed her from behind glasses. "Have you gained weight?" he asked.

Ugh!

"She has," her mother answered for her. "You're eating too much again."

Maison's cheeks flushed with shame. No, it wasn't shame or embarrassment she realized as her hands began to shake. It was because she was *angry*.

"It's probably because you've gone back to eating that junk

food again, right?" her mother went on. "I told you that stuff was garbage. I don't know why you still—"

"*Stop!*" Maison shouted. "Stop talking about me and tell me why you're here!"

Her mother's eyes widened before narrowing to slits. "Is that how you speak to your parents?" She glanced back at her father. "I have *never* been spoken to that way. And if you must know, we're here because there's a convention nearby and we thought we'd check in on you."

Maison crossed her arms over her chest. "You should've called."

"I'm your mother. I don't need to. Now do you want to tell me what exactly is going on with you and that boy?"

She shook her head. "That's none of your business."

"You're my daughter, so it is my business. Didn't I tell you never to mix business with pleasure?"

"You and Dad are both doctors, so I don't see how this is any different."

"I'm not the one sleeping with my boss's son!" her mother snapped.

Her father's eyes grew big. *"What?"*

Maison rolled her eyes and put a palm to her head. "Oh boy, here we go."

"Yes," her mother said quickly. "She spent the night with him!"

When her father glanced back at her, she was hit with the same look of condemnation he'd been giving her all her life. "You disappoint me, Maison."

You disappoint me.

They were just three words, but they'd always had such an effect on her life.

"You can't see him anymore."

"What? *No*." She would never throw away the one thing that made her happy. Plus, her mother didn't have a say in who she dated.

"If you don't, your job will be in jeopardy. Do you really think a man like him will want to stay with you in the long run? He may like you now but he will get tired of you. You should save your career while you can."

"No. Hutch isn't like that. He likes me for who I am."

Her mother walked up to her suddenly, all sleek and polished in her black dress. She looked like she was going to a funeral. "Don't be stupid, darling." She cupped her face gently and tapped her temples. "Follow your head, not your heart. You'll only get hurt."

God, why was she always such a bitch to her? She had done nothing wrong!

She did her best not to let the tears fall but Maison could already feel her heart breaking. She thought she'd managed to overcome the emotional and verbal abuse she'd suffered as a kid, but only minutes back in the presence of her parents and already she was on the verge of a mental breakdown.

"We'll find you another man," her father said, as if he were doing her a great favor. "Someone less good-looking and more to your standards. It'll be hard with you so overweight but don't you worry. Your mother and I will help you."

That had to be the final jab into her heart. And it was the most brutal.

Maison ran from the room, trying to hold in her sobs as tears rushed down her face.

TWENTY-FOUR

UTCH KEPT HIS PHONE WITH HIM ALL DAY. EVER since he'd dropped Maison off at her house, he couldn't stop thinking about her. What had happened to her? Was she okay?

When a day had passed and he still hadn't heard from her, he started to worry. She'd been so shocked by her parents' sudden appearance that any trace of happiness she'd felt had suddenly disappeared.

He knew he should hang back and let her be with her family, but the look she'd given him right before he walked away didn't leave him with much confidence. All the times she'd spoken about her parents hadn't been pleasant so he worried about what their sudden appearance would mean for her.

Hutch sat there for about ten minutes before he cursed and reached for his phone. *How the hell did other people do this*? It drove him crazy not knowing that she was all right! Quickly dialing her number, he waited to hear Maison's sweet voice. Unfortunately, the call went straight to voicemail. "Hey," he said after the beep. "Just wanted to check in on you. I hope everything is okay. I miss you," he added before hanging up.

"Oh God, you're pathetic."

Hutch looked up to find his brother scowling at him. "What the hell are you doing here?" he snapped.

Hunter shook his head, a small smile curling his lips. "Never knew you were such a sap."

"Shut up. If I recall correctly, you were the one who cried

at your own wedding."

"That's perfectly normal."

Hutch pocketed his phone and rose to his feet. As he passed his brother, he patted him on the shoulder. "Yeah, you keep telling yourself that."

Hunter shrugged him off. "Don't touch me!"

"Sorry, you're not my type."

"Speaking of type, what the hell are you doing with Maison?"

Hutch could only stare at him. "What does it look like I'm doing?" He cared for her. *A lot.* Hell, he might already be in love with her, which was ridiculous since he'd never been in love before. But there was something about Maison that made her stand out against all the other women he'd been with. He was going to see where the rest of things went between them.

"But it's Maison," Hunter said unhelpfully.

"Yeah, so?"

"She's not your usual type." In answer, Hutch flipped his brother off. But Hunter just ignored him and continued, "I'm serious. We've known Maison for years and you've never made a move on her before. What changed?"

"Maybe I have, okay?" His voice came out more defensive than he wanted it to be. Why the hell was Hunter grilling him on this anyway? He forced his voice to soften. "Maybe I want something different for myself now."

After having his dreams taken away from him, Hutch was looking for ways to be happy here in Moonrise Beach. Maison had been the one thing to bring meaning back to his life.

Hunter went silent. "Okay," he said after a while, "I can understand that. So does that mean you're in love with her?"

Hutch grinned at his brother. "You sound jealous."

Hunter rolled his eyes at him but surprisingly, he said,

"Maybe I am since my attempts at finding someone new have backfired on me."

"Sucks having a brother so good-looking, huh?" When the punch came, Hutch was too slow to stop it. *"Ow!"*

"In case you think otherwise," Hunter said, "I don't see Maison that way." Good. He didn't plan on sharing. *Not ever.* "But I did notice that you guys ran out of here really fast the other morning. What happened?" Concern laced his words.

"Her parents showed up out of the blue."

"That's weird. I didn't realize they lived close by. She doesn't mention them much."

"No, they don't live in Moonrise. I don't think she was expecting them because she looked really surprised when they called."

"Uh oh."

"Yeah. That's why I'm so worried about her. I caught a glimpse of her mother when I dropped her off. She makes Dad look like a little puppy in comparison."

Hunter blanched. "Really? Damn. No wonder why she doesn't even blink whenever Dad flips out."

"Yeah. I just hope she's okay."

"Maison's a big girl," Hunter reassured him. "She can take care of herself. Give her the weekend to sort it all out. I'm sure when you see her again she'll be fine."

Hutch could only hope so, and since she wasn't answering his calls, he'd have no choice but to take on his brother's advice and give her space.

"Hey," Hutch said as Hunter made to leave. "Did you and Dad get into a fight recently or something? I felt a little tension between you two at the beach the other night."

His brother's face showed no emotion. "No. We're all right."

It sure doesn't feel like it, he thought as Hunter left.

Maison called in sick the next day. Except she wasn't really sick.

At least not physically.

After spending the last few days with her parents, her mind was filled with poison. Even just a minute in their presence was enough to dampen her spirits and have her doubt herself like she was a vulnerable thirteen-year-old girl all over again.

It wasn't enough that her father had criticized her, but her mother had continued to belittle her and scold her until she felt like nothing more than a piece of gum she'd accidentally stepped on and had to deal with it.

For the first time since they'd left, early this morning, Maison allowed herself to breathe. Too bad the damage had already been done. She was back to feeling raw and unrefined after the brutal lashings from her parents.

Now alone, Maison allowed herself to cry in earnest. She hated hearing the words about Hutch from her mother because, if she was being honest with herself, she had thought about it too. In fact, that was exactly what had been on her mind the last time she'd been with him.

But instead of focusing on her flaws like her parents did, Hutch only saw the good things about her. She'd never been with a man who was like that. And although she certainly got nervous around him, Hutch still managed to get her to smile at him. Maison knew that she was risking a lot in being with him, but how could it be wrong when she felt so alive while with him?

Maison had no idea what she was going to do. She loved her job but she loved being with Hutch too. Her parents, however, kept grilling it into her that she couldn't have both. One day, she'd have to choose and Maison just wasn't sure how she could pick.

Rubbing the tears from her eyes, she glanced down at her phone, noticing all the missing calls from Hutch. It was clear that he was worried about her and she felt bad for not calling him back. But when she reached for the phone with the intention to call him, her mother's voice echoed inside of her head.

You're too fat, darling. And one day, he's going to see that and throw you away. Save yourself the heartbreak and leave him already.

Just like that, the desire to hear Hutch's voice faded.

Flopping back on the bed, Maison curled up into a ball and let the tears fall.

The next morning, Hutch sat at his desk at Gleam, his gaze firmly planted on the elevator doors. Every time it dinged and the doors opened, he searched for the familiar blue eyes and sweet smile he loved. But every time he was left feeling disappointed when Maison didn't show up.

What the hell? What was going on with her? He'd been worried when she'd called in sick yesterday and wasn't answering his calls, but now he couldn't shake the feeling that something was wrong. It wasn't like Maison to miss work like this.

Hutch didn't bother knocking on Matthew's office door before entering. When his father glanced up, he frowned. "What do you want?"

"Where's Maison?" he asked. "Is she not coming in again today?"

"No, she called in sick again."

"Sick? But Maison never gets sick. Did she say what was wrong?"

"No, she didn't."

"Did you even *ask?*" His father opened his mouth, but

then snapped it shut. *Son of a bitch, the guy could be so cold sometimes.*

"Do you think something is wrong with her?" he asked.

Hutch nodded. "She's not sick. Maison doesn't miss work even when she's got a high-grade fever." *It had to be her parents. Were they still with her?*

His father's eyes narrowed. "What do you know?"

Hutch shook his head. He wasn't sure if he should be telling him about her parents but if it concerns Maison's well-being, he had to say something. "Her parents showed up out of the blue a few days ago and she went rushing to see them. I haven't seen or spoken to her since and she hasn't been answering my calls or texts. I think something's up," he admitted. "Is it okay if I drop by her house and check on her?"

Matthew gave a nod. "You do that and then you call me after, okay?"

"Okay." He was out of the building in the next moment, driving way too fast to be considered safe. He only slowed when he pulled onto Maison's street.

Anticipation at seeing her again had his heart beating wildly in his chest. He practically ran for the door and waited impatiently for her to answer when he rang the doorbell.

When he could hear no movement inside, Hutch tried knocking. "Maison?" he called out. "It's Hutch. Are you in there?"

Where the hell was she? Was she out? Was she still with her parents?

When there was no response, he tried her number and froze. *Wait a minute, was that her phone he was hearing?* He leaned into the door and pressed his ear to it.

Though it was muffled, he could definitely hear her phone ringing inside.

So she *was* inside! She just wasn't answering him! Disappointment flooded him. Why was she avoiding him? Could it be that her parents were still inside, telling her to ignore him?

Gritting his teeth, Hutch made his way back to the car. He thought that in coming here, it would ease his mind. However, it had only caused his worry to increase.

He couldn't stop himself from glancing back, hoping to catch a glimpse of her through the window, but there was nothing there but the wisps of curtains.

On a sigh, Hutch slid back into his car and drove back to work in silence, the roaring in his ears the only thing he could hear.

TWENTY-FIVE

S HE WASN'T COMING.
At nine o'clock the next day, Hutch entered his father's office once again without announcing himself. Matthew didn't even glance up this time until he sat in the chair before him. "Did she call in sick again?" he asked.

"No, she didn't," his father informed him.

"Then where is she?"

Matthew finally looked up from his computer screen. "She's working from home today." *What? Why?* His questions must've been written on his face because his father said, "I'm sorry. I don't know what's going on with her and she refused to share anything to me."

"Did you ask? She didn't say what happened with her parents?"

"No, she hasn't mentioned a thing. She only asked if she could work from home today so I allowed it."

Hutch felt himself frown. "Has she requested for this before?"

"No. Never. Which makes me wonder what's going on with her. What happened when you saw her yesterday?"

"I didn't," he said glumly. "At first, I thought she wasn't at home, but then when I called her, I heard her phone ringing inside the house. Why would she do that? Why would she ignore me?"

"Maybe her parents were still around."

"That's what I thought too. But it's been *days*. Why hasn't she called me back? Even a text would be nice."

Hutch rose to his feet. He didn't like not knowing what was going on with her. "I'm going to check on her again."

"Whoa. Relax. She might actually be fine. She seemed okay in her emails to me." Hutch beat back the sudden surge of jealousy. Why was Maison talking to his father and not him? To his surprise, his father asked, "Do you want me to come with you?"

Hutch shook his head. He wasn't sure what state he'd find her in but he doubted having her boss around would help her open up to him. "No, I'll be fine. But I'll call you if I need anything."

Matthew simply nodded.

This time, Hutch took his time driving to Maison's house. He wanted to plan what he was going to say when he saw her. Knowing that she was now ignoring him, he'd wracked his brain trying to figure out what he'd done to make her act this way.

Had he said something wrong? Had he done something that she hadn't liked? He thought back to their last day together and couldn't come up with a single thing that might make her turn away. Could it be something else that was bothering her? Something her parents may have said or done?

When he arrived at her house, he rang the doorbell, waiting patiently for her to answer it. Again, there was no movement from inside the house. Hutch leaned over, trying to get a glimpse through the windows, but inside, everything remained still.

Cursing softly, he pulled out his cell phone and called his father. "She's not answering the door," he told him. Taking several steps back, he craned his head to check the second-floor windows. "It doesn't look like anyone is home."

"She's there," his father said. "I just received a work email from her."

"Could she be working remotely from someplace else?"

"I don't know," Matthew said honestly. "Hard to tell over email. But when she called the office this morning, she used her home phone, not her cell."

Hutch cursed. "Okay," he said dejectedly. "I guess I'll head back now."

To his surprise, Matthew said, "You know what, Hutch. Why don't you take the rest of the day off?"

Hutch blinked, wondering if he heard his father correctly. "But it's only nine."

"I know, but I doubt you'll be concentrating on anything else but Maison. Maybe I'll email her and ask her what's going on."

"Do it," he said, feeling desperate by the second. "You're the only one she seems to be talking to at the moment. If something is wrong, I want to know."

"Okay. But take the rest of the day off."

"Fine," he said. But strangely, he found that he didn't want to go home. He never thought he'd be so reluctant to miss work at the office. What if Maison decided to stop by?

As Hutch got back into his car, he rubbed a hand over his face. With the rest of the day off free, he thought about where he could go or what he could do. Only one person popped into his mind.

Sam.

Luckily, she was home when he arrived at her house. She'd still been in bed and he felt kind of bad about waking her. But she was in a good mood when she answered the door for him. "Hello, stranger. I thought I'd finally gotten rid of you."

For what felt like the first time in the last few days, Hutch smiled. "You can't get rid of me that easily."

"I just figured that you and Maison have been busy." At the sound of Maison's name, his smile vanished. "Uh oh, did I say something wrong?" Sam asked.

"No. It's fine." *Well, he hoped it would be.*

"You guys are still a thing, right?"

"Actually, I'm not so sure," he admitted. If they were, surely she would've called him back, right?

Sam shot him a look. "Okay, I'm not following. Tell me everything."

As Hutch filled her in on what happened, he couldn't help but feel grateful for her presence. Sam was always there for him, no matter the time or place. "Something's happened and I don't know what it is," he finished. "I just came back from her house but it seems like she's ignoring me for some reason."

Sam frowned as she swallowed a mouthful of Cocoa Puffs. "Is this unusual behavior for her?"

"Yes, it is. I have a feeling it had to do with her parents because she freaked out when they suddenly appeared at her house."

"Maybe something happened with them," Sam suggested.

"Yeah, but what exactly happened?" Hutch found it hard to let go that easily. As Sam finished her breakfast, Hutch thought about his short time together with Maison. She'd come out of her shell a hell of a lot since he'd started working at Gleam. Was she reverting back to her old ways? And if so, why?

Still that didn't explain why she suddenly wasn't going into the office. Was she that desperate to avoid him?

As Hutch contemplated the possibility of this, Sam watched him. Well, it was more like being examined. Being stared down by a PI was intimidating and Sam's emerald-green eyes weren't helping. They saw entirely too much and Hutch didn't have the strength in him to keep his emotions off his face. He hadn't wanted to admit it, but he *hurt*.

He hated being casted out and feeling this disconnect from Maison without so much of an explanation as to why. It made him feel small, and most of all, alone.

Sam got up and grabbed a beer from her fridge, placing it before him, but Hutch didn't reach for it. "Come on," she said. "It's five o'clock somewhere."

Despite himself, he laughed. "Sam, it's only ten a.m. here though."

"So what? When has that stopped you before?"

He smiled at the tough love she was giving him. "Fine." Taking the offering, Hutch twisted the cap off and took several gulps. Maybe changing the topic would put him in a better mood. "So how's work going?" he asked her.

Sam let out a long, drawn-out sigh. "That's easy to answer. It's going nowhere."

"No interesting new cases?" Sam always had funny stories to share with him.

"No. It's like I've stumbled upon a dry spell or something."

Hutch took a sip of his beer. "Let's hope that doesn't last." He already worried about her.

"Yeah, I've got bills to pay and I'm already on a tight budget."

"You need money?"

"No, Hutch. I'm not taking any of yours."

"I'm just saying, if you need . . ."

"Hutch!"

"Fine, fine."

"At least I've found something that I actually enjoy here. It'd be a shame to pack it all up just because I can't afford to stay open."

"What would you do if you have to close?"

Sam shook her head. "I don't know. I guess I could go back to school or something . . ."

"School? Honey, I school you all the time." In response, Sam raised his middle finger at him. He chuckled. "Real mature, Sam."

"Hey, I'm younger than you, Grandpa, so let me be."

"I'll let you be when you stop acting like a teenager." He pointed at her box of Cocoa Puffs on the counter.

"I'm not the one moping around like one," she shot back. The words were enough to wipe the smile off his face. "Look," Sam said, her tone sobering. "Whatever it is that Maison is going through, I'm sure she can handle it herself. And if it does have to do with her parents, it's probably best if you stay out of it anyway."

His brows knitted together. "Are you telling me to stay away from her?"

"No. I'm just telling you to give her time. If it really is as bad as you say, it's going to take more than a week to fix shit up, you know what I mean?"

Hutch drew the bottle to his mouth. "I kind of do." Except how could he stay away when he knew Maison was hurting?

Sam came around the table, giving his shoulders a tight squeeze. "If she really loves you, she'll realize that on her own and then she'll come to find you. But she can't do that unless the rest of her life is settled first."

Hutch nodded in understanding. Somehow, Sam always knew the right thing to say even if it wasn't the words he wanted to hear.

TWENTY-SIX

MAISON SPENT THE REST OF THE WEEK AT HOME. Luckily for her, Matthew was in a good mood and allowed her to do most of her work from the comfort of her own bed. But the other day he'd called her and she hadn't known what to do.

Just like whenever Hutch called her, panic seized her and she could only hold herself tight until the ringing stopped. She felt terrible for ignoring them, but she just wasn't in the right mindset to talk to anyone right now.

This time, however, she knew she couldn't ignore Matthew's calls anymore. If she did, she'd risk getting fired from her job. So when her phone rang again with an incoming call, Maison took a deep breath and reached for her phone with shaky hands. "H-hello?"

"Maison? How are you?" Matthew's voice was the gentlest she'd ever heard it and she wondered if Hutch had told him what had happened.

"I'm fine, sir. How are you?" God, she hated pretending like everything was fine when it clearly wasn't.

"Are you sure you're fine? We're worried about you."

We're. Did that mean Hutch was nearby? Was he listening to their conversation? Her heart did a little flutter as she thought of him.

"He's not here," Matthew said, as if reading his mind. "So you can tell me what's going on with you without any fear."

But that wasn't what she was worried about. She was

scared that she was going to revert back to her old self before she found the confidence in herself to be who she was.

"Maison, come on. I need you to tell me what's going on. Working from home is fine for a few days but I do need an assistant to help me out here."

Oh God, it was exactly as she had feared! He was going to fire her if she didn't come in! But how could she when she knew Hutch was going to be there? She couldn't face him again after what she'd done to him! God, she felt terrible! And worst of all, he hadn't even done anything to her to merit her behavior towards him.

Despite her best efforts, she'd allowed her parents' words to get to her and now she wasn't acting like herself after their visit.

She thought she would've handled this better. Growing out of her social anxiety and self-esteem issues had taken a long time and while they sprang to the surface every now and then, Maison could control it for the most part. However, her parents' sudden appearance had done more than just caught her off guard; it'd weakened her defenses and, now, she was back to feeling like a total loser.

Although Matthew hadn't said it, he didn't have to. She could tell that he was disappointed in her.

You disappoint me.

Her father's words hit her with a force of a speeding car. Suddenly her eyes were stinging and she was holding back her tears. A few droplets spilled past and she irritably brushed them away before focusing back on her conversation with Matthew.

"I'll come in tomorrow," she promised.

"You will? Great." He sounded relieved. "But you still haven't told me what's bothering you."

"Don't worry, sir. I'm absolutely fine." She smiled even

though he couldn't see her. "I'll see you tomorrow."

It sounded like Matthew wanted to argue, but she was glad when he simply said, "Okay, Maison. See you tomorrow."

She'd never been so happy to hang up on someone.

Okay, now that she'd made the decision to go into work tomorrow, she had to get caught up on all her work she'd missed.

Problem was, every time she attempted to get some work done, she thought of Hutch. He was yet another person she'd pushed aside for no reason. God, what was wrong with her? She'd messed up a perfectly good chance to be with him because she was too chicken to face the uncertainty of his love.

But what if her mother was right? What if Hutch got tired of her and realized that he was too good for her? Where would that leave her? While he'd be off, flirting with some other woman, she'd be stuck at Gleam, working for his father and pretending that she didn't actually love him.

Oh God, she *loved* him! *She actually loved him!*

Was that why she was so torn up about this? God, she was pathetic! She really needed to call him back, but she was worried that once she heard his liquid voice, she'd burst into tears.

Outside, rain poured down in heavy sheets and it seemed like it wasn't going to let up anytime soon. Letting out a loud sigh, Maison stared out the window. The hours had passed quickly and it was already late. She should really fix herself something to eat. But what good would food be when she felt like the world around her was breaking? Or was that just her heart falling into pieces?

Her phone rang suddenly, and as she picked it up, her heart started to pound. *Oh God, what if it was Hutch again? Should she answer?*

But the caller ID told her that it wasn't Hutch calling. She frowned as the name of the local hospital flashed on her screen.

"What the—" *Why was a hospital calling her? Had something happened to her parents?* Her stomach twisted with worry. "Hello?"

"Ms. Lane?"

"Uh, yes?"

"I'm sorry to inform you but Mr. Hewitt has been in an accident."

Her stomach bottomed out. *Matthew? Oh God.* "What happened? Is he okay?"

"His car slid off the road and hit a tree. He's unconscious at the moment but the doctors are looking after him right now. Unfortunately, I haven't been able to contact his family yet. You were the first emergency contact in the records."

"I'll call them," she said immediately. "And then we'll come over there."

"Thank you."

As Maison hung up, she had to take a moment to process everything. "Matthew . . . Oh God." She'd just spoken to him on the phone a few hours ago! She remembered how she'd been relieved to hang up on him and now look what happened! *How the hell did all this happen so quickly?*

She hastily dialed the Hewitts' residence, cursing when no one answered. "Shit!" Panic had a stronghold on her throat. *What was she going to do now?*

Grabbing a light jacket, she pulled it on before running out the door to her car. Thankfully, she'd picked it up the other day. The rain was still coming down hard and she was soaked in seconds.

Realizing that she might get into an accident herself if she didn't slow down, she forced herself to drive cautiously. Her visibility was so poor that she couldn't see more than a few feet in front of her. Because of that, it took her longer to get to the

Hewitts' house.

As she pulled up into the driveway, she caught sight of Hunter getting out of his car. "Hunter! Your father—"

"I know!" he called back, holding up his phone. "Just got the call. I'm going over there now. Have you seen Hutch?"

"No." A bolt of shame spread through her at hearing his name. She turned off her engine and joined Hunter, using her jacket to shield her from the rain.

Hunter had no such protection other than the leather jacket he wore so his hair was soaked. He shook his head. "He's not answering his phone. I came here to check if he's home. I'll go inside and check. Can you watch Owen? He's in the car."

As Maison nodded, Hunter ran to the house.

"Hey, Owen," Maison said as she turned back to the car. She slid into the seat beside him, noticing that he was clutching some kind of action figure in his hands. She tried for a smile, but it felt forced even to her. She was just too worried about Matthew at this point.

Owen's own smile was less than his usual dazzler but he did lift up his action figure to show her. Maison took it from him. "He looks cool," she said softly. "Does he have a name?"

"Hunter."

"Hunter?" Actually, now that she got a better look at it, it did kind of look a bit like his father.

When the real Hunter came running back to the car, Maison's heart stuttered a beat. Her gaze searched for Hutch behind him. "He's not in there," he said.

What? "Then where is he?"

"I have an idea." Before she could ask what he was talking about, Hunter slid back into his car and twisted in his seat to look at her. "Put your seatbelt on. We're going to go get him and then we'll go to the hospital."

"*Wait!*" As much as she knew they were in a hurry to see Matthew, she couldn't help the spike in her anxiety. *Oh God, she was going to see Hutch again!*

"What is it? Come on, Maison. We need to get to the hospital."

Realizing the situation was bigger than her anxiety, Maison forced herself to nod. "Okay, fine. Let's go."

Throughout the entire ride, she sat in the back seat with Owen in silence, watching as the houses and cars went by in the window. When she could no longer keep track of the area, she asked where they were. They'd stopped at a house in an area she didn't recognize. *Why would Hutch come here?*

"This was where I found him the last time," Hunter explained. He cut the engine and got out of the car. By now, the rain had stopped so Maison had no problem taking Owen out of the car and carrying him with her to the door.

Her eyes examined the exterior of the house. The house looked nice and tidy and it even had a really nice garden out front. For some reason in her mind, she'd pictured something far less pleasing to the eye when she remembered that this was the place Hutch had run off to whenever he was distressed.

Hunter knocked on the door, his impatience clear in the way he bit down hard on his jaw. He glanced over at her. "Are you okay with him?"

Maison smiled down at the boy in her arms. "Don't worry, I've got him."

The moment the door swung open then, they both turned to find a woman. She was tall, just a couple of inches shorter than Hunter and she stood there, looking understandably suspicious and confused. "Uh, can I help you?"

"Uh, I'm Hunter Happa-Hewitt. Is my brother here?"

The girl cocked a brow at him, studying him with sharp

emerald eyes. As she examined Hunter, Maison took that as an opportunity to take in more of her. In this position, with her arms crossed over her chest, she couldn't help but notice the woman's guns. Wow! She was fit. Like really, *really* fit. Her body was lean and had more definition than a dictionary. Maison definitely didn't want to get into a fight with her.

That was when the woman slid her gaze to her and something flashed in her eyes. Was it recognition?

Hutch suddenly appeared beside her. He was shirtless and his dark hair was messy and falling into his eyes. "Hey, what are you—" His gaze jumped to her. "*Maison?* What are you doing here?"

Maison opened her mouth but nothing came out. Dammit. She'd lost her ability to speak now that Hutch was in front of her! Thankfully, Hunter spoke before she could.

"Why don't you fucking answer your phone?" he growled. "Dad got into an accident. He's unconscious and at the hospital right now!"

Hutch blinked in shock. "*What?* What the hell are you talking about? My phone is out of battery."

Was that why he'd stopped calling her? Or was it because he was done with her and had moved on?

Hunter shook his head. "I don't know everything yet. Come on, put on a shirt. We're going to the hospital."

To Maison's surprise, the other woman said, "I'm coming too." Both brothers looked at her, but neither one argued.

God, Maison thought. *This day just kept getting worse.*

Hunter was buzzing with nervous energy. He just couldn't seem to stand still. A mixture of fatigue and worry for his father was eating at him, making him want to bark at everyone. But he knew that that would only worsen matters.

In coming here, he intended to get his brother and head to the hospital, but here he was, waiting in this chick's house for his brother to get dressed. Why the hell did he take his clothes off anyway? Wasn't Hutch with Maison? Hunter shook his head. He had other things to worry about.

"If you want, you guys can go ahead," the woman who'd answered the door told him. "I'll drive Hutch over."

Maison was already in the car with Owen. He didn't know what silent torture she was putting herself through but she clearly didn't want to be in the same room as Hutch. Did that mean things were over between them? Hunter nodded, wondering who exactly this woman was to his brother. Though he'd been here before, this was the first time he'd actually seen her.

The woman stuck her hand out. "I'm Sam, by the way."

Sam? Wait a minute. Hutch had mentioned Sam numerous times before, but—"I thought you were a guy," he blurted.

Instead of being insulted like any other woman would be, Sam smiled. "That would make my life so much easier."

Huh? What the hell did that mean? Before he could ask though, Hutch reappeared. "Okay, let's go."

"Your shirt is on inside out," Sam drawled. Amusement laced her tone.

Hutch looked down at himself. "Dammit. I'll fix it later. We have to get to the hospital."

Hunter nodded. "Let's go."

Once outside, he slid quickly into his car while Hutch rode with Sam in her car. So was Sam the reason why Hutch wanted to join the Army? Guess that explained how they were so close.

After putting his seatbelt on, he glanced back at Maison.

"Are you all right?" This was probably really hard for her right now.

She smiled softly at him but he noticed that her gaze kept returning to the other car. He had no idea what caused the separation between her and Hutch but all he knew was, he wasn't touching that one with a stick.

TWENTY-SEVEN

MAISON WAS A BALL OF EMOTION AS THEY DROVE TO the hospital. Her worry for Matthew festered inside of her until she felt like she was going to burst.

Catching that glimpse of Hutch shirtless had not only brought her memories to the surface but also her anxiety as well. And now her heart was feeling more vulnerable than ever before.

He looked surprised to see her but he didn't look particularly mad either. Naturally, he looked far more upset about the news of his father than about her. She wanted to know what had happened to Matthew, and until then, she was going to have to shelve her emotions to deal with at another time.

When they all arrived at the hospital, they'd all jumped on the staff, riddling them with questions about Matthew. Maison would've felt bad for them if she weren't so scared.

As they were led to Matthew's room, her legs started to shake and she let out a sob. They said that he was unconscious but what else had happened to him? "Oh, Matthew . . ."

Lying on stark white sheets, Matthew blended into the bedding. There were tubes everywhere and the sounds coming from the machines increased her anxiety.

And then she remembered something. Or rather, *someone*. What had Hunter said to Owen about Matthew's accident?

When she spun around, it was clear that he hadn't had the chance to explain anything because Owen's little eyes were wide with horror and confusion as he stared at his grandfather.

"Daddy? What happened to Grandpa?"

Maison tried to hold back her tears but it was hard not to show her emotion. As Hunter bent down and started explaining things to Owen, she went to sit beside Matthew.

She recalled her last conversation with Matthew when he'd asked her about coming into work. She felt terrible to have left him alone all week without so much of an explanation as to why. She'd acted so irresponsible and so unlike her that she wished she could take it all back. But she couldn't.

It was too late.

Now looking at Matthew, with his eyes closed and his face pale, he didn't look like the virile man she knew. She mourned the loss of his spirit and wished she could turn back time to avoid all this.

When she'd first started working at Gleam, she'd been afraid of Matthew. But as the days passed, she learned to grow comfortable around him. His temper and his demands became something that motivated her, and whenever she was feeling nervous or shy, Matthew had never allowed her to remain that way for long. His straight-to-the-point attitude left no room for such empty emotions, and in being around him, she'd become more resilient. If she was being honest with herself, Maison felt like the reason why she was able to overcome her childhood upbringing was because of Matthew.

And now look at him! He was lying there and she could do nothing to help him!

Everything she'd kept in for the past week came out in a rush. Although she hated crying in front of people, she found that she couldn't stop once she started. Maison cried for her parents. She cried for Hutch. And now, she was crying for Matthew.

Hands came around her to comfort her, but she couldn't

stop crying. She knew it wasn't Hutch by his scent. Hutch smelled like eucalyptus and spearmint but the man holding her smelled like expensive forest.

Hunter.

Thankful for the support, she allowed herself to rest her head against him. He was warm, and he was strong, and she could use all the strength she could get to make it through the rest of this day.

She could feel Hutch's gaze on her but he didn't move to comfort her. Maison wasn't sure what she'd do if he did. But she had noticed Sam rising up from her chair and holding her hand out to Owen. Gently, she said, "Come on, let's go wait outside."

Maison had never been so grateful for the woman until the door shut behind them. "Shh," Hunter soothed. "It's going to be okay. He's going to be fine."

"How can you know that though?" Just from looking at Matthew, she could tell that the accident had been serious. What if the injuries he'd sustained were permanent?

She forced herself to stop crying and wiped at her face. Hunter handed her a tissue and she accepted it graciously, dabbing at her nose before grabbing another to wipe her eyes. Hunter was right. Matthew was strong. She had to believe that he would pull through. She just hated seeing him this way. "I'm sorry," she announced. "I'm just really worried about him."

Hunter nodded in understanding. "We all are."

She felt terrible for breaking down like that. Instead of being concerned about their father, Hunter was fussing over her. Feeling embarrassed, she pulled back and went over to sit in a chair in the opposite corner of the room.

As Hutch and Hunter spoke together in hushed tones over their father, Maison wondered where Dacey was. She had no doubt that she'd be here soon. Should she leave? Obviously she was making this worse with her presence here. Technically speaking, she wasn't even family.

She really should give them space like Sam had, but Maison found that she didn't want to leave. The Happa-Hewitts had become as much of her family as her own parents were, except they didn't criticize her every move.

The thought of her parents once again made her glance back at Hutch. It hurt to see him again, but it pained her even more to know that he was hurting. She wished that she could go to him and talk to him. To hold him and comfort him but she couldn't. She had hurt him too.

And although it would just about kill her to keep her distance and give him space, she would have to. After all, she'd been the one to push him away in the first place.

"What have you got there, buddy?" Sam leaned over the kid's shoulder, trying to get a better glimpse of the action figure in his chubby little hands. "Is that Batman?"

"No, his name is Hunter."

Hunter? What kind of hero complex did this kid have if he thought his own father was a superhero? "Actually, I think his name is Bruce Wayne."

Owen shook his head. "No. His name is Hunter."

"Okay fine. Hunter it is." She knew better than to argue with a five-year-old. And actually, the kid wasn't that far off the mark. The movie icon did kind of resemble his father in a way. They both had dark hair and a big build, but Hunter had his sexy Asian features that Batman didn't have.

Wait a minute. *Sexy?* Since when had she started seeing Hunter as sexy? Well, he had made her take notice of him when he'd shown up at her door unexpectedly . . .

Whatever. She couldn't worry about that right now.

When Sam checked the watch on her wrist, she realized that she and Owen had been out here for more than an hour. Things inside the hospital room had gotten heavy too quickly, and while she knew that Maison had done her best to keep her emotions inside, Sam thought it was best to give them some room. That was how she had ended up in the waiting area outside with Owen.

Dacey had arrived earlier in a rush, and when she had trouble finding her father's room, Sam had helped direct her to it. A part of her wanted to go inside and check on Hutch but she really didn't want to leave the kid out here alone.

When she said she'd tag along, it'd been for Hutch. She wanted to be there for the guy, just like he'd been there for her. But Sam had to admit, she was feeling a little awkward sitting here with nothing to do.

Although she knew Maison wasn't technically family, she had a right to be there. She was closer to Matthew than probably anyone else in that room right now.

But Sam . . . well, Sam was the reason for some of the animosity between their family. She'd been the one who'd suggested Hutch join the Army with her. She knew they blamed her for planting the idea in his head. Did they blame her for the loss of his leg too?

Sam was pulled out from her thoughts when Owen suddenly got up. Sam stood too, blocking the kid's way. "Whoa, where do you think you're going?"

"I'm hungry."

Shit. She should've thought about that. "Okay then," she said, sticking her hand out. "Let's go grab something to eat." She remembered seeing something around here somewhere.

When they finally found something, Sam let the kid

browse all the food available. It was probably a bad idea she realized later on, but instead of picking out something sugary and sweet like she expected, Owen asked for a bagel.

"Okay. What kind of bagel do you want?" By the kid's expression, he had no idea what kind of bagel he usually had. "Hmm, why don't I pick for us then?"

When Owen nodded, she grinned. Sam scanned the options again.

"I want that," Owen said, pointing to a carton of apple juice.

Apple juice. What a healthy kid.

Sam straightened and spoke to the cashier. "Two everything bagels with cream cheese and two apple juices, please."

After paying, Sam and Owen walked to one of the tables. Sam unwrapped Owen's bagel for him before jabbing his straw into his juice box. As soon as she gave the bagel to him, Owen dug into it like he'd never seen food. "Still hungry?" she asked when he'd finished. "You still have one half left."

Owen shook his head.

"Okay. Let's save it for later, okay?"

Owen nodded, picking his Batman toy up again.

"Hey, there you are," a voice called out. "I've been looking all over for you." Sam swirled around to find Hunter standing behind her. Before she could say anything, he settled down beside his son, rubbing the top of his head. "Looks like you're all fed and happy," he said. Then he turned his dark eyes on her. "Thank you for taking care of him." He reached back to pull his wallet out. "Let me pay you back."

Sam reared back. "Oh no, don't worry about it. It's on me."

"Are you sure?"

"Yeah, it's just a little snack."

"Oh, well. Thank you." Hunter put his wallet back into his

pocket. "And thank you also for what you did in there. Maison was a little embarrassed after but she shouldn't be. We're all going through the same thing."

Sam nodded. "I understand." As awkward silence stretched between them, she couldn't help but notice how smooth the guy's voice was. It was so liquid; it seemed to flow over her.

God, what the hell was wrong with her? Since when did she get all dreamy-eyed over a guy's *voice*?

She should really go before she made a fool out of herself. Standing up, Sam grabbed her trash from the table. "Owen still has half his bagel left," she told him. "I was going to keep it for him for later but maybe you want it. You must be starving."

Hunter nodded. "I am. Thank you."

"Anyway, I think I'll go now. Can you tell Hutch to call me when he gets the chance?"

"Wait. You're leaving?"

"Yes. I have a client to meet," she lied. Sam tossed her garbage in the nearest trash bin and said her goodbyes to Owen.

Just as she was about to walk away, Hunter called out for her. "Sorry," he said. "I don't want you to take this the wrong way but I gotta ask, what is it that you're doing with my brother?"

The question took Sam by total surprise. But should it really? Considering how much time she and Hutch spent together, most people would assume things about them.

"We're not sleeping together if that's what you're thinking."

"You're not?"

"Nope. Never have. Never will."

Hunter looked adorably confused. "So if you're not then what exactly—"

"We're just friends."

Hunter's laugh was deep and rough. "Okay. Sorry. It's just that I noticed that he and Maison—"

"Hutch loves her, okay? I think he has loved her for a while now, but whatever she went through recently has torn them apart. I don't know her side of the story, but I do know that Hutch is heartbroken over it. I'm just hoping that there's a happily ever after somewhere there for the two of them."

Hunter nodded. "Yeah, they're perfect for one another," he agreed. "And I'm sorry about thinking there was more between you and him."

For the first time since he showed up at her door, Sam smiled. "Don't worry about it. I'm used to it. Bye," she said for the final time.

"Bye, Sam. Take care of yourself."

Don't worry, she thought. *She always did.*

TWENTY-EIGHT

UTCH OSCILLATED BETWEEN WANTING TO PUNCH something and wanting to drop into the fetal position and cry. He'd been through a hell of a lot during his time in the Army, but nothing got his heart racing and his gut churning like seeing his father lying in a hospital bed, his eyes closed with various tubes sticking out of him.

The doctor had come in and explained everything to him and his siblings, but Hutch still couldn't wrap his head around it. Apparently, Matthew had been on his way home when he discovered a problem with his brakes. Despite taking precautions, Matthew had swerved on the slippery road and hit a tree. The entire car had crumpled upon impact, but luckily there had been people nearby who had seen it all happen and had called for emergency help right away. Hutch didn't even want to think about how much worse it would be if his father been alone with no one to assist him.

Despite the fact that the doctor had said not to worry, Hutch couldn't help himself. While he and his father hadn't been very close, in the recent months, they'd been getting along a lot better. Sure, Matthew still grated on him and still occasionally treated him like he was still a mischievous fifteen-year-old, he'd also started treating him like a normal colleague after he started working with them. Even more, Hutch found himself turning to his father when he'd been concerned about Maison.

God, seeing her again was like getting shot in the chest with an M4. He couldn't hide his surprise when she *and* Hunter had appeared outside of Sam's house. At first, he thought they were there for him, but when he got the news about Matthew, he understood. Maison would only come see him if it concerned his father.

All hope of rekindling what they had disappeared. At first, he thought that they may still have a chance, but one look into Maison's blue gaze and he could see no love for him in her heart anymore. Had she really gotten over him that quickly?

It wouldn't be the same for him. No. Hutch was pretty sure that he would never feel this way about another woman again.

And that was why it was important for him to keep his distance. Hutch wasn't sure he could trust himself if he got too close to her again.

Maison was sitting in the hospital's waiting room, anticipating Hunter's return. He'd gone to check on Owen after speaking to the doctor. *God, it'd been so horrible!* She hated hearing how Matthew had gotten hurt. Hutch and Dacey were still inside with him but she found that she couldn't stay. The silence was becoming unbearable and she was finding it more and more difficult to be in Hutch's presence.

She hated that she couldn't talk to him. But what would she say to Hutch anyway? Should she keep the conversation strictly about his father? Or should she also apologize for her actions too? She felt terrible but she also wasn't sure it was the right time to express that.

God, everything was just so fucked up! Her parents were right. Mixing business with pleasure only complicated things and now Maison worried how things would be between them. There was just no way that Hutch could forgive her for pushing him away.

Hunter arrived then with Owen in tow. He moved to Matthew's hospital room first, opening the door and pushing the kid inside first before returning to her side. Maison looked up at him in confusion. "What's going on? Is everything okay?"

Hunter sat down in the chair beside her. "I should be asking you that question. Why aren't you inside with the rest of them?"

"I just needed some air."

Warm brown eyes scanned her. "You okay?"

"I'm not sure," she admitted.

"Do you want to talk about it?"

Maison lifted her head, feigning innocence. "What do you mean?"

"I mean, what's going on between you and Hutch?"

"Nothing is going on between us."

Hunter sighed. "Okay, let me rephrase that. What *was* going on between you and Hutch?"

Now it was her turn to sigh. Dammit. She had no idea how to proceed. She was the one who had fucked up, of course, but admitting that only made her feel worse. And she really didn't feel comfortable talking about this with Hunter.

Hunter sighed. "Fine. Let me tell you what I know and then you can fill in the blanks. You guys started working together at Gleam Enterprises and somehow you two got involved." He paused, eyeing her carefully. "How am I doing so far?" Maison nodded to his question but she kept her mouth shut. "You two started to get serious and then—"

"We were never serious," she cut in. "And, to save you from continuing, I was the one who screwed things up. My parents showed up out of the blue and it threw me off course. I realize it sounds really stupid and minor, but seeing them again brought some of my childhood issues back to the surface."

Hunter nodded as if he understood. After a moment, he said, "I think you should talk to him."

Maison shook her head. "I can't. He probably hates me now."

"He'll hate you even more if you continue ignoring him," Hunter shot back. Her frown deepened. "Look. He may be mad right now, but Hutch won't hate you forever. In fact, I think the guy actually loves you." Her eyes flew open at that admission. *What? How could that be?*

Hutch . . . in love . . . with her?

Impossible.

"So, as a guy looking out for his brother, *please,* just talk to him. We've had enough heartbreak for the day."

At the words, she looked up at Hunter. He looked tired, but more importantly, he looked concerned.

Damn, he was right. She was letting her fear stand in the way of her own happiness. And if her parents hadn't shown up, she was pretty sure she could say with confidence that she was in love with Hutch too. But they'd fallen apart so much since then. How could they ever go back to the way things were?

Hunter rose and headed for the hospital room. But he stopped and looked back at her. "Do you want me to ask him to come out so you can talk in private?"

The suggestion made her stomach clench but Maison forced herself to nod. "Yes, that would be great. Thank you." She would have to apologize someday. Might as well do it now.

With a reassuring smile, Hunter slipped back into the room. As the door closed behind him, Maison could picture him talking to Hutch. What would Hutch say when he told him she was waiting out here for him? Would he come out? Or would he leave her out to dry?

Her entire body began to shake with her fear. Not even

deep breathing could ease the growing panic inside of her as she waited to see if Hutch would come out to talk to her.

When the door opened, Hutch worried it might be Maison returning. But it was just his brother coming back. "You all right?" Hutch asked him. The guy looked exhausted, but he wasn't sure a dozen hours of sleep would do him any good. Like him, his stresses would keep him awake.

"I am, but I know you aren't."

Hutch frowned. "What are you talking about?"

"Maison is outside waiting for you."

Hutch blinked. *"What?"*

"You heard me."

"She's . . . outside?" *Waiting for him?* He knew she'd gone out for a bit, but he figured it was because she had to go to the bathroom or something.

"Yes, genius. So go out and talk to her."

Hutch frowned. "Wait a minute. Where's Sam?"

"She left. She said she had a client to meet. But you better hurry. Maison looks impatient."

Maison wanted to talk? Okay. Okay, he could do this. "Did she say what she wanted to talk about?" *She didn't want to talk about what happened, did she?*

Hunter gave him an *are-you-really-that-stupid* look. "What do you think?"

Okay, so he was stalling. But that was because he was nervous. He had no idea what Maison was going to say to him. Did she want to make up or break up with him?

Hunter groaned and scrubbed a hand over his face in frustration. "For God's sake!" he cried. "She wants to apologize, okay? Now go outside and *talk to her.*"

"Okay, okay, relax. I'll go talk to her." But as he walked

to the door, his pulse skyrocketed and his muscles stiffened. Drawing in a breath, he braced himself. "Okay," he told himself. "You can do this."

On a breath, he opened the door and peered outside, finding a woman with dark brown hair, sitting alone. *"What the—"* He probably stood there for too long staring because the woman looked up and shot him a confused look. "Ah, sorry." *Where the hell was Maison?*

He turned back into the room. "What?" Hunter said, seeing his confusion. "What happened?"

"She's not there."

Hunter was already moving towards the door. "What do you mean she's not there? She said she was going to wait for you." He spun around in a quick circle once in the waiting area, eyes searching for Maison. "What the hell? She was right *here!*"

Hutch stood by the door, mouth pursed together in a line as disappointment filled him. Why did it not surprise him to learn that Maison had bolted once again?

TWENTY-NINE

S HE WAS SUCH A PUSSY! WHY HAD SHE DONE THAT? Hunter had done everything for her and all Maison had to do was wait outside for Hutch but she couldn't even manage that without falling into a panic attack!

Was she so much of a coward that she couldn't give Hutch the explanation he deserved? Not only had Maison screwed this up for them the first time but also she knew she was making this worse by not confronting him. *What the hell was wrong with her?*

Although she wasn't in the best of moods, Maison still went to see Rissa. Having the teen around usually cheered her up. Plus, she wanted to know how the dance went.

But when she arrived at her house, she was surprised to see another woman answering the door. She looked so much like Rissa that she stepped back a step. "Maison? Hi, I'm Florencia, Rissa's mother. Please, call me Flo." Maison tried to hide her surprise. *What was Rissa's mother doing here?*

That was a stupid question. She lived here. But in all the times that she'd visit, Flo had never been around.

"Hello, Flo." Shaking off her surprise, she reached out to shake her hand.

Flo smiled at her. "I really want to thank you for what you've done for Rissa. Without this program, Rissa would never have found you and would never have made it through this school year. You've been such a positive influence on both her attitude and behavior that I don't know how I could ever repay you."

"It was my pleasure. Getting to know Rissa has been such a wonderful experience. And actually, in offering her advice, I've learned a few things myself. You have an amazing daughter."

"I know I haven't been around here much but that's going to change. I'm starting over. I don't want to miss out on the opportunities that I have here with Rissa. Sooner or later, she's going to be an adult and I want her to have a role model she can look up to."

Maison smiled, loving what she was hearing. "That's amazing, Flo."

The other woman beamed. "I know I have a long way to go, but I want to start fresh." Flo suddenly looked emotional and Maison felt like she was on the verge of tears herself. But then Flo jumped into action before they both started crying. "Here, let me get Rissa for you."

As she called for her daughter, Maison quickly dabbed at her eyes. God, she'd been an emotional wreck all week, but at least this time her tears weren't because she was sad or heartbroken.

Rissa had a huge smile on her face as she came down the stairs. "Hey, Maison!"

Maison felt her mood brighten instantly. "Rissa! How are you?"

"Good."

"How was the dance?"

"It was *awesome!*"

"You had fun?" She worried that she would still be upset about not having a date.

"Yes! Jasmine and I danced *all* night. And we even got to stay out afterwards."

Her smile widened as Rissa's excitement filled the room.

"I'm a little jealous now," she admitted. "I could use a girls' night out." Especially after everything that had happened to her.

"Maybe you two could have one before we go," Flo said.

When Rissa turned to her mother, her smile faded. Maison frowned. What did she mean by *before we go?*

When the girl turned back to her, her expression almost looked apologetic. Her voice softened and Maison realized that she was holding something in her hands. "I have something for you . . ."

"Oh."

Looking down at what she'd given her, Maison realized it was a Polaroid picture of Rissa, looking all dressed up and glam in her dress. She was smiling brilliantly at the camera and Maison grinned at the confidence that oozed from her. "Wow," she breathed. "Rissa, you look absolutely beautiful."

The teen blushed. "Thanks. I want you to keep it. You know, so you don't forget me."

Maison's smile faded and she shook her head. "I don't understand. Why would I forget you?"

Rissa's voice was sad when she said, "We're moving."

"Moving? *Why?*"

Flo spoke up first. "Rissa's father will be released soon and we're going to try and be a family again."

Oh, wow.

She should be happy for them. No, she should be *ecstatic!* But instead sadness filled her. Did this mean she would never see them again? "Can't you try and be a family *here?* Do you guys really need to move away for that?" She wasn't ready to let go yet. Not when she'd lost everything else already.

"I want a fresh start, Maison," Flo said. "It would be so easy to fall back into old habits if we stay here. I want a completely new life. One that doesn't involve prison sentences."

"But what about Rissa?" Hadn't she moved enough in her lifetime that she deserved to stay in a school for more than one year?

"Rissa is okay with it, right?" Flo glanced at her daughter. Rissa looked so much like her; it was uncanny.

"It's okay, Maison," Rissa said. "I *want* to go."

Another argument was on her lips but Maison snapped her mouth shut. Flo was right. There would be too much temptation around here, and if they had a shot at starting a brand-new life, why not take it?

Still, that wouldn't erase the fact that she was going to worry about them. But Maison couldn't ask them to stay for her sake. Somehow, she'd just have to learn how to deal.

The tears she'd been holding back earlier threatened to spill again, and this time, Maison didn't stop it. As she started to cry, Rissa did too. *Why was everything falling apart around her?*

As Rissa held her, Flo stepped back, giving them the space for them to say their goodbyes. This was likely the last time Maison would see her and that knowledge only made her sob harder. "Be good, okay?" she said when she finally found her breath. She wiped a tear from Rissa's cheek. "And remember what I said . . ."

Since the first moment they'd met she'd been trying to tell the girl that she was beautiful and intelligent and that she didn't need to follow what other people did in order to feel included or cool.

The girl's her bottom lip quivered but she did nod. And although she hated saying goodbye, Maison knew she was going to be all right.

After a while, she forced herself to stop crying and smile at this girl who she'd quickly come to love as a real sister. "Here."

She grabbed one of her business cards from her planner and scribbled down both her personal email and number on the back. "Don't lose this, okay? Call me any time you want."

Rissa took the card and clutched it tightly in her fist. "Thanks. I will."

On a breath, Maison turned to Flo, pulling her into a hug before heading for the door. She didn't know Flo well, but she admired the woman's courage. A lot of changes would be coming their way and she hoped that their family was strong enough to survive it.

Maison paused at the door to look back at the mother and daughter standing together. She was scared for them, but feeling scared wasn't always a bad thing.

She hoped that life treated them well. She believed that they would get the fresh start that they deserved, and she hoped that they realized that they were stronger when they were together than they were apart.

Today's trip hadn't gone as planned, but in coming here, Maison realized a few things about herself. She'd become so reliant on getting her parents' approval that she hadn't sought out ways to try to overcome it. Instead she'd allowed herself to wallow in her own self-destructive thinking and pushed those she cared about away from her.

If she wanted things to change for the better then she had to take her own advice. She had to stop running away from people and fully embrace who she was. And in order to get over her parents' influence on her, she had to start seeing herself as beautiful and intelligent again.

Maison smiled. Once again, Rissa had taught her another life lesson that she wouldn't have figured out if it weren't for her.

With a last parting goodbye, she stepped out of the

Ferlito-Joneses' household and started walking back to her car, clutching the photo of Rissa tightly to her chest.

* * *

When she reached home, Maison went to her living room and pulled out one of her old picture frames. For years it sat unused on her bookshelves simply because she had nothing to put inside, but it was finally going to be used for the first time today. As she placed Rissa's beautiful picture inside, she smiled. It fit perfectly inside the frame and Maison thought it would look beautiful on her coffee table. She was definitely going to miss her dearly but she was also glad that Rissa was going to have the fresh start she always dreamed of. As Maison set the picture down on her coffee table, the doorbell rang and she turned to answer it.

Once she swung the door open, her mother stepped through without warning. *"What the—"* A second later, her father followed. Maison gaped at their presence. "What are you doing here?" She thought they'd left already.

Her mother waved her hand in her face. "Stop asking silly questions."

"We've come to check on you," her father said as he made his way to the couch.

Huh? What was she, twelve? She didn't need babysitting!

Her father leaned forward and frowned at the picture frame in front of him. "Maison, who is this?"

Maison jumped forward. "Hey, don't touch that!" She didn't want their dirty hands touching something so precious to her.

But her mother reached for it before she could. She examined it like it was one of her X-rays. "Who is this girl?" she asked after a while.

Maison considered lying but then decided against it. "She's my Little Sister."

"*What?*" Her mother looked shocked. "Explain."

Maison sighed again. "I'm in a Big Sister program and she's my Little Sister."

Some of the outrage had dimmed from their expressions but her parents still didn't look happy. "Oh," her mother huffed. "Well, I guess that's nice of you." She looked down at the photo of Rissa and frowned. "Where is this photo taken?"

"It's at one of her school dances."

"Where's her date?"

Maison thought of Boone. Of the heartbreak that he'd caused Rissa. "She didn't have one." *Didn't need one.*

"Humph. That's not surprising. Look at her. She's skin and bone!" Her mother's tone was one that Maison was very familiar with.

"Let me see," her father said. When her mother handed the picture frame over to him, he laughed. "Why don't you try handing over some of your fat to her so that the two of you can actually resemble normal, healthy human beings?"

Maison felt heat start to rise in her body. As her mother chortled at her father's cruel joke, she asked, "Does she have an eating disorder or something?"

Ugh! They were terrible! How could they say such a thing about an innocent girl?

Fury erupted within her. For thirty years she'd allowed her parents to verbally abuse her, to call her cruel names and to let them dictate her life, but she wouldn't allow the same thing to happen to Rissa!

Maison stomped across the room and snatched the picture frame from her mother's hands. "Give that to me!" Her mother gasped. "Rissa does *not* have an eating disorder. She has a body that is perfect for her age group! What is wrong with you people?" she snarled. "How can you two sit here talking bad about an innocent teen who has done nothing to you at all? Do you two get off on being so cruel to others?"

"Maison!" her father snapped, coming to his feet. His own anger had risen to match hers. "You do not get to speak to us that way! Apologize at once!"

"No," she snarled, matching the same venom in his voice. "I've had enough of you two and your nasty words! I won't listen to it any longer!" Her eyes began to well up as emotions ran rampant within her. "For all my life, you've made me feel worthless and ugly and I went around thinking that all of it was true! But I'm not actually any of those things. I'm perfectly fine the way I am and I've found people who like me for me!"

"Ha!" Her mother laughed cruelly. "Like who?"

"The Ferlito-Joneses and the Happa-Hewitts," she shot back.

"They're lying to you." Her mother took a menacing step towards. "They feel bad for you, so that's why they tolerate you."

Maison shook her head. "That's not true. Matthew has become a great friend of mine. *A life-long friend.*"

"Really," her mother drawled. "What about that boy then? Have you seen him again?" Maison's mouth snapped shut and her mother grinned wider, sensing triumph. "Don't make me say that I was right again. He was too good for you and he was going to realize it sooner or later."

Emotion welled up inside of her but Maison refused to cry. "He loves me," she whispered. "And I love him."

Her father scoffed. "If that's the case, then where is he now?"

Her mother stepped forward again. "Come on, darling."

Her tone was mean and condescending. "Wake up and see what's around you. Can you really believe that they'd really like this?" She waved a finger at her body.

"They do. But even if they didn't, there's no need for me to change who I am. And I certainly don't need your approval before I can feel better about myself." Maison stormed towards the door and flung it open. She was sick of thinking she was inferior. From now on, she was going to take back her life and live it how she wanted to. *"Get out,"* she snarled. For a moment, her mother just blinked at her. Her father looked equally shocked. *"Get out!"* Maison screamed, finally reaching her breaking point. Her parents jumped into action, startled out of their wits. Supreme satisfaction filled her as they ran out the door. "Until you realize just how much you've hurt me, don't ever think about showing up here again!" She slammed the door in their shocked faces, feeling no remorse.

God, she hated them! They had riled her up so much that all she could hear was the blood roaring in her ears. She still couldn't believe what had just happened or what she'd managed to say, but after all those years of keeping her mouth shut, she had finally boiled over and had finally said what was on her mind.

Maison didn't expect that they'd try to get in touch with her again soon, but she hoped that when they did, they would have the decency to apologize for everything that they'd put her through. If they weren't aware of her hurt before, then they were now.

Maison knew that although she was now standing up for herself, things wouldn't change overnight, but already she was feeling a hundred times better for doing it.

From now on, there would be no more busting her butt, trying to please others. There would be no more working herself to the bone, and definitely no more feeling self-conscious when she had no reason to be. She had to kick those nasty habits to the curb before she could take back control of her life and focus on the people she cared about.

Once she managed that, the world would be hers.

THIRTY

Apart of Hutch felt guilty for not going with his siblings to visit their father at the hospital in the morning, but for his own sanity, he just needed to be alone.

Maison would likely be there again and he wasn't sure what he would do if those blue eyes met his. Not only had she left him but she'd ditched him too. He'd appreciated his brother's efforts in trying to smooth things out between them, but it was clear that Maison didn't want to. Why run from him otherwise?

No. He wasn't going to put his heart through that again. If anything happened to Matthew, Dacey or Hunter would give him a call. But he wasn't going to wait around in the same room as Maison if he could help it. He had tortured himself enough the last few days worrying about her already.

Today he was just going to take a breather and try to center himself. Normally, he'd go over to Sam's house whenever he was feeling like this. But he didn't want to burden her with such a heavy load. If what Hunter said was true and she'd gone to meet with a client the other day, then that meant she'd finally found a job that interested her. He wasn't going to take her away from that just so she could listen to him complain about his shitty life. What else could he do to take his mind off things?

He could go back to the gun range. He'd enjoyed his time there and the simple act of focusing on one target made the rest of the world go blissfully blank.

Yes, that was what he was going to do. Hutch jumped out of bed and quickly changed into some jeans and a T-shirt. Then he grabbed his keys and headed for his car.

Not only did he plan on working his aggression out, but he also planning on forgetting the world.

"Hey, have you heard from Hutch today?" Dacey asked.

Maison looked up from her planner she'd been decorating. "Huh? Uh, no." Actually, she hadn't heard from Hutch in a while but she wasn't going to bring that up right now.

Hutch's sister frowned. "That's weird. I texted him earlier to see if he wanted me to bring some take-out home but he hasn't replied yet. That was hours ago." It was already nearing the end of the day and Maison could see the worry in her friend's eyes.

"Maybe he's still sleeping," Hunter remarked as he picked Owen up and held him in his arms. They'd been with Matthew all day, and although Maison knew miracles didn't happen overnight, she was hoping for some good news today. So far, however, there was no change in him.

"It's nearly five in the afternoon."

"You know Hutch. That guy can sleep through anything."

But the words did little to ease her friend. As a matter of fact, Maison was concerned about him too. After her cowardly move the other day, she wanted to apologize to him in person but he hadn't arrived with Hunter or Dacey this morning. And now that he wasn't answering his sister's texts, she worried that something had happened to him. Surely he'd check his phone if he wanted to keep tabs on his father's condition, right?

"I'm going to go look for him," Dacey decided.

"I'll come with you," Maison added.

"Wait, what about Dad?" Hunter cried.

"You stay here. We'll go look for him."

"Do you even know where to look?"

That stumped Dacey. While she was more than capable of running out of here, she wasn't sure where to start looking. For that matter, neither did Maison. Hunter sighed. "Okay, how about this? Why don't you guys stay here with Dad and Owen and *I'll* go look for him."

Dacey started to protest. "But—"

"What if Dad wakes up?"

"Oh fine," she said but she clearly wasn't happy with it. "But take Maison with you."

Maison smiled at the sound of her name.

"All right, Maison," Hunter drawled. "Grab your things. Let's go find my brother."

* * *

Maison felt her anxiety begin to rise as she and Hunter walked up the steps to Sam's home. She felt terrible for coming here again unannounced but this was where Hutch would likely be hiding out if something was bothering him.

Hunter rapped on the door. "Sam?" he called out. "It's Hunter. I'm looking for Hutch. Is he there?"

The door swung open a few seconds later and Sam walked out wear a pair of ripped jeans, a simple tank top, and wet hair. *Had she just come out of the shower?*

Maison had no idea why she was so surprised to see the other woman again. Perhaps it was her appearance. Sam looked strong and vital with her long hair and tattoos whereas Maison didn't look like she had an ounce of toughness in her. It made her want to turn away like a dog with its tail between its legs.

No, she couldn't do that. She had to be strong. But her heart was already beating hard at the thought of seeing Hutch again. Squarely her shoulders, Maison asked, "Is Hutch with you?"

Sam shook her head. "No, he isn't. Why? Is something wrong? How's Matthew doing?"

"Matthew is fine," Hunter informed her. "Well, he's still in the hospital but Hutch hasn't been answering any of our calls. Have you heard from him today?"

"No. I tried calling him earlier but he hasn't called me back. Is he not at home? I assumed he'd be at the hospital with you guys so I didn't think much of it."

Hunter shook his head. "He's not there."

"Where could he have gone then?"

"I really thought he would be here," said Hunter.

"Hmm, well if he's not at home or at the hospital, then I think I know where he might be," Sam said. "Let's go."

They all filed back into the car but this time Maison gave her seat up to Sam. Since she was the one who knew where they were going, she would need to give Hunter the directions. Sliding into the back seat, she tried not to let her anxiety get the best of her. *Where the hell had Hutch gone?*

When they finally pulled up to the large building, Maison's eyes went wide. "A gun range? Why would he be here?"

"I showed him this place not too long ago," Sam explained. "I have a feeling he'd come here if he was feeling down. Do you want to wait here or come inside?"

Maison *hated* guns, but her worry for Hutch was strong. "I'm coming. Wait for me!"

As they entered the establishment, Maison wasn't surprised to see that everyone knew who Sam was. They greeted her with big smiles, and when she asked if Hutch was around, they were quick to nod. "Well, he was here," one man said. He had a burly chest and a heavy dusting of facial hair. "But I think he left about two hours ago."

"*Two hours ago?*" Sam looked annoyed to have missed him. "Well, if he's not here, then where the hell could he have gone?"

"Do you think he has gone back to the house?" Maison asked.

"Let me try calling him again," Hunter said. But when he shook his head a few minutes later, Maison felt her worry amplify. *Oh God, where was he? And why wasn't he answering any of their calls?*

She thought about what she knew of Hutch and where he might go to find some peace. She'd thought they'd find him with Sam since he always seemed to run to her when he felt troubled, but was there someone else who he'd confided in recently? Someone else that he cared about and felt comfortable with?

For a while, she'd consider herself a good listener. As she got over her anxiety around him, she'd opened up to him about her feelings, and in return, Hutch had done the same. But those days were long gone and she'd ruined all those moments with her actions.

Maison recalled the day that she and Hutch had left work to grab some breakfast together. He'd taken her to get some ice cream after and told her that she was extraordinary. At the time, she hadn't believed him but now she would kill to experience that moment again.

It was then that it hit her and she gasped. "I think I know where he is!"

The sun was on its descent after another long day. As Hutch sat on the ground admiring the view, he tried not to think about the yellow and blue hues of the sky and what they reminded him of. Somehow, no matter how much he tried to not think of her, everything reminded him of Maison.

Blue like her eyes.

Yellow like her hair.

And just like that, he felt his chest twinge with pain.

Hutch thought that in going to the gun range he'd be able to lose himself, and for a couple of hours, he had. But when the adrenaline had passed and his beating heart had slowed, he was once again hit by the empty feeling in his chest.

He'd come here, to the special place where he could be alone but still be with Maison. This was where he'd taken her after feeding her breakfast. Further down the road, he'd bought her ice cream and then brought her here. They'd made out in his front seat of his car for a little bit before moving to the back. That was when Maison really started to blow his mind. She'd been so sweet. So sexy. That was when he first realized that she was going to be different to all the other women he'd been with. Hutch suspected that was the very moment when he'd started to fall in love with her.

If he could change reality, he would find a way to make Maison his. Permanently. Because nothing was worse than feeling this way without her.

Hutch let out a loud sigh. No one would hear him here, but even if someone did, he didn't care. All he cared about was what he was going to do when he had to face—

"Hutch?"

He turned out the sound of his name. "Maison?" His heart clenched hard in his chest. "What the hell are you doing here?"

But instead of answering him, Maison ran forward and launched herself into his arms. Hutch couldn't do anything else but hold tight as her softness pressed against his body. *God, he missed her. He missed her so much!* "Hutch, I'm so happy you're all right. I was *so* worried." *What was she doing here? Had she come looking for him?* Her lips turned up in a smile. "I knew you would be here."

"You did? How?"

"Because I want to relive this moment again too." Her beautiful blue eyes started to well up with tears and her smile faded. "Hutch, I'm sorry. I didn't mean to push you away. It's just the thing with my parents hit me harder than it should've and my confidence was rattled a bit. I started to doubt myself again and . . ." she trailed off and her body started to shake. Hutch could do nothing else but hold her tight to his body. "I-I was afraid of embarrassing you," she finished on a whisper.

Hutch reached out and gently lifted Maison's head so that she was gazing into his eyes. He made sure he maintained eye contact with her when he said, "Why would you ever embarrass me? You are the most beautiful, intelligent, most extraordinary woman I have ever met. I should be the one feeling embarrassed to be standing here with you."

Maison grabbed his hand and shook her head. "No, don't think that. You're more than I could ever ask for in a man. I feel terrible for what I did to you. Do you forgive me?"

He still couldn't believe that Maison was here, back in his arms again. He thought he'd lost everything when he'd lost his leg. But despite his missing limb and his bad attitude, Maison loved him anyway. It caused him to believe that there could be other things to live for other than chasing his passion. Sometimes, it was enough to live for the people you loved too. "Of course I forgive you. I could never stay mad at you, Maison. I love you."

Maison let out a sob, and when she shut her eyes, a single tear slipped past. Hutch bowed low and kissed it away, drawing his lips over hers. "I love you, Maison," he whispered again. "More than anything in the entire world. Will you marry me? I promise to spend the rest of my life trying not to embarrass you."

Maison pulled back as her eyes flew wide. "Wait, what? You want to—"

"Marry me," he said again. "I don't have a ring or anything but I'll get you whichever one you want. Just promise yourself to me and—"

"Yes."

Hutch froze. "Yes?"

Maison laughed at his expression. "Yes, you fool. Of course I'll marry you!"

"Oh, thank God," he breathed, crushing her to his chest. Inside, his heart was bursting with happiness. When he kissed her again, he poured every drop of love he had for her in that kiss. Maison Lane always worked hard, but she never did anything for herself. Now he was going to spend the rest of his life spoiling her so she didn't have to.

The sudden sound of something pulled them apart. When Hutch glanced behind Maison, he realized that his brother and Sam were standing by his car. Sam was in the process of doing a dramatic slow-clap while Hunter was fighting a smile. His own lips turned up in a grin. "Way to ruin the moment, Sam."

"Sorry," she drawled. "I just couldn't pass it up." She shook her head at him. "I can't believe you proposed to a girl without a ring! It's a good thing Maison is sweet or you would've gotten your ass turned down!"

This time, Hunter laughed out loud.

Hutch clutched Maison to his chest and gazed down at her. "Yeah. Good thing she loves me, huh?" Maison slapped him across his chest playfully. He caught her hand, bringing her fingers to his lips, kissing her ring finger. "Don't worry," he whispered. "I fully intend on getting you a diamond, Snowflake."

Maison grinned up at him. "I'm not worried. As long as I have you, I have everything I want in the world.

EPILOGUE

HUNTER HAPPA-HEWITT SAT BY HIS FATHER'S bedside in the hospital, feeling—and probably looking—worse than he'd ever felt before.

He was tired. *No, he was exhausted actually.* Like every single parent was familiar with, caring for a child was hard work. He just hadn't expected it to remain this difficult now. Despite being divorced for a few months already, he thought that things would ease up, but that clearly wasn't happening. In fact, it seemed to get harder every day.

Today was proving to be one of the more difficult days.

Hunter stared down at his father, seeing so much of himself in the man. They shared the same strong jaw and hairline, but while Matthew had the green eyes that reflected his Scottish roots, Hunter had his mother's rich, brown eyes. Out of all his siblings, Hunter would say that he was the closest in temperament to his father. Sometimes his brother even claimed that they shared the same mind sometimes. His sister, Dacey, kept saying that he wanted to grow up to be just like their father. But it wasn't true at all. Hunter never wanted to follow in Matthew's footsteps.

When Matthew had last asked him to take his place as CEO of Gleam Enterprises, he'd already known the answer he'd give him. The answer would always be *no*.

No matter how many times his father asked, Hunter had no intention of running a multimillion-dollar company. He just couldn't see himself sitting behind a desk all day. It just wasn't what he wanted for himself. But his father had never stopped asking him to take his place.

In the past, he never once felt remorse for turning him down but, now, as he stared down at his father, Hunter wondered what would happen if he'd said yes.

As if knowing he was thinking about him, his father made a noise. It wasn't a big one but it was enough to make Hunter freeze. He watched on with bated breath for another movement from his father. When Matthew's lips moved for a second time, Hunter shot to his feet. *Holy shit! Was he coming to?*

He immediately called for the nurse, feeling his heart shift into overdrive. *"He moved!"* he cried when the nurse came in. *"And I think he might even be trying to speak!"* Dammit, he wished his brother and sister were here to see this! But they'd already gone home for the night with Owen. Only he had stayed behind.

The nurse's eyes darted to the patient but Matthew was suddenly still. Hunter frowned and leaned in. "Hey, what happened? Dad, you all right? He moved, I swear," he said to the nurse. By her expression, it was clear she didn't believe him. "Come on, Dad. Wake up!"

Hunter willed his father to do it again, to lift a finger or to open his eyes—*anything!*—but when minutes passed and Matthew remained as still as a corpse, the nurse said to him, "I think you should get some rest." Her tone suggested that she thought that he may be hallucinating. But Hunter was absolutely positive that his father had moved. Why wasn't he now?

When Hunter was alone again, he settled back in the chair and dropped his head into his hands. He hadn't been hallucinating. He might be tired but that wasn't enough to get him to start hearing things.

For a long moment, he stared at his father, seeing no

movement but the slight rise and fall of his chest as he breathed.

Dammit! He shot to his feet and ran a hand over his face. Maybe he *was* tired. He should just head home. Owen would be waiting for him but Hunter hated the idea of leaving his father here alone. What if he woke up again and no one was around?

A sound froze him in place and when he looked down at his father again, he realized that his eyes were open. *"Dad!"* He was by his side in the next instant. *"Dad! You're awake!"*

See! He wasn't seeing things!

A rush of relief spread through him. He was never happier to see those green eyes staring back at him. "Where am I?" Matthew rasped.

"You're in a hospital. You were in a car accident. Do you remember what happened?" Matthew shook his head. "That's okay. The police are . . ." Hunter trailed off as his father's mouth opened. It looked like he was trying to say something. "What is it?" he asked, leaning forward to hear him better.

"Don't—" He was clearly struggling to speak. Matthew licked his lips and Hunter immediately went to grab him a glass of water.

After taking a sip, Hunter prompted him again. "Don't what?"

"Don't let Clive . . . take my place . . . at Gleam."

"Clive?" Hunter frowned. Out of all the things his father could say to him, why would he say that? "Why not?" Clive was already taking care of things in his father's absence. He'd been doing it for a few days already.

Matthew shook his head. *"You . . .* you have to do it."

Hunter reared back. *"What?" No way!*

"You," his father said again. Speaking was obviously still a hardship for him so Hunter told him to relax.

He couldn't believe this! There was no way he could take his father's place as the CEO! Clive was much more suited for the role. Why was his father still pushing this on him? Was this his way of trying to get him to do what he wanted?

Maybe one of his siblings could step in. At least they would have some experience working there already.

He wondered why his father didn't want Clive Davenport, the man he'd started the company with, to cover for him while he was recovering. Had something happened between them? Had it something to do with accident?

He opened his mouth to ask but then realized that Matthew had dozed off again. *Shit.* He was torn between wanting to wake him so he could ask more questions and leaving him to rest. The poor man definitely needed it. He couldn't even finish a proper sentence without struggling. Hunter would let him rest then. There was no use trying to pry words out of him when he clearly wasn't feeling well enough yet.

In his frustration, Hunter decided that it was best that he head home. At least now he could tell his siblings that their father had woken up.

Or should he? What would he tell them? Should he reveal what his father had said to them too?

Hunter got into his car and tried focusing only on the road ahead of him. He should be thrilled to tell his siblings that their father had woken up, but why then did thinking of Clive suddenly give him such a cold feeling in his chest?

MORE THAN THIS

Moonrise Beach, Book Three

Hunter Happa-Hewitt's life has never been more stressful. With his divorce behind him, he thought that life with his five-year-old son would be easier. But now his father is in the hospital and has asked him to take his place as the CEO of Gleam Enterprises, a part that he has no interest in playing. Hunter is about to refuse when he suspects that his father's accident perhaps wasn't really an accident at all. Now, he will do everything in his power to learn the truth.

No one is more surprised than Sam Cosi is when she finds the sexy billionaire in her office, asking for her help. Although this isn't her usual MO, Sam can't say no to the job—or the man. But working alongside Hunter proves difficult, especially as she can no longer hide her feelings for him.

Can love still bloom in the midst of mystery? Or will their love run out when they discover the truth that binds them?

Be notified when new titles are released by subscribing to my newsletter at www.anajolene.com

RESURRECTION

Glory MC series, Book Four

When the president of the club goes missing, Beck Caulder, one of Glory MC's sergeant at arms, is the one to strap on his anti-radiation gear and go in search for him. Problem is, Knuckle has a hit on him, which means Beck won't be the only one on the lookout.

When Beck discovers that the president is hiding in Westborough, the most dangerous place in Ward Four, he has no choice but to run headlong into Slasher territory. There, he encounters Devine Blaise, the raven-haired beauty, covered in leather and tattoos. With her killer bod and equally killer instincts, Devine quickly becomes Beck's dream woman. Too bad she's also the mercenary hired to take out his club's president.

Equally matched in determination and skill, the chase soon becomes a battle of the most deadly as Beck and Devine try to take each other out. This should be easy for the club's sergeant at arms, but resisting the killer becomes the hardest battle he's ever fought—and the only one Beck fears he can't win.

Be notified when new titles are released by subscribing to my newsletter at www.anajolene.com

ACKNOWLEDGMENTS

This book was definitely a labor of love. So much time and effort has been put into it and I have many people to thank because of it.

First off, thank you to Sissy for once again providing your insight and opinion. I appreciate you being there for me.

Thank you to my editorial team, Karen Schmauch and Judy Zweifel for helping me make this the best book it can be. And also Stacey Blake for putting it all together and making it look pretty.

Many thanks to my parents for believing in me and telling me not to quit. I will continue to work hard.

And lastly, thank you to the readers and bloggers who have shared their love of my books to others. You are helping me make my dreams come true.

ABOUT THE AUTHOR

Ana Jolene is the author of the Glory MC series, a New Adult Dystopian and the Contemporary Romance series, Moonrise Beach.

Growing up as a rebellious kid didn't allow for much reading time. It wasn't until Ana was in university that she found her passion for books and has since then devoured every book placed before her. Ana holds a B.A. in Psychology and has worked in both IT and Administration. But she's had the most fun in the bookish world, working as a reviewer, columnist, and assistant to multiple sites and best-selling authors.

Ana currently lives in Toronto with her family and an extremely lazy Shih Tzu whom she adores. To learn more about Ana and her books, please visit her website www.anajolene.com and subscribe to the newsletter to be notified of the hottest new releases and giveaways!

Connect with Ana:

Twitter: @ anajoleneauthor

Facebook: www.facebook.com/anajoleneauthor

Instagram: www.instagram.com/anajoleneauthor

Website: www.anajolene.com

Other titles by Ana Jolene

Glory MC series

Glory

Origin

Nirvana

Resurrection (Coming Soon)

Moonrise Beach series

Close To You

Sweet As Sin

More Than This (Coming Soon)

www.ingramcontent.com/pod-product-compliance
Lightning Source LLC
Chambersburg PA
CBHW030410030726
47497CB00002B/563